rawhead

Author of four previous novels, including *The Secret Sexist* and *From Stockport with Love*, Mancunian writer David Bowker now lives in Cambridge.

rawhead

DAVID BOWKER

PAN BOOKS

First published 2002 by Macmillan

This edition published 2003 by Pan Books
an imprint of Pan Macmillan Ltd
Pan Macmillan, 20 New Wharf Road, London N1 9RR
Basingstoke and Oxford
Associated companies throughout the world
www.panmacmillan.com

ISBN 0 330 49231 4

1 3 5 7 9 8 6 4 2

A CIP catalogue record for this book is available from
the British Library.

Typeset by SetSystems Ltd, Saffron Walden, Essex
Printed and bound in Great Britain by
Mackays of Chatham plc, Chatham, Kent

To my English teachers with apologies

Acknowledgements

Thanks to Robert Kirby for the idea. Millsy for the bad language. Jane and Gabriel for everything. Kevin and Sandra Childs for being loyal friends. Ra Page for encouraging me to write about Manchester.

Love to Simon Delaney, Peter Lavery, Sinead O'Connor and anyone else who's Irish.

All of the authors quoted in this book have inspired me.

Special thanks to Dr Moad of the King's College Archive for permission to view the M. R. James papers.

The line from 'Living Doll' Words and Music by Lionel Bart © 1959, reproduced by permission of Peter Maurice Music Co. Ltd., London WC2H 0QY.

phone calls. Despite Billy's persistence, Boswell had sworn that he had more chance of buggering the prime minister during *Question Time* than of talking to Malcolm Priest.

And now, without warning, the villain who ruled Manchester and regularly sent senior officers in the Greater Manchester Police on well-deserved Caribbean holidays had elbowed his publicist aside and was phoning Billy at home, late at night, when the writer was drunk and dangerously low on self-esteem.

'Have you just woken up?' Priest asked him. 'You sound a bit, you know . . .'

'To be honest, I was having a wank,' Billy lied, hoping to sound like a bit of a character.

Without pausing for breath, Priest said, 'Who about?'

'What do you mean?'

'I mean, who were you wanking about?'

'That's a bit personal, isn't it?'

Priest snorted. 'Well, you fucking started it. You were the one who was pretending to be all trendy and up-front by saying you were a wanker.'

'I wasn't pretending. And I'm not a wanker.'

'Tell you what, you're not a writer, either,' said Priest. 'I saw that piece you wrote about alcohol abuse among the cast of *Coronation Street*. Know what? You write like a cunt.'

'That's because I'm only read once a month.'

Priest didn't laugh. 'That article gave offence to many people, including my mother.'

'Why? Is she in *Coronation Street*?'

'No. She's a recovering alcoholic.' There was a long silence. 'Anyway, most of the journalists we deal with are from London. I thought it might be nice for a change to talk to someone from Manchester, someone who doesn't know much and might not have too many preconceptions about who I am and what I stand for. A dickhead like you, basically.'

'I see,' said Billy, aware that he was being tested.

'So what's this interview going to be about?' snapped Priest.

Billy had a feeling that Priest already knew the answer. He said, 'Malcolm Priest. Who he is and what he stands for.'

'Correct.'

They met at the Moroccan, Priest's exclusive restaurant in Deansgate. It wasn't a lunch date. Billy wasn't important enough for that. He'd been told to arrive at ten a.m. Predictably, Priest kept him waiting, oozing through the revolving door shortly after eleven in the company of a tall, sullen tool with a typically bad Manchester haircut. Billy had been warned about the tool, but not the haircut.

But the worst surprise was Boswell. As a veteran of countless celebrity profiles, Billy knew it was a terrible sign when publicists insisted on babysitting their clients. It meant that the publicist distrusted the journalist and was concerned that the interviewee might be compromised in some way. Fair's fair, Billy wouldn't have trusted himself either. But coming from a creep like Boswell, this was a serious insult.

The publicist was a small, wiry man with a beard and steel-rimmed spectacles. He smiled all the time or, rather, grimaced nervously as if he was afraid of being hit. The fact that he was sitting next to Malcolm Priest may have had something to do with this.

The tool perched on a tall stool by the bar, sulking and eating peanuts from a dish. Billy, Priest and Boswell occupied a table by the window. Priest sat with his back to the window, enabling him to take in Billy, the restaurant around him and the entrance to his right at a single glance. Priest was about fifty-five, of medium height, with enormous hands and shoulders, a big belly and no neck. He stank of cigars and expensive aftershave. With his garishly dyed chestnut hair and unfeasibly rosy cheeks, he appeared to have received a makeover from the same under-taker that had humiliated Billy's Uncle Ted.

As is the case with many hardened criminals, Priest's face was almost comically brutal. But what prevented you from laughing, apart from the obvious desire to escape physical pain, was the sheer presence of the man. It wasn't so much charisma, as an all-pervading psychic stench that emanated from his massive frame in slow, steady waves and proclaimed: 'I could hurt you. I would probably enjoy hurting you. I hurt people all the time.'

Billy was a little frightened of Malcolm Priest. When Billy was frightened, he attacked. The interview got off to a bad start. His first question was, 'Who's your favourite philosopher?'

Priest stared at Billy, very much as one would stare at a spunk stain on a hotel bedspread. Twenty seconds passed before Priest spoke. 'Are you a Jewboy?' he said. 'I don't mind. I'm just asking.'

'None of your business,' said Billy.

'That question you asked me. It struck me as a very Hebrew type of question. Don't get me wrong. I've nothing against Jews. I just think they should go back to the Old Testament.'

Noticing that the tape was running, Boswell chipped in with: 'Mal isn't a racist.'

'Racialist?' said Priest, mishearing. 'How could I be racialist? I've done more for work-shy immigrants than any other bastard going. I've given millions to boys' clubs in the Manchester area. I've even raised money for a charity that makes cups of tea for dying queers. How could I be prejudiced? I'm asking you. How?'

'I don't know,' said Billy carefully.

'I suddenly thought of all the people who'd crossed you and won't be getting out of bed ever again.'

Priest held up his fist. 'Most ordinary tossers don't go in for violence. If they do, they stop if they're bleeding or if they've made the other fucker bleed. Now, that's the difference, you see. Because I don't stop. I carry on 'til the other bastards have got no fucking blood left. But I'm warning you: if you write that down, you'll get the same.'

Rather stupidly, Billy said, 'How do you know you'd win?'

Priest frowned. 'What are you on about?'

'If you tried to kill me, how do you know you'd win?'

Priest laughed incredulously. 'You fucking what?'

Tight-lipped, Boswell said, 'That's it. The interview's over.'

Priest held up a hand to silence his publicist. 'Just one fucking second. Let me get this clear in me mind. Are you saying that if we had a fight, you and me, face-to-face . . . are you saying you could take me?'

Billy lowered his gaze, having read somewhere that gorillas were provoked by direct eye contact. 'I'm making no special claims for myself. You're a big guy. But, you know, I might get lucky. People *do* get lucky.'

Deadpan, Priest said, 'Not people like you.'

Of all the gangster's taunts, this proved to be the

most effective. In his heart, Billy Dye had always felt cursed. Billy was strange, and strangeness was a curse in itself. He didn't wear women's clothes, or lust after animals, or smear himself with strawberry jam whenever the moon was full. But virtually every day he thought about all the people who had died and turned into spirits. He also wrote horror stories. Few people think about the spirits of the dead and fewer still read horror stories, so the market for Billy's books, and indeed Billy himself, was alarmingly small. By suggesting that the writer was not lucky, indeed would *never* be lucky, Priest was echoing Billy's deepest fear.

There was a long silence, which Billy broke by asking his final question: 'Have you any unfulfilled ambitions?'

Priest considered this for a moment. 'Yes,' he said eventually. 'I'd like to burn the city of Liverpool to the ground.'

'Why?'

'What do you mean, why? Have you never been there?'

That night, at his old, crumbling house in Albert Road, Billy played the interview back twice. After the first hearing, he felt dirty and ashamed. It seemed to him that he'd let Priest off lightly, allowing fat Mal to dodge all but his most trivial questions. In

bones and fine, chiselled features. He was a detective constable in the drug squad, who was unlikely to be promoted in his lifetime because of his aversion to responsibility and his advanced cocaine habit. Tony had just come off duty. Early that morning he'd been entrusted to unload a vast hoard of illegal substances from the safe and drive them to the incinerator. But only half of the consignment had perished in the flames. The remaining half, inexplicably, had remained in the boot of Tony's Vauxhall Cavalier, and was now on sale to his family and friends. But today Billy wasn't buying.

'You can afford it,' mocked Tony.

'Tony,' said Billy. 'I probably could afford it if I wanted to. But I've gone off drugs. I don't like the associations.'

'Which association? The "Association of Corrupt Police Officers"?'

'I mean I distrust my reasons for taking artificial stimulants.'

Tony sucked so hard on the spliff that it shrank by a full inch. 'Bill, you're just depressed because your bird's walked out on you. But you know, I have to be honest, Nikki may have been nice-looking, but she had no tits. So in some ways, it's really a blessing.' Tony meant this kindly, but Billy wasn't impressed. Tony persevered. 'What reasons?'

'Eh?'

'What reasons do you distrust?'

'Well, you know, even with dope, I used to get little insights.'

Tony looked sceptical.

Billy said, 'I'm talking about listening to a stream and hearing music ... seeing trees as shimmering living beings.'

'Oh, for fuck's sake.'

'You've never experienced that? You've never got into trees or music by smoking dope?'

Tony laughed and shook his head. 'I think you're missing the whole point of drugs, Bill. They're not for getting into things. They're for getting *out* of things. That's why they're called *recreational*.'

Billy was on the verge of making a winning point about 'learning through play' when he realized that he wouldn't win, because Tony wouldn't know what he was talking about. Billy had given Tony signed copies of all his books, but his friend had never been able to finish them. Tony's primary criticism was that the stories started well, but then Billy always had to ruin things by bringing the dead to life. Tony, who had seen numerous corpses in the course of his police career, had never yet known one to rise from the mortuary slab. Because of this, he thought Billy's books lacked realism. Tony, without knowing it, was an existentialist, believing that people were born, lived rotten lives, then died.

Billy believed this too, but he also believed that when their rotten lives were over, the spirits of human beings lived on. In other words, Billy believed that we possess the potential to be rotten for all eternity. At the beginning of the twenty-first century, it wasn't fashionable to believe in eternal life. It was only considered hip to take drugs, to be under twenty-five and to be somehow connected with either the music business, Hollywood or the fashion industry. In that order.

Tony and Billy were sharing a joint in a wine bar in St Anne's Square. Billy had bad memories of this bar, because it was here, in 1985, that he had picked a fight with a Manchester group called New Order. That unhappy meeting had represented Billy's first job in journalism. New Order had just released a new album, which Billy hadn't bothered to listen to, on principle. The band's manager had refused to give Billy a free copy and Billy, being poor, didn't want to waste money on a record that he instinctively knew would be crap.

The band, hostile from the outset, quickly realized that Billy hadn't heard their newest dirges. Bass player Peter Hook accused Billy of asking dumb questions and Billy challenged him to a fight. Peter Hook, who would probably have won, didn't take him up on the offer. Billy went away and wrote an article about how badly he'd got on with New Order.

Despite this, Billy didn't hate New Order, feeling that they had merely prejudged him as he'd prejudged them. However, he despised the wine bar that had witnessed his worst-ever performance as a journalist, feeling that the bar had stood by while he made a tit of himself and done nothing to intervene. Billy was funny that way. He could forgive people, but not places.

'So you're really giving up dope? I don't believe you.' Tony seemed to find this notion irritating.

'I'm just sick of feeling ill,' said Billy. 'I go to bed tired and wake up tired. I'm knackered all the time and I'm only thirty-two.'

'It's normal to be knackered,' argued Tony. 'Every bastard in the CID is knackered.'

Before answering, Billy stared at a miniature Christmas tree that was standing on the bar. The tree represented the proprietor's sole attempt at seasonal decor. As well as being ugly and misshapen, the tree was about nine inches tall, and draped in a single strand of tinsel. It was a veritable 'Reader's Wife' of Christmas trees. Finally, Billy said, 'Of course you're all knackered. You spend all your free time drinking, smoking and masturbating to hard-core pornography.'

'Not just our free time,' admitted Tony. 'If you're undercover, like I am, you tend to masturbate on duty. In fact, it's required behaviour.'

'Well, you know, I'd just like to know what it feels like to be *healthy*.'

Tony nodded to the whisky and soda in Billy's

children of tattooed scum. He'd been ripped off at the Hacienda and chased down Oxford Road at two a.m. by angry murderers with nothing to do.

Manchester made Billy feel alive. It was where he belonged. If outsiders criticized his city, Billy automatically leapt to its defence. And so it was that criminals from Manchester interested him more than criminals from anywhere else in the world.

A week before Christmas, the same week that Billy's girlfriend left him and his fourth novel came out to absolutely no reviews, he received an unexpected phone call from Malcolm Priest. Like many of the city's native inhabitants, Priest was obese with rosy cheeks and continued to support Manchester City Football Club in the face of all the evidence. But Priest was a famous gangster. His gang, the Priesthood, controlled Greater Manchester and Priest, it was said, ruled his men with Procrustean might.

The voice on the phone matched the photographs Billy had seen: wheezy, high-pitched, thick with phlegm and bravado.

'I believe you've been trying to get a fucking, whadyacallit, interview with me,' Priest ventured flatly.

This was true. Like most people of low character, Priest had a personal publicist, an embittered ex-teacher called Boswell who used his inability to form lasting relationships as an excuse for failing to return

1

Although every word of this story is as true as despair,
I do not expect people to believe it.
'Man-Size In Marble', E. Nesbit

Billy hated Manchester. He hated Piccadilly Station, the Royal Exchange Theatre and the way the windows didn't open in the Malmaison Hotel. He hated TV presenters from Manchester, especially Tony Wilson. He hated Manchester United, Manchester City and all their supporters. He hated popular Manchester double acts including Little and Large, Brian and Michael, Stalker and Anderton. He hated the Arndale Centre, before and after the IRA bomb. He hated Manchester's soot-blackened buildings, its unwelcoming faces, the promise of imminent drownings that drifted up from its reeking canal.

But hating Manchester was Billy Dye's God-given right, because he was born there. He'd grown up inhaling Father Christmas's beery breath in Lewis's department store. Perverts had stalked him in Piccadilly Gardens. At Belle Vue he'd been spat on by the

hand. 'I notice you're not giving up booze. Isn't booze unhealthy?'

'I'll give up booze eventually.' (Tony was already jeering.) 'One vice at a time.'

They were silent for a while, each entering that gloomy period of daytime drinking when life seems to consist of nothing but headaches and urinals. Tiring of the silence, Tony said, 'Had any exciting adventures lately?'

Flattered to be asked, Billy told his friend how, the previous month, he'd scored an exclusive interview with Malcolm Priest. 'It was weird to be close to someone so evil. And, you know, it struck me what a pure life I lead. I mean, I've never even had a parking ticket!'

'You've never had a fucking car.'

'No, listen, listen . . . I always imagined I was living life on the edge. But you know what? It was the edge of a pedestrian crossing. And I never stepped over the edge until I'd looked right, looked left and right again. I thought I was Jim Morrison. It turns out I'm fucking Tufty!'

'Who?'

'Tufty? The road safety-conscious squirrel who ran the Tufty Club? Oh, forget it.'

'You must at least have been busted.'

'Never. I haven't been in any real trouble since I was at school.'

'What trouble was this?' asked Tony, suddenly reminding Billy of all the police officers who'd ever stopped and searched him. ('This may seem like a funny question, sir, but would you happen to have a criminal record?' *Yes, Officer. 'Crazy Horses' by the Osmonds.*)

'My best mate stabbed someone.'

'Nice mate.'

'He was a lot nicer than the stupid bastard coppers who came round to question me about it.'

Tony didn't think this counted as trouble. Then Billy told Tony about the damning article he'd written about Priest. Tony's mouth dropped open. He thought this was *real* trouble. 'You're joking, aren't you?'

'No.'

'Then you're insane. You've got to be. He'll fucking kill you.'

'He wouldn't dare.'

'What makes you say that?'

'The power of the press.'

Tony was stunned by his friend's naivety. 'What power? When Priest puts out a contract on you, do you think the NUJ is going to post a picket line outside your front door?'

'No . . . he's not going to be bothered by a shitty magazine article.'

'Billy, wake up. We're talking about a guy who'd

Billy was confused. 'So why are you talking to me?'

'Because you once wrote a very nice article about an old Man City player called Francis Lee.'

'You're joking, aren't you?'

'No. Francis happens to be a hero of mine. He played for the club in the days when City were kings.'

Billy was amazed. 'So that's why I'm here? Because I got pissed in a bar with an old footballer?'

Priest sneered broadly. 'Well, you're certainly not here for your good looks.' There was a silence. Priest made a great show of looking at his watch. 'Five fucking minutes and he's already run out of questions.'

'How do you think you gained a reputation as a gangster?'

'God help us,' said Priest wearily, pausing to light a slim panatella. 'How the fuck do you think, you gormless twat?'

'So you're an habitual law-breaker?' said Billy. This wasn't the way Billy talked normally. He was quoting from an old *Thomas the Tank Engine* video, just to see if Priest noticed. But Priest obviously wasn't a *Thomas* fan.

'In the past I've broken the law. I hold my hand up,' Priest pronounced, exposing a plump, pink palm. 'I was born and raised in Hulme. It's a poor area. When we were kids, we had nothing. We didn't know we had nothing, because everyone around us had nothing. It wasn't my mam and dad's fault. They were good people who worked hard all their lives. And what reward did they get for their efforts? A few fucking pennies.'

There followed a dull, sentimental speech about how Priest's father had died tragically young at the age of sixty-seven, and had therefore not lived to see his son get a director's box at Manchester City. 'The old fella never saw me make it big. He would have been proud. I've got more money than anyone in the fucking history of Manchester. I've got a fucking yacht that's wider than Oxford Road. I could move to Portugal tomorrow if I wanted to. I could fucking *buy* Portugal. I could buy anything I like, including you.'

'So you like me?'

Priest laughed. 'You fucking what?'

'You just said you could buy anything you liked. So you must like me.'

'I can't fucking stand you, you ugly twat.'

'Do you admit to being a criminal?'

'I am *the* fucking criminal, pal. There's no one else.'

'And you've got a gang. Called the Priesthood.'

'Gang! It's a fucking *movement*.' He smirked at Boswell, who was lost in his own dismal thoughts. The tool smiled and nodded, as if to say, 'Nice one.'

glared down at him, then at Priest, waiting for a sign, any sign, that his boss wanted the journalist dismembered. But Priest, smiling like a malignant Buddha, dismissed his employee with a single shake of his head. Visibly deflated, the tool retreated.

Hoping to ease the tension, Boswell opened a packet of McVitie's Ginger Nuts and offered one to Billy. Billy didn't like ginger nuts, but ate one anyway. 'So how would you describe yourself?' he began tentatively.

'Very fat and very ugly,' Priest replied. 'How would you describe yourself?'

Unable to think of an original reply, Billy said, 'More popular than Jesus.'

Then Priest surprised Billy by saying, 'That's a fucking lie for a start. *No way* are you fucking popular. Your only mate is a *copper*. Which, let's face it, is equivalent to having no mates at all. No one likes you.'

Struggling to retain his composure, Billy said, 'I'm the sort of person who's only popular in retrospect.' He suddenly remembered to feel indignant. 'How do you know nobody likes me?'

'I made enquiries. And what I found out was that you're a fucking pauper. The only reason you've got a roof over your head is that your grandma died and left you her fucking house. You're a cheeky, annoying little prat.'

Priest detected the nuance. 'What do you mean you don't know?' he demanded.

'Mal isn't prejudiced. No way is he,' insisted Boswell.

'Don't think you can be fucking clever with me, pal,' warned Priest mildly. 'I named this restaurant after a wog. Moroccans are wogs, aren't they?' To prove his point, he handed Billy a promotional book of matches bearing a crude caricature of an Arab in a fez. Trying not to laugh, Billy slipped the matches into his pocket.

'I'm telling you,' Priest expounded. 'You could be any nationality sitting there and I wouldn't turn a hair. Wouldn't matter one iota. In fact, the only reason blacks don't come here is they can't afford white man's prices.'

Billy glanced at the tape recorder, glad that he was getting all this down.

Priest saw the look and leaned forward, or as far forward as his belly would allow. There was no malice in his eyes, just candour and mild amusement. 'A friendly warning, pal. Don't get on the wrong side of me. You wouldn't want me as an enemy, believe me.'

The words left Billy's mouth before he'd had time to think. 'I certainly wouldn't want you as a friend.'

Boswell turned as pale as a giro. The tool on the stool, who hadn't appeared to be listening, suddenly bounced off his perch and strode over to Billy. He

Priest rose slightly and leaned in Billy's direction, so that his paunch rested on the white tablecloth. He leant so close that Billy smelt his stinking cigar breath. Priest said, 'Which part of "fuck off" don't you understand?'

'How much money have you got?' Billy asked Priest.

'A fuck of a lot more than you.'

'It shows, does it?'

'It bloody does,' said Priest. 'In fact, when you walked in here, I thought you were about to sell me the *Big Issue*.' Priest nodded to the black skull ring on Billy's finger. 'I mean, look what you've got on your fucking hand! Looks like it came from a lucky bag.'

Billy yawned. But Priest hadn't finished. 'Who's this article for?'

'*Blag*. It's a men's fashion magazine. '

Boswell nodded in enthusiasm. 'A good mag. No two ways about it.'

Priest couldn't have cared less. 'And what'll you get paid?'

'Depends how long the piece is. Maybe five hundred quid.'

'Is that all? I wouldn't get out of bed for that.'

'Have you ever killed anyone?'

Priest smirked. 'Ooh! What a seamless segue! How did me saying I wouldn't get out of bed lead to you asking me that?'

'Yet you've only been to prison once,' said Billy. 'Why *is* that?'

'Because I've got money and people are afraid of me. So I've always been able to find sad silly arse-holes who'll do my time for me. But if you write any of this down, you'll spend Christmas in a fucking coffin.'

'So you don't want to talk about crime. What *do* you want to talk about?'

Without warning, the evil, comical face assumed an attitude of piety. 'I've done a fuck of a lot for charity. It's about time the press and the public took notice of the fact.'

For the next eight minutes, Priest talked about his work for the handicapped. Not the people he'd personally helped to handicap, but those little kiddies in leg-irons that all born bastards profess to love. 'It breaks my heart,' Priest concluded, 'it breaks my heart to look at those kids. But someone's got to do it.'

After a disrespectful silence, Billy said, 'Would it be fair to say that you've got friends in the police?'

'I have friends everywhere, pal. I've been lucky. No doubt about it.'

'And did you send Derek Parks, Deputy Chief Constable of the Greater Manchester Police, to Jamaica after his wife died?'

'Fuck off.'

'Is Mr Parks a friend of yours?'

11

called out the Gas Board many times. A succession of disgruntled men had turned up to investigate the suspected leak. Nothing had ever been found. Billy had long resigned himself to the fact that whereas some houses smelled of toast or violets, his stank of gas and dog turds.

Billy made himself some tea. His favourite brand was Twinings Lady Grey, but he was ashamed of drinking a beverage with such an effeminate name, so he stored the tea in a PG Tips tin. While the tea was brewing, he glanced at the clock. It was five past four. Paul Tinker, editor of *Blag*, would just have returned from lunch. Billy picked up the phone and dialled Tinker's direct number. Tinker picked up the phone and said what he always said: 'Editor.'

Billy gave his usual response. 'I'm not the editor. I'm just a poor bastard who writes for the editor.'

'Dye,' said Tinker, recognizing at once his only northern contributor. Although Tinker came from Hull, the few pages of his magazine that actually contained articles were mainly filled by public school boys and London yobs. 'I never thanked you for the gangster thing. Good work. I've been meaning to talk to you about it—'

'That's what I was ringing about. I wonder if it's too late to make a few tiny adjustments?'

Tinker grunted as if he'd been punched in the gut. 'Well, it is really. The mag's already out.'

Billy felt dizzy. For a split second he saw himself

25

on a hospital ventilator, grief-stricken relatives sobbing and praying by his bedside. 'It's what? Say that again.'

Talking over him, Tinker said, 'We put it out early so we could all enjoy Christmas more. But listen . . . can't talk now. I'm in the middle of a meeting. I'll call you soon and we'll sort out a lunch. When are you next in London?'

But Billy had already replaced the receiver. He went into his front room, turned on his PC and opened the file that contained his interview with Priest. Finding it difficult to breathe, he reread the article at speed, willing it to be as hollow and anodyne as an interview in *Hello!* Unfortunately the piece was even more scurrilous than he'd remembered.

It was no use pretending. Tony was right. Billy had been foolish. He had performed a hatchet job on a man who was famous for despatching his enemies with a hatchet. What had he been thinking of? Was his life really so miserable and unfulfilled that he'd unconsciously contrived to end it?

He had no escape route planned. He had no money and no car. His first blind instinct was to go and stay with his sister Carole in Disley. He and Carole didn't get on. She thought he was a lazy, foul-mouthed nihilist who shirked responsibility. He thought she was a fat-bottomed traditionalist who admired the queen. They were both right.

2

I fled in vain. My evil destiny pursued me as if in exultation,
and proved, indeed, that the exercise of its mysterious
dominion had as yet only begun.
'William Wilson', Edgar Allen Poe

Tony waved his hand in front of Billy's face. 'Hello?
Anyone home?'

Billy coughed out a cloud of perfumed smoke and
absent-mindedly passed the spliff back to Tony.
Tony noticed the glazed expression in his friend's
eyes and gave Billy a nudge. 'Bill? You OK?'

Billy shivered. 'Yeah. I just had this really weird
rush. I thought I saw something . . .'

Tony laughed dismissively. 'Like I said, it's one-
hit-shit. Which is why it's going for one thirty an
ounce.'

'I can't afford it,' said Billy.

'One twenty and I'm robbing myself.'

'Tony, how could you be robbing yourself? That
shit didn't cost you anything. You fucking *stole* it.'

Tony was a small, angular man, with high cheek-

short, Billy thought that he'd failed as a journalist. Now failing as a journalist is not necessarily a cause for self-reproach. One can fail as a journalist and still succeed as a human being. Yet Billy, who expected too much from himself, felt that he'd failed on both counts.

But later, listening again with a couple of shots of rum under his belt, he realized that if he left in all the things Priest had warned him to leave out, the article could be salvaged. Fuelled by alcohol and misguided enthusiasm, he set to work. By two a.m. the article was complete. It contained all the bragging, the insults and the blustering threats and was more than enough to consolidate Malcolm Priest's reputation as a vicious parasite. Elated, but too pissed to stand up, Billy lay down on the sofa and closed his eyes.

Despite Carole's conformity, or perhaps because of it, she had invited him to stay with her for Christmas. His sister had heard about Nikki walking out on him and without saying so, obviously pitied him. Billy, who was proud, found sympathy profoundly insulting and had already turned the invitation down.

Yet suddenly the prospect of spitting out date stones in Disley seemed very attractive, or at least more attractive than the prospect of spitting out teeth in Levenshulme. The house in Albert Road was neither cosy nor comforting. He'd always been scared of the attic. And what about that shadow by the wardrobe in his bedroom? He had often awoken in the night and mistaken the shadow for his dead grandmother. It wasn't his grandmother, it was only a shadow. But it troubled him.

He stashed some clothes into a holdall, remembering at the last moment to pack his mobile phone and the Christmas presents he'd bought for Carole's boys. As an afterthought, he took his notebook and a pen. After all, he was supposed to be a writer. Then he locked up the house and stepped out into the freezing fog.

He could barely see for more than three yards in any direction. Cars crawled by at ten miles an hour, their approaching lights like spreading yellow stains in the murk. All the way to the station he kept glancing behind him, convinced that someone was following him. Then he reminded himself that it was only five in the evening, and that wherever he walked, there would be people before and behind him. But where were they? In the fog, the world seemed silent and empty.

On the station platform, he began to feel the cold. He was wearing a leather jacket that was two sizes too big for him. Refrigerated air circulated freely between its lining and his thin sweater. The train was twenty minutes late and when it arrived, it was crowded to capacity.

But Billy was reassured by the tightly packed strangers, their shopping bags and their knackered end-of-day faces. None of them looked like Priest or his minions. They were mostly ordinary, unremarkable citizens who would leave the world as anonymously as they'd entered it. Then again, none of them would set fire to an enemy's pubic hair with a blowtorch.

Because of the fog, a journey that should have lasted an hour took ninety minutes. As the train pulled into Disley Billy began to feel safe. He found it impossible to imagine Priest's men roaming this predominantly middle-class village on the rim of the Derbyshire hills.

Walking out of the station he felt a familiar sense of loss. Steve Ellis, the friend he'd told Tony about, had lived in Disley. Steve had been adopted by an affluent couple. Shortly after his arrival at Manchester Grammar School, Steve had adopted Billy. Steve was the hardest kid in school. Billy was the cheekiest. Steve used to beat up sixth-formers, and Billy made jokes about them when they were lying on the ground.

But there had been a sensitive side to Steve that few had known about. He was obsessed with finding his real mother, and fantasized endlessly about where she lived and what she might be like. He loved classic stories of the supernatural and could quote verbatim from his favourite novels, *Dracula* and *Frankenstein*. He was acutely perceptive and always knew what those around him were thinking and feeling.

Billy and Steve had been as close as two boys can be without kissing. Their lives and dreams were interfluent. The skull ring on Billy's finger had been a birthday present from Steve. The ancients believed that the ring finger was connected directly to the heart. The ache that Billy felt when he touched the ring lent credence to this myth.

Billy had only seen his old friend once since the night of the stabbing. They met one night in a city centre pub when Steve was out on parole. Steve had been surrounded by slightly younger boys, the kind of kids who tattooed the back of their hands with a pin and a ballpoint pen. Billy had been alone. Steve's greeting had been a nod and a slightly contemptuous smirk. The smirk seemed to say: 'I stabbed someone. I went to prison and survived. I'm harder than you'll ever be.'

Billy's sister lived in an affluent, leafy avenue near Lyme Park. As Billy approached Carole's house and saw the Christmas lights hanging in the trees at the end of the drive, he began to wonder whether he'd done the right thing. He rang the doorbell. Carole, always older and more twitchy than he remembered, opened the door. She was surprised but genuinely pleased to see him. Her husband Roger emerged from the kitchen to shake Billy's hand before offering him a can of Boddingtons.

Billy drank the beer in the living room, under the Christmas tree, while his nephews, Mark and Chris, proudly informed Billy that they'd found a review of his last book. 'It was on the internet,' enthused Mark, the elder. 'It said it was really bad.'

Chris corrected him. 'No, it just said it was boring.'

'Well, thanks, guys,' said Billy. 'I suppose it must be quite a thrill for you to have such a successful uncle.'

Later that evening, true to form, Billy began to outstay his welcome. When the boys had gone to bed and Carole was busy in the kitchen, Roger poured a brandy for Billy and himself. Billy's brother-in-law had a round, florid face that looked as if it had never needed shaving and a full head of immaculately white hair.

Roger, a scoutmaster, mentioned that he was getting a biography of Baden-Powell for Christmas. Baden-Powell, according to Roger, had always done his duty. Billy reminded Roger that on one occasion, Baden-Powell had hanged a man for stealing a goat. 'Ah,' said Roger, 'that only illustrates my point.'

'I wonder if he awarded himself a "hanging badge",' mused Billy.

'He did his duty,' reaffirmed Roger stiffly.

'But why did the man he hanged steal the goat in the first place?' wondered Billy. 'Maybe his family were starving and he felt it was his *duty* to feed them.'

'Now, let's be careful,' said Roger. 'We're talking about a great man, here.'

'So why did Baden-Powell hang him?'

Carole and her husband went to bed at ten o'clock. Billy went to bed half an hour later, feeling about twelve years old. Mainly because he was lying in a bed that belonged to his twelve-year-old nephew. The bedroom walls were covered with *South Park* posters and pictures of Manchester United strikers. So there he was, a grown man, asleep in a child's bed in a warm, middle-class house that was swaddled in silence and fog.

Billy lay awake for a long time, thinking of the terror and disbelief that must run through a man's mind when he thinks he's in for a flogging and learns that he's actually going to be executed. And it occurred to him that although he wrote horror stories, nothing he ever imagined was quite as horrible as reality. With this unhappy thought, he fell asleep.

When he awoke, there were two men standing in the room. Big men in expensive overcoats. Billy recognized one of them as the bruiser from Priest's restaurant. The other had bright ginger hair, a dimpled chin and a vaguely apologetic expression. 'Mr Dye? I'm Graham Wain. Also known as the Beast. I work for Mr Malcolm Priest and he's very keen to talk to you.'

'What the fuck . . . how did you get in?'

The Beast nodded at his companion. 'This is Heidi. He's got a way with locks.'

Billy was now wide awake. He felt sick with fear, yet still found it in himself to sneer. 'Heidi? Like the little Swiss girl?'

'Fucking watch it,' warned Heidi, colouring instantly, like an exotic fish.

Billy was now wide awake. The Beast coughed and smiled politely.

'Get dressed, would you? Best not to keep Mr Priest waiting.'

'My mum always advised me not to go anywhere with strange men. Especially in the middle of the night.'

The ginger man wrenched open the curtains. Daylight seared Billy's eyes. 'It's eleven o'clock in the morning.'

'You idle prat,' added Heidi.

Billy suddenly remembered his sister and her family. 'If you've hurt anyone in this house, I'll fucking—'

The Beast held out a restraining hand. His voice was soft and guttural. Billy had to strain to hear what he was saying. 'Hey! Hey! No one's hurt nobody. Your nice clean relatives have fucked off to the shops in their nice shiny people carrier. There's only us here. Now get dressed, there's a good lad.'

Billy said, 'Any chance of a bit of privacy?'

The two thugs left the room, keeping the bedroom door ajar so that they had a view of Billy's window. He dressed slowly, scanning the room for some kind of weapon. All he could find was a small dark hunk of mineral, a souvenir from the Blue John mine. Someone had once told him that a fist, sufficiently weighted, can break an opponent's jaw. Billy now saw an opportunity to put this theory to the test. He wrapped a sweating palm around the rock and stepped out onto the landing.

Outside the fog had lifted. It was a grey, overcast day. A mud-spattered Jag was parked in front of the house. Priest's men walked on either side of Billy, dwarfing him, carrying themselves with the uniquely irritating nonchalance that comes of a lifetime of gazing down at the top of people's heads. When they reached the car, Billy let a pound coin fall from his pocket to the ground. As Heidi looked down, Billy swung back his arm and bashed the rock as hard as he could against Heidi's temple.

The gangster's eyes widened in surprise, but he didn't fall. Instantly, almost as a reflex, he lashed out with the back of his hand and sent Billy sprawling. At first the Beast was too startled to react. Then he guffawed, amazed by Billy's preposterous behaviour.

Heidi had hit Billy hard. So hard that for a few moments the ground beneath him felt as comfortable and welcoming as a sprung mattress. He lay there for a few moments, recuperating while the Beast struggled to restrain Heidi, who was eager to finish what Billy had started.

'I'll rip his fucking head off!' said Heidi through clenched teeth.

'Heidi – will you – will you quit it? Malcolm wants him in one piece.'

Billy felt sure that this could only mean one thing. Priest wanted to do the job with his own sweet hands.

The Beast separated the lump of crystal from Billy's fingers, regarded it with a frown and dropped it into his overcoat pocket. Then he steered Billy, now too dazed to resist, into the back of the car. Billy sat back in the squeaking upholstery as Heidi cursed and examined his face in the rear-view mirror. A purple lump had appeared above his right eye. He caught Billy's reflection in the mirror and swore dark vengeance.

As the car moved off, the Beast, trying not to laugh, turned to Billy. 'You're a bit of a rum cunt, aren't you? Are you on drugs or something?'

It was Christmas Eve. The traffic on the A6 was almost at a standstill. A family trudged by: father, mother and a young boy. The father feigned a kick at the child's arse and the mother slapped her husband on the back. As the father laughed, he peered into the crawling Jag, looking straight into Billy's eyes.

It crossed Billy's mind to gesticulate wildly, shouting, fighting, screaming for help. But he couldn't be bothered, feeling that such a display would be beneath his dignity. Worse, there was a strong possibility that the stranger would dismiss Billy's frantic antics as irrelevant, none of his business.

The Jag turned off the main road and swept through the wrought-iron gates of Lyme Park. Billy was puzzled by this. Lyme Park was a tourist attraction, a public place. If Priest was waiting for him here, surely he was rash to the point of insanity?

But the park was almost deserted. Only sheep and

deer witnessed the car's languid approach. Billy knew the winding road that led to Lyme Hall from his childhood. He had always associated it with holiday outings, ice creams and picnics. Not mutilation or violent death.

As the car passed under Cage Hill, Heidi gently applied the brakes. All three men got out of the car. Billy tried to make a run for it, but Heidi, anticipating the move, grabbed his jacket just in time. The Beast started to laugh again. 'He doesn't like us much, does he?' Heidi kept hold of Billy's coat, using it to propel him forward. 'Walk,' commanded Heidi. The Beast chuckled softly to himself.

Billy was really scared now. The cold, damp Derbyshire air, lightly scented with sheep shit, froze his face and ears as they climbed. Lyme Cage, a grim conical watchtower on the summit of a gently sloping hill, was a local landmark. As a boy Billy had been frightened of the Cage, without ever knowing why. And now he knew. This was where he would lose his life or, if he was lucky, his face.

When they reached the summit, a familiar stout figure emerged from the concealed side of the tower. It was Malcolm Priest, wrapped in a voluminous sheepskin overcoat. His vindictive face was framed by a fur-lined trapper's hat and he was smiling. His cheeks were bruised blue by the biting cold. Billy looked down and was startled to see that Priest was accompanied by a dwarf. He looked again and saw that it was a child, a little girl of about seven. She was fair-haired with blue accusatory eyes and a prim, delicate mouth.

'My granddaughter,' explained Priest proudly. He took the child's gloved hand and squeezed it.

Billy was flooded by a relief so profound that he could have walked over to Priest and kissed him. This wasn't an execution or a punishment beating. It was something else entirely. Heidi shoved Billy forward. Billy skidded in the mud, almost losing his balance. When he saw this, Priest turned to the girl. 'All right, my love? You go and play. But stay where I can see you.'

The child wandered off. Priest walked up to Heidi and gave him an insulting slap on the chest. 'Hey! What's going on? Keep your hands to yourself, you stupid bloody article.'

'He *attacked* me, Mr Priest.'

'I don't care. The size of you and the size of him?' Priest stood on tiptoe, grabbed one of Heidi's jowls and twisted it fiercely. Heidi, who was by no means a weak man, blushed and cowered. Then Priest turned to the Beast. 'And you, you big ginger twat! You're supposed to be in charge.'

The Beast extended his hands in an attitude of helplessness.

Priest turned his back on the two men. 'Go! Out of my sight, the pair of you.'

The two tall thugs marched stiffly down the hill.

Priest looked at Billy for the first time. 'Come on then.'

'Where're we going?'

Priest grimaced. 'Do you mean they didn't tell you?'

Billy said, 'I thought I was in some kind of trouble.'

Priest showed a fresh surge of anger. 'I've got morons working for me. Morons!'

'I don't mean to be picky, but I think you'll find they're imbeciles. They're not bright enough to be morons.'

Priest forced a laugh as he rejoined his grand-daughter. 'This is Judith. She and I are special friends, aren't we, petal?'

The girl glared at Billy and nodded solemnly, as if daring him to disagree.

Priest's Rolls-Royce Silver Seraph, with the regis-tration plate MALP1, waited in the car park. Judith sat in the front beside her grandfather. Billy had the back seat to himself. A miniature TV screen had been installed in the rear of the front passenger seat. Priest produced a flask of steaming oxtail soup, filled a cup and passed it to the girl. Then he did the same for Billy. 'So,' said Priest, raising his cup to Billy, 'thanks for writing that smashing article.'

'Ah. Well, the less said about that . . .'

Priest craned his neck to look into Billy's eyes. He looked puzzled. 'Didn't you think it was any good?'

'Why? Did you?'

'I think it's great. The best bit of journalism I've ever seen done about me. What's more, everyone I know says the same. I know I took the Michael a bit, and I must say you ask for it. But, you know, fair's fair, you did a fine job of reporting and I'd like you to work for me.'

Billy had a flash of déjà vu. The soup, the plush car, Priest's beaming face. He'd seen it all before. 'What? As a gangster?'

Priest showed a flicker of his former malice. 'No. As a writer, you gormless get.' Then, remembering that he was supposed to be wooing Billy, not insulting him, he quickly added, 'Yes, I'd like to offer you a job. I want you to write my autobiography.'

'I'd love to,' said Billy, without thinking.

Even though this news pleased Priest, his eyes remained cold, dead and soulless. 'In that case,' he said, 'I'd like to give you a little present. For Christmas.'

Priest passed the writer a cheque for £3,000.

'Is this a bribe?' asked Billy breathlessly.

'Call it a present,' said Priest with an unlikely smile. 'For Christmas.'

Judith kneeled on her seat and looked at Billy's face, giggling with delight at his pleasure and astonishment. Her face was transformed. She looked like a different child. Billy held the cheque in both hands and wondered.

3

*Yes, I think he has all the possibilities of a distinguished
criminal . . . I should be sorry for anyone who got
into his bad books.*
'Casting the Runes', M. R. James

When he realized that he was going to live, the
world briefly seemed very beautiful to Billy Dye. The
bleak muddy grass of Lyme Park, the Derbyshire
sky, the flesh beneath his fingernails – all were
presented anew in colours so intense they hurt his
eyes. Artificial stimulants aside, the world hadn't
looked so good since he was thirteen years old and
Gabrielle Town, the best-looking girl in Manchester,
had let him touch her perfectly round breasts on the
back row of the ABC Deansgate. For a whole week
Billy's world had shimmered with visionary light.
Then she had finished with him and the shadows of
ignorance and sleep had returned.

Billy saw that he himself was responsible for these
shadows; that with an effort of will he might live in
courageous happiness rather than buckle under the

dead weight of anxiety and bitterness that wearied his soul and fouled the taste of every waking day. But, as on TV, normal ugliness was resumed as soon as possible. In the space of fifteen minutes, the window that had opened inside him closed again and Billy awoke to the fact that he was lunching with a murderer at a pub in High Lane.

The pub was called the Red Lion. Because of the presence of his granddaughter, Priest was on his best behaviour. There was no swearing, very little boasting and Priest made only one threatening remark, this to the landlord. In a voice that resonated through the bar, Priest said, 'No offence, pal, but if the food we ordered doesn't turn up in one minute, I'll let the whole pub know you're wearing a wig.'

They passed an idle ninety minutes, after which Priest offered Billy a lift back to his sister's house. Billy declined, claiming to need the exercise. Before they parted, Priest opened the boot to get his de-icer and exposed a stack of magazines: about twenty copies of *Blag*. 'I got a good supply in,' he explained. 'For friends and business contacts, you know.'

'I haven't seen it myself yet,' Billy commented.

The hint wasn't lost on Priest, who pressed one fat, glossy magazine into Billy's arms. 'Happy Christmas. I'll be in touch in the New Year.'

As soon as Priest had driven away, Billy went back into the pub, ordered a shot of Rémy Martin, perched on a stool at the bar and read the article that had so impressed Manchester's number one. Its resemblance to the piece Billy had submitted was minimal.

The editor, afraid of offending a known psychopath, had halved a three-thousand-word exposé by excising all Priest's threats and racist gaffes and leaving him to describe, at length, his tireless work for charity and all the things he would have done for his father had the old man lived. It was an apologia for a monster, and it had Billy's name above it.

In a further act of unctuous homage, the article was complemented by a glossy photo-spread that Billy hadn't known about. It showed Priest modelling suits by an up-and-coming bespoke tailor while two attractive anorexics draped themselves over the gangster's broad shoulders and planted lipstick kisses on his fat, Manchester bastard face. Billy was both amused and relieved. By butchering his work, Paul Tinker had saved Billy's life. It was the first and last time Billy Dye would ever be grateful to an editor, for anything.

Billy didn't cash Priest's cheque. At least, not at first. He began by consulting his agent, Rosie Silkman. She was a large, pear-shaped woman with a small, apple-shaped head. Rosie had an office above a massage parlour in Soho. Billy often met red-faced civil servants on the stairs. On that rainy January day, the day that Billy Dye and Rosie Silkman met for the very last time, Billy felt certain that Rosie would urge him to tear up Priest's cheque and return to the serious, honourable business of writing novels that nobody read.

They had lunch at an Indian restaurant that was just around the corner from Rosie's office. Rosie and Billy were the only customers. After bringing Billy up to date with the achievements of her more successful clients, she fixed him with a basilisk stare as he was choking on an onion bhaji and said, 'Of course, you'd be absolutely crazy to turn down a chance like this. Um, I know you're not crazy, at least I don't think you are, which is why you'll say yes.'

After a fit of coughing, followed by several gulps of mineral water, Billy protested, 'But I don't do biography. I'm a horror writer.'

'Horror doesn't sell. As you know only too well.'

'Stephen King sells.'

Casually, with her mouth full, Rosie said, 'But you're not Stephen King.'

'Thanks, Rosie. Thanks for that marvellous vote of confidence.'

'Now, don't be silly. There's no shame in being versatile.'

'What the fuck are you talking about?'

'Exactly that. You write horror books, um, you're

a bloody good writer, um, world class in fact. Do you doubt for one second that I think that?' (Billy shrugged ungraciously.) 'But, um, look you've got more than one string to your bow, you're a journalist, you're perfectly capable of the discipline involved, um, plus I think I could get you a decent deal. '

'It'd have to be fucking gigantic.'

'Well, all I'd say to that is the biggest isn't necessarily the optimum.'

'What the fuck does that mean? Am I the only person alive who thinks you talk total bollocks?'

Billy and Rosie had established a recurring neurotic pattern: she as the overbearing mother, he as the rebellious ungrateful child. In fact, Billy was four months older than Rosie, although he would never have dreamed of telling her. She sighed and shook her head. 'You can be such a pain.'

There was a silence. A sulky waiter visited the table to refill their glasses with mineral water. At last, Billy spoke. 'So you really think you could sell a book about Malcolm Priest for lots of money?'

'Probably.'

'How much?'

She flicked back her hair brusquely. 'It isn't an exact science.'

'Rosie, why is it that whenever I ask you about money, you always act as if I'm asking personal questions? I am, of course. But as they're personal to me, there's really no fucking need for you to be offended.'

'I'm not.'

'Right, then. How much will you try to get?'

'Um, well, um, that would depend on, um, how big the publishing house was.'

'Rosie, did you know you say "um" a lot?'

'Do I?'

'All the, um, time.'

'And you wonder why you're not more success-ful?' asked Rosie wearily.

'Rosie, with you as my agent, why on earth would I wonder that?'

The insult struck home. The very next day, Rosie Silkman rang Billy at home and told him that if he ever spoke to her like that again, he could find a new agent. Billy desperately wanted to tell her to go fuck herself. But he didn't want to risk it. He was fairly certain that no other agent would have him.

An agreement was reached with depressing alacrity between the Rosie Silkman Agency, Priest's lawyer and Rathbone, Lewis & Fry of Bedford Square, Lon-don. Billy took the publisher's name as a favourable omen: Matthew Lewis was the author of a famous Gothic horror story called *The Monk*. Basil Rathbone starred in *Son of Frankenstein*. Fry's Turkish Delight was a well-known chocolate bar.

When he read the contract, Billy was astonished. This time Rosie Silkman had excelled herself. Malcolm Priest would grant Billy a weekly interview until Billy had ghostwritten his life story. While Billy worked on the book, Priest would pay two hundred and fifty pounds a week to Rosie Silkman, from which she would extract ten per cent plus tax. When the book was completed, it would become the joint property of Priest and his publisher. Billy would receive no credit for its authorship. Nor would he receive income from any feature film or Malcolm Priest cuddly toys that might result from the book's success.

As a deal, it stank. Billy didn't care. He would gladly have written the book for nothing. Although he despised himself for it, he was thrilled by the prospect of mixing with real gangsters.

The interview sessions took place at Priest's ranch-style bungalow in Knutsford. The house was situated in a wide, graceful avenue lined with larch trees and 'for sale' signs. At first, Billy didn't appreciate the significance of the 'for sale' signs. Knutsford was one of the most affluent towns in Cheshire. The writer Elizabeth Gaskell had modelled Cranford on Knutsford. One hundred and fifty years later, the town was still as snobbish, narrow and pretentious.

Malcolm Priest didn't know any of his immediate neighbours.

But they knew him.

Priest hated the ritual of talking into a tape recorder as much as Billy did, so to lessen their mutual boredom, the interview sessions sometimes overflowed into the wine bars and restaurants of Knutsford. As they sat at all the best tables, Priest abandoning his customary swagger as he fought to recall names and places from his family's past, Billy was very conscious of being stared at. Mostly by married women with sleek hair and gold jewellery that matched their tans. Everyone knew Priest, so to be seen with him, to be actually seen *interrupting* him as he stumbled over a fact, gave Billy an intoxicating taste of influence and power.

Malcolm Priest, like a pop star or a member of the royal family, never had to pay for anything. His address book bulged with the names and business cards of terrified associates who were eager to supply him with all the electrical goods, furniture, flowers, chocolates and alcohol he could ever need.

Since the demise of his marriage, Priest only had sex with prostitutes, or 'stinks' as they were known in the Priesthood. From the outset he made it clear that he could provide Billy with all the porn, drugs, or stinks he needed. 'All you have to do is ask. I persecute any bastard who steals from me, but ask and ye shall receive.'

Billy explained that he was trying to give up drugs and that porn had given him up. 'But if you could find me a beautiful, intelligent woman who's sexually compatible with me and never boring, I wouldn't ask for another thing.' Priest found this statement too abstruse, so ignored it and resumed his soliloquy. 'You want a gun? I'll get you one. DVD player? I'll get you two . . .'

His house possessed eight lavatories. There was a games room, where poker, pool and darts were played into the small hours, always for money. There were giant ashtrays in every room. The ashtrays were intended to be decorative as well as functional. 'See the Bell's Whisky one?' he said to Billy at their first session, 'it's shaped like a fucking big bell, see? You don't get that kind of craftsmanship any more.'

There were photographs of Priest's luxury yacht all over the house. Moored off the Algarve, the vessel was named the *Uncle Joe*, after Joe Royle, Manchester City Football Club's manager. To be offered a holiday aboard the *Uncle Joe* was at once an accolade and a damning curse: a guarantee that you would never be out of debt to Malcolm Priest for as long as you lived.

Although Priest had no taste, he was rich enough
to hire people who had. But he had a low opinion of
interior designers. 'They're all lezzies and bum boys.'
He'd filled his house with red leather armchairs and
had all the floors carpeted in dark brown to camou-
flage the piss and shit stains left by his mother's
incontinent toy poodle. The poodle was called
Lucky. 'Lucky not to have been tied up in a sack and
dropped in the fucking river,' remarked Priest.

The first time Billy met Priest's mother, she was so
startled that she almost dropped Lucky. The dog
snarled at Billy through bared yellow fangs. Because
Billy dressed like scum, Mrs Priest and the poodle
wrongly assumed that he *was* scum. Malcolm and
his boys may have robbed and terrorized law-abiding citizens. But, unlike Billy, they went to good
tailors and they always looked clean.

A fleet of classic cars crowded the curved gravel
drive. There was a Sunbeam Lotus, a Triumph TR7
and a Jaguar XK. The Rolls-Royce Silver Seraph that
had chauffeured Billy out of Lyme Park was complemented by a rose pink Corniche. When Billy was
late for their first interview because his bus hadn't
turned up, Priest lent him a five series BMW with a
dented wing but only thirty-five thousand miles on
the clock. 'You can use it while we're working on the

book.' (Priest pronounced the words 'book', 'cook', 'hook', 'took' and 'look' to rhyme with puke.)

Priest had a nasty and suspicious nature. To test the loyalty of those around him, he constantly laid traps around the house. On Billy's second visit to Knutsford, he went for a shit and found seven ten-pound notes pinned to a dartboard that was hanging on the lavatory door. He knew instinctively that the money had been left there as bait.

As a way of saying 'fuck you', he took another tenner from his own pocket and added it to the other seven. A week later, to Billy's annoyance, the extra tenner had gone but there was a fifty-pound note lying under the kitchen table. This time, he left the money untouched.

The house smelled bad, because Priest's mother insisted on doing the cleaning herself. She was seventy-eight and had poor eyesight, so she always missed the patches of poodle piss on the carpet. Every surface in Priest's two-million-pound house was sticky to the touch. Priest didn't want to hurt his mother's feelings by hiring a cleaner. Instead he waited until the old woman had gone to her weekly meeting of the Clover Leaf Club, then ordered a couple of his men to scrub all the lavatories. Billy never heard anyone complain.

Apart from Billy, no one complained to Priest

about anything. That was the secret behind all the free gifts. They weren't so much gifts as offerings to placate a vengeful god. The Beast, who took Billy under his wing, claimed that four years ago Priest's brother-in-law had borrowed Priest's Daimler and crashed it into a brick wall. The brother-in-law, who happened to be a builder, built Priest an indoor swimming pool as a 'thank-you present' for not killing him.

Blake Terry was Billy's publisher. He'd edited all four of Billy's novels, which explained why all existing copies were stacked in a warehouse in Luton. He was a plump man in his thirties. The tip of his nose was shaped like an arsehole and his face always wore a slightly surprised expression. Surprised, perhaps, that it had an arse for a nose. Blake never returned Billy's calls and seemed to take it for granted that Billy would never earn royalties or be favourably reviewed in a prestigious publication.

Blake's name was engraved on a brass plaque at a table in Artie's restaurant in Covent Garden. It was at this table that he and Billy had their final conversation. There were four other names on the plaque. One of them was Windy Miller, an alternative ventriloquist who talked through his arse. Billy asked, without much hope, whether the company ever planned to promote his books.

Blake took a mouthful of the house red and dabbed his mouth with a napkin. 'Well, that's what I wanted to talk to you about,' he said.

'Yeah?' Billy put down the bread roll he'd been chewing and waited, fully expecting the worst. Blake saw the look on his face and held up a hand. 'No, we're not getting rid of you.' As an afterthought, not wishing to raise false hopes, he added, 'I was wondering how you'd feel about waiting a while. Seeing how the new book performs before we commission another.'

'How can it perform?' demanded Billy. 'We're virtually the only people who know it exists.'

'It's not just you. Horror isn't selling,' said Blake.

'Nothing sells if it's not in the fucking shops.'

'Now, now—'

'It's called business. A company manufactures a product and publicizes it. A company that tries to sell something that nobody's fucking heard of has little chance of success. But Blake, you go one step further than that. You try to sell books without even putting them in the shops.'

Blake's voice rose by half an octave. 'I resent the implication that I'm somehow to blame for the general lack of interest in your work. Do you seriously think I *want* books to fail?'

'No. But the facts speak for themselves. I've never had a book launch. Not one penny has been spent on promoting my work anywhere on the face of the earth. And the combined advances for all four of my novels add up to less than a nurse earns in a year.'

Blake swallowed more wine and banged his glass down belligerently. 'If you want me to pay for this meal, I suggest you hold your tongue.'

'Did you know your nose is shaped like an arsehole?' asked Billy.

Besides the Beast and Heidi, there were only four other men in the Priesthood's elite inner circle. Priest's second-in-command was a broken-nosed melancholic called Stavri. Stavri wore Armani and radiated faint disappointment, perhaps because he had always wanted to be Sicilian and was actually Greek. He was a laconic man who rarely acknowledged Billy's presence. In his youth, he had exhibited a taste for setting fire to people. Because of this, Priest and the others called him Chef.

Most of the driving was down to Lol Shepherd, a thin, genial man in his fifties who was obviously no hard man – his nerves were so bad that he shook constantly. But he became steady behind the wheel of a car and had made himself indispensable by having no vices, being a fast, efficient driver and always doing exactly what he was told.

Newey was a stocky, unsentimental ex-soldier who had served in Ireland and had a huge nose, small angry eyes and a bright red complexion, partly because he drank too much, partly because he was consumed by bitterness and impotent rage. He had a grudge against the army, the Irish, the government and Billy. The only time Billy was rash enough to wish Newey good morning, the ex-soldier spat on the carpet at Billy's feet.

This didn't matter. The carpet was already filthy and Newey wasn't popular. His colleagues couldn't even be bothered to think of a nickname for him. They just called him Newey. Then there was Albert 'Doc' Docherty, the oldest of the hired hands, a huge ex-professional wrestler with a sonorous voice and a fist-flattened face. Before snobbery and ignorance had banished wrestling from British TV screens, Doc had faked matches with the best of them. 'Jackie Pallo? Now, he was a cunt. Mick McManus? An even bigger cunt. Big Daddy? A big fat cunt . . .'

Doc was, without a doubt, one of the most ignorant human beings that Billy Dye had ever encountered. Doc claimed, in all seriousness, that Prince Edward had left the Royal Marines because he didn't like the colour of the beret. He also maintained that people with Down's syndrome all died at the age of twenty-one. 'It's a shame, it is. The poor bastards just get fatter and fatter,' explained the Doc. 'When they reach their twenty-first birthday, they explode.'

Most of the time, Doc was like a jocular uncle. He wore golfing cardigans and was the only member of Priest's team to show interest in Billy's writing. He asked what kind of thing Billy wrote about. 'You know,' he marvelled, 'that must be one of the hardest things, to put it all down. I mean, I could tell a few stories but I couldn't really write 'em down – because I can't really write.'

Unprompted, Billy gave Doc a paperback copy of his first masterpiece, *Complicated Monsters*. Doc seemed impressed. 'I'll look after it but I won't read it,' he explained respectfully, 'because I can't really read.'

Priest had a son, a son he adored, whom Billy never met. The other gangsters spoke highly of this invisible heir. Even Doc, who thought most people were cunts, had to admit that Malcolm Priest Junior was a 'good lad'. Junior managed Diva, Priest's trashy nightclub in Salford Keys. It was mainly on his recommendation that the raw recruits, known as the altar boys, were introduced to the organization.

Without exception, the new boys were greedy white trash, bejewelled and cynical, with comic-book names that made them easy to remember.

For example, Dogman was a rugby-playing hulk with no hair, teeth or manners. He owed his name to the almost mayoral gold chain he habitually wore around his neck. A well-educated boy from a sedate south Manchester suburb, Dogman specialized in organizing heavy-duty protection for people that didn't deserve it. His hobbies included busting skulls and gambling. His favourite colour was red.

Below the altar boys were the 'sops', the eager losers who acted as runners and tea-boys for the real gangsters, often working for years without the slightest hope of promotion. Soppiest among them was Bryan Edwards, a twenty-something bad boy from Rusholme who had started his criminal career by setting fire to litter bins, slowly graduating to burglary and petty theft before landing his job as a trusted nobody. He was lean and wiry with boyish blond hair and freckles. He had no eyebrows because he'd accidentally burned them off freebasing crack. The resultant scar tissue gave him a permanently puzzled look.

Bryan had sidled his way onto the edge of the Priesthood in the time-honoured British way: by working for nothing. After a few months of voluntary work, Malcolm Priest Junior had taken him on as a cloakroom attendant at Diva. Since then, Bryan had showed up at Priest's home almost every day, delivering parcels, taking them away, or simply sticking around for a game of pool and the chance to hang out with the big boys.

Bryan thought Billy's vocation was risible. 'A fucking pen-pusher, you poor sad bastard! While the rest of us are out drinking, there's you sitting at home at your little desk. You're mad, you, Billy.'

*

Billy liked Bryan. He was dishonest without being at all vicious. Since his teens, Bryan had associated with hardened criminals, yet he showed no sign of becoming hard himself. He was friendly, in an open, foolish way that Billy found oddly touching. One night, out of the blue, Bryan offered to treat Billy to an Indian takeaway in exchange for a lift home. 'Me car's broken down and I can't afford to take it to the garage, Bill.'

Billy parked outside an Indian restaurant in Longsight and waited. After about fifteen minutes, Bryan emerged with the food and a bottle of cheap champagne. 'I thought you were broke,' said Billy.

'I am,' admitted Bryan. 'I had to borrow some feed.'

'Who from?'

Bryan flashed Billy a sly grin. 'Fat Mal. He doesn't know it yet.'

'What are you talking about?'

'You know the seventy notes he keeps pinned to that fucking dartboard in the bog? I got tired of looking at it, Bill.'

Billy couldn't believe it. 'Bryan, you're crazy. He'll know it was you.'

'Why?'

'Who else'd be stupid enough to take it? You've got to promise me you'll put it back first thing tomorrow.'

'All right, all right.' Bryan was taken aback by the

level of Billy's concern. 'No need to have a shit about it.'

Bryan directed Billy to the grim council flat in Ardwick that he shared with a nineteen-year-old girl and their one-year-old baby. They lived at the top of a flight of concrete steps that every drunk in Manchester appeared to have pissed on. A faded Bart Simpson sticker was hanging off the front door. Inside, the flat was small and covered in brown stains. So was the baby. Bryan's girlfriend was called Leanne. She was fair-haired and pretty with large, resentful eyes.

The baby was a girl, but looked like a fat, bald old man. Bryan called her 'Marlon' after Marlon Brando in *Apocalypse Now*. As he was bringing in some plates from the kitchen, he glanced at his daughter and whispered, 'The horror. The horror . . .'

The champagne made Bryan talkative. 'Next time you're on the internet, tap in "Empire porn". It's this massive site owned by Fat Mal, and the fucking free stuff is out of this world: big tits, small tits, fat fannies, grey fannies. Really good quality filth to suit all tastes. But to get to the really hard stuff, you've got to be a member. Shouldn't be a problem, membership's free, but guess what? They need your credit card number. Not 'cause they want your cash, you understand, but 'cause they wanna check your age and whatnot.

'So picture this poor twat, desperate for a wank.

What does he do? He thinks "I'm in England. I'm a fucking Englishman. No one would dare to cheat me. The rights of Englishmen are sacred." So he taps in his credit card number and up comes his free personal ID number, which he also fucking taps in.

'But, oh dearie me! A notice flashes up saying: "Invalid ID. Please refer to server." Well, of course, the poor bastard isn't going to tell his server that he's a porn addict, so he lets the matter drop. Lo and behold, next month he finds that Bulldog Enterprises has taken fifty notes out of his account.

'Well, at first he's as sick as a cunt. But then he thinks, fuck, I'm hardly going to take the bastards to the small claims court. Not for fifty, I'm not. Me wife'd find out I was a pervert, and so would the judge. If I went to the cops, they'd laugh at me. So I won't do anything. I'll treat it as a lesson. I just won't give me credit card number to pornographers ever again, as long as I fucking live.

'Billy, it's the perfect crime. And it happens every day, hundreds of times. Each time, Priest is making another fifty quid. And that's what he does with everything – drugs, sex, guns, you name it. He takes calculated risks. He cheats people who think they're doing something wrong, because he knows they won't dare go to the law. And that's why Malcolm Priest is fucking loaded.'

*

According to Malcolm Priest, everyone he'd ever met, including policemen, prison officers and rival criminals, had respected him for his courage, integrity and peerless fighting ability. 'Wanna know my technique? "Gut and nut." Hit 'em in the belly. When they bend forward, nut 'em in the face.'

Priest had already christened his memoirs. 'Say the name Malcolm Priest and what's the first thing that springs to mind?' he had asked Billy excitedly. 'Manchester. Malcolm Priest *is* Manchester. So I reckon we should call our book – my book – "Mr Manchester".'

By mid-April, Billy had completed the first draft of an opening chapter of *Mr Manchester*. It read more like *Mr Shit*, aping scholarly tradition by including irrelevant and tedious details about Priest's grandparents and the price of a loaf of bread in Salford in 1924. Priest's Uncle Roy, his mother's younger brother, had been a conscientious objector during the Second World War. Priest's earliest memory was of his mother throwing a potty of baby Malcolm's piss over her cowardly brother in the yard of their terraced slum in Hulme.

After reading the chapter, Priest invited Billy to dinner at the Moroccan. Just the two of them, sipping ice-cold Manhattans at the very best table. Priest said, 'If it's as good as that all the way through, we can't go wrong.'

'But nothing happens.'

Priest instantly took offence.

'What do you mean nothing fucking happens? Malcolm Priest is born in those fucking pages. That's a momentous event in the history of Manchester. I'm somebody, pal. For every penny you've got, I've got a twenty-pound note. My name is known in New-castle, Leeds – all over the fucking globe. Now, when *you* were born, *that's* when nothing happened.'

'Cheers,' said Billy.

Billy raised his glass. Priest, relenting slightly, gave Billy a troubled look. 'What do you mean, nothing happens?'

As tactfully as possible, Billy explained the problem. 'It's as if you're trying to present yourself as a model citizen who's been unfairly vilified by a snobbish and unjust society.'

'So?'

'You say you don't steal, that you only stole from shops as a kid.'

'That's right.'

'According to you, you're not violent, either. Yet I happen to know why you went to prison when you were seventeen. You blinded a man in a fight.'

'Aw, that was just youthful high spirits.'

'You don't feel bad about it?'

'He fucking deserved it.'

'Why?'

'I called him a liar, but he just wouldn't see it.'

'Well, he wouldn't see anything if you'd blinded him, would he?'

Priest eyed Billy moodily.

'What are you telling me?' said Billy, smiling. 'That you're just a gentle, peace-loving citizen, trying to get along?'

'All right,' Priest conceded. 'I'll admit that, over the years, I've been occasionally forced to defend myself against a few idiots who've attacked me for no reason. Now, sometimes I hit 'em a bit too hard. My trouble is that I don't know my own fucking strength.'

'And you've never hit anyone who didn't deserve it?'

'No.'

'Have you ever chopped anybody's hands off with an axe?'

'That's such a stupid fucking question that if you repeat it I'll kill you.'

One night, the Beast asked Billy for a favour. The Beast had been ordered to go to Ringway Airport to pick up a parcel. Would Billy mind going along for the ride? Billy consented readily, hoping that the Beast would give him some background for the book.

On the way, the Beast stopped at a late-night chemist to buy a pack of Durex. Knowing that he was divorced and single by choice, Billy asked the Beast what he needed condoms for. 'I treat myself to a posh wank now and then,' the Beast confided in his low, husky voice.

Billy asked the Beast what he thought of his employer.

'Off the record?'

'But of course.'

'You're a lying little piece of shit, William.'

'I know. But what do you think of him?'

'I've got no complaints. He's a boss. All bosses are the same.'

'But do you *like* him?'

'Well, you know, maybe I'm getting mean in me old age, but I'm not that aware of liking anyone.'

'Has he ever taken anyone out?'

'Yes. Last Sunday. He took his mum to Brookside Garden Centre.'

'Oh, very droll.'

The Beast smiled. '"Taken out" is what wankers say.'

'Thanks.'

'We prefer "reaped", or "burned". The favourite is "boxed".'

'*Boxed?*'

'Yeah. Kill more than one, it's called a "boxed set".

Kill someone to make an example of 'em, it's a "presentation box". Kill a witness? "Witness box". Kill a nigger? "Chocolate box".'

"Kill Princess Anne – a "horse box".'

'You're getting the idea.'

'Has Mal ever "boxed" anyone?'

'Not to my knowledge.'

'So how did he get a reputation as a mad axeman?'

The Beast sighed. 'What you've got to understand is this, Bill: we lads on the wrong side of the law tend to exaggerate. If a fella gets his face cut and needs a plaster, we say he's had his arms and legs chopped off with an axe and been left to bleed to death in the gutter. Makes life a bit more interesting, you know. It'd be a dull world without a few stories.'

'You're taking the piss, aren't you?'

'Well, maybe a bit. But being serious, now, how do you think Mal's managed to stay out of prison for so many years? It isn't that he's law-abiding, is it? He just avoids doing anything that can be traced back to him. So he doesn't box people, the blokes he surrounds himself with don't box people. We're clean, Bill.'

The Beast honked his horn at a wobbling cyclist.

Billy said, 'Have you ever broken anyone's legs?'

'Nah.'

'So what do you do when someone owes you money and won't pay up? Go round and make faces at them?'

'Billy, what're you asking me for? It's not me you're writing about. Know what I mean? If you read about Elton John, you don't want to know who makes his wigs for him.'

'Elton John wears a wig? You're kidding me.'

The Beast laughed. Then Billy wiped the smile off his face. 'What's happened to Bryan?'

The Beast tightened his grip on the steering wheel. 'Dunno what you mean.'

Billy said, 'I haven't seen him for weeks. I thought maybe something had happened to him.'

'Ah, you don't want to waste your time worrying about that light-fingered little twat.'

'I didn't say I was worrying about him. I just want to know where he is.'

'Who do you think I am?' said the Beast indignantly. 'His girlfriend? How the fuck should I know?'

Billy waited a day, then walked to Ardwick and climbed the piss-darkened stairs to Bryan's council flat. It was early evening. At first, he thought he'd got the wrong address. The windows were all broken and boarded up. Then he saw the Bart Simpson sticker on the door. Billy knocked a few times, then rang the bell on a neighbouring door. There was no answer, so he tried again. The letter box opened and Billy heard an old woman say, 'Marian? Is that you?'

'It's not Marian,' said Billy. 'I'm looking for the

people who used to live next door. Any idea where they've gone?'

'Did they have a baby?'

'Yeah. That's them.'

'No, love. I don't know them, I'm sorry.'

'Any idea what happened to the windows?'

'Windows? What about me windows?'

'Not your windows. *Their* windows. They're all smashed.'

'Oh, that happens all the time round here, love.'

The flap of the letter box closed softly.

As he was descending, Billy noticed drops of dried blood on the steps. Blood is a common enough sight on the streets of Ardwick but Billy began to worry. He walked back to Levenshulme in a trance, convinced that Bryan had been murdered, and that Priest had ordered his execution.

As he walked past a Jag that was waiting at a set of traffic lights, the passenger window rolled down and the Beast leaned out. He seemed truly delighted to see Billy.

'Billy! Mate! Where you going?'

'Home.'

Doc leaned over the wheel and gave Billy a wink. 'We're off for a pint. What say you come with us? Then we'll run you back.'

'Thanks,' said Billy. 'I'm not in the mood.'

'Aw, go on,' urged the Beast. 'It'll be a laugh.'

Billy hesitated. On an impulse, he opened the rear passenger door and got in.

'Where do you fancy?' the Beast asked Billy.

'I'm not bothered.'

'We know a nice little pub,' said Doc.

'The Doc likes the landlady's tits,' explained the Beast. 'He's hoping to give them a full medical examination.'

'Anywhere'd be fine by me,' said Billy.

Doc asked him how the book was going.

'A bit slow,' admitted Billy.

'Hurry up and fucking finish it, will you?' urged the Beast. 'Then we can sell the film rights to Hollywood.'

'That's right,' said Doc. '*The Malcolm Priest Story*. Starring Al Pacino as little Malcolm.'

'Harrison Ford as "The Beast",' added the Beast.

Doc raised one hand from the wheel to frame his name in lights. 'The leading role of "The Doctor" to be played by lookalike Tom Cruise.'

'But who's going to play Billy?' mused the Beast.

'How about Madonna?' suggested Doc.

'Fuck off,' said Billy.

They drove to Didsbury, not to a 'nice little pub' but to a large, smoke-filled mausoleum. The gangsters made fun of Billy's trousers but refused to let him buy a single round. Aglow with Guinness and warm, ribald company, Billy forgot about Bryan and began to relax. A young man with Down's syndrome, wearing a flat cap and carrying a shopping basket, passed by their table on his way to the exit. He smiled shyly at Billy and gave him a 'thumbs up' sign.

Billy nudged Doc. 'Better duck. He might explode at any moment.'

The Beast laughed. Doc shook his head in disapproval. 'You wouldn't laugh if it happened to you.'

The Beast admitted that in the seventies he had worked the northern cabaret circuit as a singer. 'Graham Wain didn't sound classy enough, so I called myself "Wayne Graham". Clever, eh? For a laugh, I'd always end it with: "For God's sake, get 'em down".'

'I bet that brought the house down,' said Billy. The Beast, unaware that he was being mocked, said, 'Without fail. You see, it's not enough to get up and sing. You have to develop a durable act.'

'Exactly. You do. Yes, you do,' agreed Doc, cheering up. 'Like when I was "Man-Eater".'

'When you were *what*?' said Billy.

'"Man-Eater",' Doc repeated. 'In me wrestling days, I used to dress up in a kind of tiger rug. "Man-Eater, the Jungle Terror"? I appeared as Man-Eater for three and a half years.'

'Wasn't a very durable act then, was it?' commented Billy.

Billy went to the gents. The lavatory was empty. He stood at the urinal, wanting to pee so badly that he couldn't. While he waited, he deciphered a question that someone had scrawled across the white tiles in front of his face. 'Call that a dick?' the message read.

The door leading out to the bar crashed open. Billy glanced around to see the Beast standing in the doorway, blinking foolishly. 'Oh, you're there. What've you been doing? You've been fucking ages.'

'Since when have you been so concerned about my welfare?' asked Billy, puzzled.

Unable to provide an answer, the Beast shuffled over to the neighbouring urinal. Billy finally managed to piss, so that the two men stood side by side, peeing in harmony like schoolboys. 'Well, isn't this cosy?' said Billy.

The Beast grunted, unwilling to commit himself.

They returned to the table to find that Doc had ordered double brandies all round. The Beast lost interest in his drink after the first sip and tipped the rest into Billy's glass. Billy didn't realize how pissed he was until it was time to leave. He could barely stand. Doc and the Beast had to escort him to the door.

They helped him into the car. The Beast slotted

The Eagles' Greatest Hits into the stereo and proceeded to sing along with 'Hotel California'. As if this wasn't depressing enough, they were heading for Withington Hospital, where Billy's gran had died. Billy was feeling dizzy and ill. The white crosses of Southern Cemetery glided by on their left. 'Where are we going?' asked Billy. 'This isn't the way home.'

'You're looking a bit poorly,' said Doc sympathetically.

They circled the huge, sweeping cemetery and stopped at a set of locked iron gates. Doc got out of the car, produced a key and unfastened the padlock. The car eased through the gates. Doc locked the gates behind him and climbed into the car.

'So what're you planning to do?' said Billy. 'Bury me?'

'No offence, Bill,' said the Beast, 'but we don't want you puking in the car.'

After a short ride down a curved, tree-lined drive, the car drew to a halt before a vast panorama of graves. The graves appeared to be suspended in utter blackness. 'What're we stopping here for?' protested Billy, finally realizing that something was wrong.

'You want to be sick. So why not be sick here?' said the Beast.

'In a graveyard?'

'What's wrong with that?' asked Doc innocently. 'It's nicely out of the way. You don't want people to see you being sick by the side of the road, do you?'

'Take me home,' said Billy. 'I'll be sick there.'

The Beast took a flashlight from the glove compartment and turned it on. Then he got out of the car, walked to Billy's door and opened it. Billy looked at him doubtfully. 'You're not planning to shoot me or anything, are you?'

The Beast sniggered. 'Shoot you?' He turned to Doc. 'Did you hear what he said?'

Nodding, Doc roared with laughter. 'He's fucking parallel!'

'I think the word you're looking for is "paranoid",' slurred Billy. He eased himself out of the car, staggering slightly as he attempted to steady himself. 'Whoa!' said the Beast, placing a paternal hand on Billy's shoulder.

Billy shivered. A light wind hissed in the trees. The pale stars were veiled by a thin haze of cloud. The gangsters led Billy down a narrow path flanked by cracked tombs and gleaming headstones. An unwholesome stench of damp earth and decay filled the air. Doc walked in front of Billy. The Beast walked behind him. Billy suddenly stopped, leaned over and puked all over someone's last resting place. 'What a world,' he spluttered, warm beer and brandy trickling from his nose.

When he'd finished, the Beast held him upright and said, 'If you feel that way, Bill, why stick around?'

Taking this as a cue, Doc turned, raised an enormous fist and punched Billy in the bridge of the nose, shattering the bone. Billy fell to the ground, swearing. His eyes filled with involuntary tears. The pain was acute.

'Think you're funny, do you?' roared Doc. 'Laugh at that!'

Stunned, Billy looked up at the Beast, waiting for him to intervene. The Beast shook his head with an air of finality. Then Doc waded in, bellowing insults as he delivered blows to Billy's head, ribs and back. 'You fucking bookworm!'

Billy curled up in a ball, face down, shielding his skull with his hands while he waited for unconsciousness. Then a vicious, deafening explosion cleaved the air, echoing and rebounding from tomb to derelict tomb. At first, Billy thought he'd been shot. He raised his head and saw that neither Doc nor the Beast was holding a gun. Both men were staring past him, into the dark.

'Better move,' whispered the Beast.

'I just want to see him. See if he's real,' said Doc.

Something whistled past their heads, instantly followed by the crack of a second shot. The gangsters shuffled nervously.

'Better go,' said the Beast. Doc was still hesitating.

'Move!' urged his companion. The two men turned, walking with deliberate slowness so as not to lose face. When they were out of sight, and only then, a shape rose above the gravestones up ahead.

It was a pale orb, floating in the darkness. It quickly became apparent that the orb was a light grey hood, worn by a man with a long, lean body. The gunman moved with speed and grace, ignoring the path and using the graves as stepping stones. In moments, he was at Billy's side.

The hood had two narrow eye-slits, through which its wearer gazed down at Billy. He wore dark clothes and a long, flowing coat. He was silent and perfectly still. The folds of his coat flapped gently in the breeze. He was holding a revolver with a peculiarly long barrel. The gun hung loosely at his side.

'Who the fuck are you?' said Billy.

By way of reply, the gunman extended his arm and pointed the weapon at Billy's head. 'Get up,' he said softly. 'I want to show you something.' The man spoke with a mild London accent.

With difficulty, Billy hauled himself upright. Blood ran down his throat and streamed onto his jacket. The hooded man guided him through the graves to the feet of a pale stone angel, its hands clasped in prayer. They stood there for a long time, the wind crying, the muzzle of the gun icy cold against Billy's cheek.

'What the fuck am I supposed to have done?' asked Billy. 'I don't even know what I've done.'

A shooting star slashed the sky's face. Billy was shaking with fear. Then the gunman spoke again. 'Do you know where you are going, and what you are going to?' he asked.

It was a literary quotation. To his amazement, Billy recognized the source. '*Dracula*,' he said with authority.

'What?' For the first time, the stranger betrayed his humanity. He lowered the gun and took a step to one side. 'What did you say?'

It was all Billy needed. With courage born of sheer desperation, he turned and ran. He had no idea where to run to. The cemetery seemed to stretch for miles in every direction. His only concern was staying alive. Blood from his nose streamed down his chest as he charged blindly through a maze of tombs. There was no shout, no gunshot, only the sound of his own breath, rattling urgently in his skull.

Billy had been running for less than a minute when he caught his foot on a twisted tree root. The impact catapulted him into the air. He landed hard, smashing his knee on the edge of a raised sarcophagus. Almost weeping with the pain, he sank behind a large grave. A Star of David was carved on the marble headstone. Billy pressed his face against the symbol and blood dripped steadily off his chin onto the hallowed earth.

After what seemed like a long time, Billy raised his head above the stone, searching for his would-be

executioner. Jagged graves grinned at him through
the gloom. There was no sign or sound of pursuit.
Then Billy heard a sniff. He turned to see the muzzle
of a gun pointing down at his head. The hooded
man was standing behind him. He had circled Billy
and hunted him down in the darkness, without noise
or apparent effort.

'Shit,' said Billy.

He wasn't ready to die. His life so far had been a
disappointment. But he preferred disappointment to
death. He was rocked by a hot surge of emotion,
anger that was close to elation. If this was the end,
fuck it. He was damned if he was going to beg for
his life.

Billy's voice shook as he made his farewell speech.
'Go on then, you useless piece of shit! Men with
guns, boys with guns, weak ignorant foul-smelling
twats who feel big because they have the power to
kill people.'

He waited. The gunman remained motionless.
Cold drizzle began to fall on Billy's face, so that he
had to squint to see his executioner.

'Old people, women and children shitting themselves with fear, just because some spineless wanker
like yourself is pointing a fucking gun at them. Go
on! Shoot! I'll be dead but you'll always be a useless
cowardly bastard—' There was a soft click. Billy
covered his head with his hands and screwed up his
eyes, waiting for the final scorching flash of light

that would signify the end of his days. Nothing happened. A strong hand grabbed Billy's left wrist, wrenching it away from his head. Billy looked up. The gunman had lowered his weapon and was peering down at the ring on Billy's left hand. Then he spoke. 'Billy?'

Billy stared.

'Billy Dye? From Manchester Grammar?'

'Yeah?'

The gunman made a noise, something between a laugh and a snort. He reached up and snatched the hood from his head. It was too dark to see the face. But the shape of the skull silhouetted against the sky was at once familiar. A tingling sensation rose from the nape of Billy's neck to the crown of his head.

'Billy, it's me.'

4

That was the last thing Billy remembered before blacking out. When he opened his eyes it was still dark. He was lying in a narrow bed in a Romany caravan, long and wide with an arched ceiling. The shuttered doors, locked and bolted, were by Billy's head. An oil lamp burned on a small drop-leaf table at the far end of the caravan, where the man who had been ordered to kill him was now seated, calmly shuffling cards. The silence was eerie and absolute.

On the opposite wall hung a tastefully framed copy of an old print: a stunning etching of a winged man falling through space. A long high shelf, tightly crammed with books, ran the entire length of the caravan. There was another shelf above Billy's head, so heavily laden with books that it dipped precariously in the middle.

Billy peered under the duvet that covered him. He was in his vest and underpants. His head was pounding. The blood on his shirt had seeped through to his vest, so that he appeared to have the flag of Japan on his chest. A tight dressing covered his injured knee. The knee throbbed with a low, deep pain. Billy tried to sit up, then felt his head falling backwards, as if his skull was anchored to the pillow. His host glanced over and saw that Billy was awake. Languidly, he gathered up the cards to form a deck, wrapped them carefully in a small square of fabric and placed the bundle on a shelf by his head. Then he picked up the lamp and walked over to Billy.

He had a gaunt face under dark brown hair, razored close to the scalp. Apart from the shape of his head and the length of his limbs, he barely resembled the boy that Billy remembered. He was built like a marine: no flab, no sign of bodybuilding, just functional muscle and sinew. Years of savagery and isolation had frozen his old friend's once-expressive features into a cold, brutal mask. It was now the face of a dangerous animal, but for the eyes: metallic blue blazing with energy and intelligence.

'Steve, this is bizarre. I can't believe it's you.' Billy's voice sounded thick and unfamiliar.

'Yeah.' The word carried a trace of regret. The voice, in contrast to the face and demeanour, was unexpectedly gentle.

'The kid who used to beat up prefects in his lunch break?'

A sullen stare. 'You shouldn't talk, Bill. Try to rest.'

'Where are we?'

'In a field.'

'Would Priest—'

Anticipating the question, his host said, 'He won't find us.'

He watched Billy calmly, hardly blinking and scarcely appearing to breathe.

'You've changed,' said Billy.

'It's been a long time.'

'So how did you know it was me?'

'Because you're the cheekiest bastard who ever lived.' The eyes smiled. 'People don't usually insult me when I'm pointing a gun at them.'

'Where'd you get the London accent?'

Pulling the quilt up to Billy's neck, he said, 'In London. That's where I learned my craft.'

'Craarft,' mimicked Billy, immediately feeling stupid for doing so. Unwilling to question his friend further for fear of what he might hear, Billy changed the subject. 'And is this really where you live, Steve?'

'No one calls me Steve any more,' said the other man, patiently. 'I'm Rawhead now.'

Billy started to laugh but had to stop. His face hurt too much. None the less, he had to admit that his friend's new name suited him. Rawhead. It was an old, old term for the bogeyman. Steve Ellis was a boy's name. There was nothing remotely boyish about the man at Billy's side. But there was more than a touch of the bogeyman.

'Where is this place?' asked Billy again.

'Somewhere safe.'

Billy raised his hand to his nose, found it was covered by an enormous sticking plaster and winced. 'What've you done to my conk?'

'I reset it.'

'You *what*?'

'It was pointing the wrong way. I had to reset it.'

'I didn't realize you'd had a medical training.'

'I haven't. I just grabbed hold of it and gave it a twist.'

Billy laughed, then groaned. He was sweating with pain.

Rawhead came to a decision. He went to a shelf and took down a small bottle of clear fluid and a disposable syringe. 'What's that?' demanded Billy suspiciously.

'Morphine. I think you could use a shot.'

Billy didn't argue. Skilfully, Rawhead inserted the needle into Billy's arm. In seconds, Billy was overwhelmed by a delicious sensation of peace and well-being. 'Where are we?'

Concerned, Rawhead looked down at him. 'You've already asked me that.'

'What was the answer?' said Billy. He closed his eyes, waiting for a reply that never came.

Billy slept. It was the kind of deep, nourishing sleep that he used to enjoy as a boy when he was in bed with a cold while all his friends were at school. There were no dreams. When he awoke, sunshine was streaming through one of the tiny windows. Rawhead was on his feet, stripped to the waist. He was cooking an omelette in a large pan. The smell of the eggs made Billy feel sick again. His throat was so sore he could barely swallow. It took all his energy to sit up in bed.

Rawhead stepped over to his side. 'Morning.' The voice flat, unemotional.

'Where did you sleep?' said Billy.

'There's a van outside with a mattress in it. How are you feeling?'

'My knee's broken.'

'No. Just badly swollen. It isn't your knee that worries me. How's your head?'

'It fucking hurts. All of me hurts.'

'I think you've had a bit of concussion, Bill.' The way he talked, it was as if he and Billy had never been separated. 'You need to take it very slow and easy.'

'How do I look?'

Rawhead held up a small oblong mirror. Billy scarcely recognized himself. Although Rawhead had cleaned off most of the blood, his nose and face appeared to have been inflated with a bicycle pump. His eye sockets were livid purple bruises, through which his eyes, bloodshot slits, peered wearily. 'I look like the Elephant Man,' croaked Billy.

'Don't flatter yourself,' said Rawhead quietly. He sighed and frowned a little as he said, 'The old guy – what made him do that?'

'I've no idea. I mean, I thought he liked me.'

Rawhead shook his head. 'That wasn't right. You were mine. They weren't supposed to touch you.'

'You mean you wanted to break my nose all by yourself?'

The question seemed to take Rawhead by surprise. He stared at Billy for a while without answering. A phone rang, the sound ugly and jarring after the profound silence. Rawhead stepped over to the bookshelf and picked up a mobile. 'Yep? Yeah ... It's all done ... No trouble at all ... The usual arrangement ... None ... Fine.'

Something about Rawhead's manner, the way he turned his back on Billy, told him the call was from one of Priest's men. Billy tried to construct the whole conversation in his head. 'Yep?' *It's me. Did you take out the rubbish?* 'Yeah. It's all done.' *No trouble?* 'No trouble at all.' *You want it paid straight into your account?* 'The usual arrangement.' *No problems, then?* 'None.' *I'll be in touch.* 'Fine.'

After hanging up, Rawhead dabbed himself with a towel and donned a sweater. Then he tipped his omelette onto a plate, pulled a chair up to Billy's bedside and started to eat. He ate like he did everything else: slowly, contemplatively, as if time was of no importance to him.

'Was that about me?' asked Billy.

Rawhead nodded.

'You had to lie? Because of me?'

Another nod.

'You were hired to kill me?'

'Yep.' Matter-of-fact, offhand, no hint of apology.

The insanity of it all made Billy reel. 'Steve,' he breathed, shaking his head.

Rawhead shrugged.

'Couldn't you have been a carpenter? You were always good at woodwork at school.'

Silence.

'So you're letting me go?'

'I don't really have a choice.'

'Why?' Billy laughed, then groaned and clutched his jaw. 'Because I've read *Dracula*?'

'You know why.'

'I haven't got a fucking clue.'

Rawhead shrugged. 'We're brothers,' he said simply.

'We're *what*?'

'I believe you heard me.'

Billy said, 'Well, listen. I'm glad you feel that way. But I have to be honest: just because we were close once, doesn't mean we're close now. I mean, we're strangers, Steve.'

'Stop calling me Steve.'

'Well, I can't call you "Rawhead". I'd die of fucking embarrassment.'

Unoffended, Rawhead chewed a mouthful of food, trying to explain the situation to himself as well as to Billy. 'What are the odds against what happened tonight? They must be astronomical. Know why I quoted *Dracula* to you? Because last night was the eve of St George's day. Remember what it says in the novel? "Do you not know that tonight, when the clock strikes midnight, all the evil things in the world will have full sway?"'

Billy nodded. 'Do you usually quote the classics before you kill people?'

'No, that's just it, I don't say anything. I just get the job done as quickly and cleanly as possible.'

Billy snorted in derision. 'A true humanitarian.'

The jibe struck home. The metallic eyes glinted. 'Maybe you'd rather have been hung from the ceiling with a meat-hook through your ribs? There are people who'd have done that to you gladly, for a fraction of what I'll be paid. It could have taken you days to die.' There was a long silence while

RAWHEAD

Rawhead gathered his thoughts. 'No. It was destiny that brought us together tonight. Not coincidence. Destiny. Priest wanted you dead, so he asked me, not realizing that, this time, he was asking too much.'

'Yes. But why?'

'You really don't know?'

'No.'

Rawhead looked down at his hands. 'When we were kids, you refused to testify against me. You wouldn't believe how often I've thought about that over the years.' He looked up, searching Billy's face. 'You were a boy, for God's sake. You must have been scared. But you didn't talk. That blew my mind, Bill. It still does.'

It was true.

In his memory, Billy saw himself as a teenager sitting with his parents, crying and shaking his head while a bullying, lard-arsed constable tried to frighten the truth out of him. Billy could still remember the policeman's name. PC Griffiths. Bad breath and BO armpits that stank like powdered vegetable soup. 'What did you see?' Nothing. 'I'll ask you again. What did you see?' I didn't see anything. 'You're lying to me, William. Look at your mother. Look what you're doing to her. How can you sit there, knowing that a lad's in hospital, knowing you're breaking your poor mother's heart, and not tell me what you saw?'

Billy studied Rawhead's face. 'I didn't know you knew.'

'I knew. '

'I thought you blamed me in some way. The last time you saw me you ignored me.'

Rawhead didn't believe he'd heard Billy correctly. 'What time was that?'

Billy told him about the night in the pub. Rawhead frowned, unable to remember. 'Are you sure it was me?'

'Yep.'

'It doesn't matter. Everything I've said is true. Whether you believe it is up to you.'

They were silent for a long time.

Then Rawhead said, 'Anyway, what happened? How did you get mixed up with Priest?'

'I'm a writer.'

'Yeah?' Rawhead was wearing the expression that Billy had grown so accustomed to, the slightly sceptical, oh-you-poor-bastard look that was usually followed by the question: 'Had anything published?' Rawhead didn't ask the question. But he was definitely thinking it. Billy told him about the novels and thought he saw pleasant surprise in the killer's face. 'And they're published under your own name? Billy Dye?'

'*William* Dye.'

'I've never seen them. And I read a lot. As you can

see.' He gestured to the shelves. 'Just never come across anything by you.'

There was a silence while Rawhead finished eating and Billy reflected on the misfortune of being a local author who was hardly represented in a single local bookshop or library. It was funny, really. So why wasn't he laughing?

Rawhead placed his plate on the floor and leaned back in his chair with his arms folded. 'What does you being a writer have to do with Priest?'

'He asked me to ghost his life story.'

Rawhead sniffed contemptuously. 'He won't have told you the truth.'

'That's what I've been finding out.'

'And you don't know why he wanted you dead?'

'No. Do you?'

Rawhead shook his head slowly. 'It could have been anything. He turns on people like that.' He snapped his fingers. 'I heard that he once had someone killed for breaking wind.'

'What?'

'A guy farted in front of Priest's mother. She was offended, so Priest had the guy killed.'

'Who killed him?'

'I don't know.'

'Could it have been you?'

After some consideration, Rawhead gave a minimalist shrug.

Billy marvelled at him. 'You kill people without finding out what they've done?'

'They don't give me reasons and I don't ask.'

'But aren't you even curious?'

'No. After all, they might only have farted. That's not much of a reason. So I'd rather not know.'

Rawhead got up to pour himself some coffee, then returned to his chair. 'So anyway, Bill, you'll have to write your books under another name now.'

'What are you talking about?'

'What I say. You're supposed to be dead. So I'd rather you used a pseudonym from now on.'

'Why can't I just go to the police?'

'And tell them what?'

'That Priest tried to have me fucking killed!'

'Billy, I'm the only proof that he wanted you killed, and I haven't killed you, so where's your proof?'

Billy hadn't thought of this.

Rawhead added, 'I live cheaply, Bill. I've done well. I mean it. It's amazing what you can put away by putting people away. In a couple of years, I'll be able to retire. But if Priest finds out what I've done, I'll be out of business and you'll be dead.'

'So will you.'

'He might have a slight problem there. He doesn't know what I look like.'

'He's never seen you?'

'Not without the hood. Nor have any of his men.'

'Don't you feel stupid, standing there with a fucking bag on your head?'

They stared at each other in silence, until Billy exploded with indignation. 'Look Steve, I can't give up my life just because some fat bastard takes a dislike to me.' He paused. 'Can't you talk to him? I'm asking you, as a favour.'

'And say what? "Look, that hit you paid for: I couldn't do it because I used to go to school with the guy."'

'Makes pretty good sense to me.'

Rawhead shook his head slowly. 'You don't understand, do you? Priest is like a warlord. He can't be seen to fail or to look weak, not if he wants his army to follow him. It's a matter of pride, you see. Men in his position can't afford to make mistakes, and they certainly can't be seen to forgive and forget. If he knows you're alive, he'll devote time and energy to having you killed.'

'Oh, this is fucking crazy,' said Billy. 'I just want to go home.'

'You shouldn't swear so much, Billy. It doesn't make a good impression.'

'What kind of impression do you think you make? You're a fucking hitman, for Christ's sake! And that's exactly what you fucking look like. No – I'm going home. To my own bed.' Billy tried to sit up, but he

felt so weak and dizzy that even this modest objective was beyond him. Sighing heavily, he flopped
back onto the mattress.

Rawhead poured water into a glass and offered
Billy two painkillers.

'Can't I have more morphine?'

'No, it's addictive.'

Resentfully, Billy swallowed the pills. 'Take me
home, would you?'

Rawhead gazed at him, looking about as sympa-
thetic as a man with such a face could look. 'Billy,
you haven't got a home. Not any more. You've got
to go far away and hide somewhere where Priest
won't ever find you.'

Billy still couldn't take it in. 'You make it sound
like a fairy tale.'

'Yeah. That's about right,' acknowledged Rawhead. 'I'm the huntsman who spared your life. Priest
is the wicked Queen.'

Billy sighed. 'You realize that makes me Snow
White?'

Billy slept for a long time. When he awoke, it was
dark and he was alone.

As the horror of his latest misfortunes descended
anew, he wrapped a quilt around his shoulders and
limped over to the table, where the oil lamp was
burning low. There was a handwritten note on the

table, with a key resting on it. Beside this stood a bottle of mineral water, a glass and a small phial of painkillers. There was also, surprisingly, a bottle of Rémy Martin, half full.

The note, reproducing the advice given by the seven dwarfs to Snow White, read, 'Don't answer the door to <u>anyone</u>.' The words were written in a huge, spidery scrawl. Billy barely recognized Steve's handwriting. It had always been bad. But not as bad as this.

Billy looked for his clothes, but couldn't find them. He searched in a narrow chest of drawers, found some clean socks, underpants and a T-shirt and put them on.

It felt like early morning, somewhere between three and four. The silence and the stillness were intense. Billy unlocked the door and opened it. Cold damp air hit him in the face. The caravan was parked on the rim of a large field, with a white Mercedes van beside it.

Billy hobbled down three wooden steps into the field itself. Above, an evil orange moon glared through a dark bank of cloud. Billy took a badly needed piss. With the unsettling feeling that he was being watched, he went back inside.

He swigged some water to quench his thirst, then opened the brandy and sniffed it cautiously. Satisfied that it was indeed champagne cognac and not battery acid, he poured two inches of pale gold into the glass and swallowed it down with a brace of pain-killers. Then he turned up the oil lamp and looked around him.

His attention was immediately attracted by the books. Books that Billy knew and loved. He hobbled to a shelf and took down a lovingly bound copy of *Ghost Stories of an Antiquary* by M. R. James. He opened the book and read:

Edward Arnold, London 1904.

His spirit levitated as he realized he was looking at a first edition of the finest collection of ghost stories ever published, with four original illustrations by James McBryde. As Billy's eyes scanned the shelves he was filled with genuine awe. Rawhead's collection of rare books was enviable. Under any other circumstances, Billy would have stolen the lot, there and then.

There was a section of Zen and Taoist classics: the *I Ching* or *Book of Changes*, the Richard Wilhelm translation – the only version worth reading; *Tao-te-Ching* by Lao Tzu stood side by side with the infamous *Book of Five Rings* by the seventeenth-century Japanese swordsman Musashi Miyamoto.

The other M. R. James first editions included *More Ghost Stories of an Antiquary* and *A Warning to the Curious*. On the same shelf stood *The Empty House and Other Ghost Stories* by Algernon Blackwood and

RAWHEAD

In a Glass Darkly, a classic collection by Joseph Sheridan Le Fanu, whom M. R. James greatly admired. Billy plucked the precious volumes from the shelves, took them down and began to read. The brandy and the painkillers kicked in and soon, despite the savage awfulness of his predicament, Billy was momentarily transported to a better, darker world.

As he opened *More Ghost Stories*, a folded square of blue paper dropped to the floor. Billy picked it up and unfolded it. It was a handwritten list, a top ten painstakingly transcribed in blue ballpoint. Beneath the heading 'The Ten Scariest Stories' was penned the following:

1. 'Oh, Whistle And I'll Come to You' by M. R. James

2. 'The Monkey's Paw' by W. W. Jacobs

3. 'The Wind' by Ray Bradbury

4. 'The Facts In The Case of M. Valdemar' by Edgar Allen Poe

5. 'The Speckled Band' by Sir Arthur Conan Doyle

6. 'The Mezzotint' by M. R. James

7. 'The Signalman' by Charles Dickens

8. 'Lost Hearts' by M. R. James

9. 'Schalken the Painter' by J. S. Le Fanu

10. 'The Empty House' by Algernon Blackwood

Finally, at the foot of the page:

Anyone who argues with this is dead! Steve
and Billy! 1982!

Billy recognized the list. He'd made it himself,
twenty years ago. Yet, apart from the small, fat,
schoolboy writing, the list might have been compiled
yesterday. Billy would not have made a single
adjustment to their selection, even though he had
spent the past two decades searching ghost-story
anthologies. Truly frightening stories, stories that
instil actual fear in the reader, are as rare as miracles.

The writing paper was also familiar. It was a
sheet of his mum's pale blue Basildon Bond, used
only for informing distant relatives of deaths in the
family. Billy was astonished that his old friend had
considered the list worth keeping. Then again, everything about the caravan and its obsessive neatness
suggested a life of lonely hermitage. What if Billy
was the only friend that Steve had ever had?

When Steve, aged twelve, had first arrived at
Manchester Grammar, Billy had taken the piss out of
his East Anglian accent; the way he said 'oi loik'
instead of 'I like'. Steve had promptly beaten the shit

out of him in the playground, then stood over Billy as he lay dazed and bleeding on the ground. 'Do you give in?'

'Oi'd loik to. But oi can't,' Billy had answered.

The sheer audacity of this, coming from a scrawny little twat with blood all over his school shirt, won Steve over. From that moment on, he was Billy's friend and protector.

The couple that had adopted Steve weren't like Billy's parents. They were young and relaxed, and interested – genuinely interested – in what Steve and his friends had to say. Steve called them Pam and Philip, and encouraged Billy to do the same. Steve said he was always walking into rooms and catching them snogging. Billy couldn't imagine his own parents snogging, not even when they first married. And as for sexual intercourse: good God, it didn't bear thinking about.

Every summer for three years Billy had stayed with Steve at his house in Disley. The Ellis family lived in a house that was shaped and decorated like a ship, with overhanging beams and bare polished floorboards underfoot. Steve's parents worried about the amount of time that Steve spent on his own. Billy, always popular with parents that didn't have to live with him, was readily accepted by the couple. Perhaps they hoped that Billy might exert a positive influence on their son. Billy seemed to be the only person who could make Steve laugh.

It had been Billy who had introduced Steve to the classics of supernatural literature. Steve was the kind of lazy bastard who liked books but seldom read one. Billy had lent him his paperback copy of *Dracula* and Steve was immediately hooked, racing through the book in a matter of days. His favourite bit involved Dracula crawling out of the castle window and climbing down a wall, face-down. That was Billy's favourite bit, too.

Next, Billy had lent Steve his copy of *Ghost Stories of an Antiquary*. The cover had a blurred photo of a woman with her head back. It was probably meant to look like a ghost, but it just looked like a snapshot taken by an incompetent arsehole. Exhibiting consummate good taste, Steve had not judged the book by its cover and became an M. R. James fan.

Billy had been so pleased, he'd given the book to Steve as a present. To Steve, who had been neglected and abused in various children's homes since birth, a cheap paperback was a treasured possession. He kept the M. R. James collection by his bed, and insisted on reading the best tales aloud to Billy, who had already read them himself, many times. Steve was quiet and reticent, but when he read, his voice would boom with theatrical conviction.

The first story Steve read aloud was James's classic 'Lost Hearts'. Its creator had disparaged this tale, considering it one of his lesser efforts. But although there are more frightening yarns, to Billy 'Lost Hearts' remained the most beautifully written and constructed ghost story in the English language. It tells of an orphaned boy who goes to live with a rich old uncle, unaware that his uncle is a black magician with a nasty habit of sacrificing adolescents and devouring their hearts. The nephew's life is saved when two of the old man's previous victims, a boy and a girl, return from the dead to wreak a suitably grisly revenge.

Billy had listened on the bed while Steve paced the floor, acting out all the characters, living and dead. When the rendition was over, Pam and Philip, who had been listening outside the door, broke into hearty applause.

Then Steve had started crying. 'What's wrong?' asked Billy. Steve had tried to explain. 'All these ghosts – Dracula, Frankenstein – the children in "Lost Hearts" – they're like me.'

'Are they fuck.'

'I'm not like you, Billy. I'm outside.'

'Outside what?'

'Everything.'

At the time, Billy had dismissed Steve's words as a youthful boast, designed to impress. Yet, with hindsight, the boy appeared to have shown exceptional self-awareness.

Steve was not sadistic or vengeful. He was lethal in a fight, but he only fought when he had to: that is, when schoolboy honour demanded. Shortly after

Steve's fifteenth birthday, a rugby-playing sixth for-mer had challenged him to a fight on the playing field. Half the school had turned up to watch. It was over very quickly.

Steve punched the older boy once, in the mouth, knocking out both his front teeth and sending him crashing to earth. The sixth former had been so shocked and demoralized by this that he instantly capitulated. Then, in keeping with school etiquette, the two pugilists shook hands.

On the night of the fifth-form disco, things had been different. The fight had taken place in the school car park. A boy from a local comprehensive had called Billy a fairy. Steve leaped to Billy's defence. The kid was feeling brave because he had three mates with him. Steve could probably have beaten them all with his bare hands.

Instead, he'd pulled a knife and thrust it deep into the kid's stomach. While his friends fled, the kid had curled up in a ball on the tarmac, whimpering, the knife handle protruding from his gut. Steve stayed at the scene, staring at the dark pool spreading out around his victim. A gym teacher rushed up and pressed his fingers against the wound to staunch the flow of blood. Finally, the Deputy Head had arrived to drag Steve away by his hair.

The wound wasn't as serious as it looked. The boy survived. But that wasn't seen to be the point. Steve had committed a shocking crime for which he exhibited no remorse, and Manchester Grammar had been quick to disown him. 'The motto of this school,' said the Head, taking assembly the following Monday morning, 'is *Sapere Aude*. Which means, need I remind you, "Dare To Be Wise". What happened last Friday was anything but wise. It was cowardly, it was unjustified and it was unforgivably stupid . . .'

When Steve was put away, Billy had felt the need to visit Pam and Philip, just to tell them how sorry he was. So he squandered half his weekly 'spends' on a train ticket to Disley. Philip answered the door. At the sight of Billy, his face clouded over. Briefly, almost tersely, he'd informed Billy that it wasn't a good time, that he and Pam were about to go out.

Billy knew that wasn't true. He could read the mistrust and disillusionment in Philip's face, as if he and Pam felt that Billy must be partly to blame for Steve's dramatic fall from grace. The unfairness of this still haunted Billy, who, after all, had lost his best friend. Billy had been as shocked by the stabbing as anyone. He had no idea that Steve even owned a knife. The first time he'd ever seen it was when it was sticking out of the kid's belly.

5

*This man belongs to me! Beware how you meddle with him,
or you'll have to deal with me.*

Dracula, Bram Stoker

Sunday was Doc's day off, the day he mowed his lawn and drove his wife to the supermarket. It was the one day of the week when he behaved like a normal person. Doc and his wife Phyllis had lived in the same comfortable, detached house in Crowton Avenue, Sale for the past thirty years. In that time, he'd been a thief, a doorman, a wrestler, a debt collector, an armed robber. After all that, working for Priest was a piece of piss.

Most of the time, all Doc had to do was stand around looking menacing. But if trouble loomed, he could still hack it. Although pushing sixty, he was prodigiously strong. He was capable of snapping a man's arm without breaking into a sweat.

Doc's local was called the Pelican. He drank there every Sunday evening. He was well liked. The landlord thought he looked like a comedian from the sixties: a big, broken-nosed cockney called Arthur Mullard. People chatted to Doc, bought him drinks, respected him without fear. No one here knew him as Doc. They all called him Albert.

That morning, because it was Easter Sunday, Doc had given his wife a box of Dairy Milk and taken her to Chatsworth House. It was a beautiful sunny day. Chatsworth was supposed to be the country seat of the Duke and Duchess of Devonshire. So why was it in Derbyshire? Doc didn't know. There was a waterfall and a maze and naked statues: the kinds of things that Phyllis loved and Doc thought were boring and effeminate. But he hadn't grumbled once, not wishing to ruin her day out. They'd had lunch in the cafe and shared a bar of Cadbury's Fruit and Nut with a hungry squirrel.

Phyllis had worn a dress from Manchester's newly opened branch of Marks & Spencer. The old branch had been blown apart by the IRA. Its replacement was reputed to be the biggest Marks & Spencer store in the world. It seemed fitting that Phyllis had bought a dress there, because she had the biggest arse in the world. Doc didn't mind, he liked big arses. Phyllis was his idea of a good woman. She ironed his shirts, asked no questions and kept the house tidy. In return, all she asked was that she should never have to socialize with Malcolm Priest or anyone like him.

Phyllis didn't like Doc working for Priest, had

hinted that she thought he was too old. Doc knew she was scared of seeing him crippled. She hadn't said so, but he saw it in her eyes when he came home late. She wanted him to retire. But what would he do with himself if he was stuck in the house all day? Die in his armchair, wearing his slippers? It was hardly a fitting end for 'Man-Eater, the Jungle Terror'.

He'd always wanted to work for a man like Priest, a real gangster. Priest was loyal to those he admired and he admired the Doc, ever since seeing him wrestle Giant Haystacks in Leeds back in the seventies. Doc had never actually been in the ring with Giant Haystacks, but wouldn't have dreamed of sharing that fact with Priest. Malcolm didn't like to be contradicted.

Doc hadn't been planning to beat the shit out of Billy Dye. It had just been one of those magical, spur-of-the-moment things. Nor did he have any qualms about delivering him into the hands of Priest's favourite reaper. Doc's only regret was that he hadn't done the job himself. He'd done the same before, to better men than Billy Dye.

Dye had been a smug bastard, always sneering with his mouth or his eyes. Thought he was special because he'd written a few poxy books. Doc had nearly puked when Billy presented him with a signed copy of one of his novels. Who did the little bastard think he was? Jeffrey Archer?

RAWHEAD

And now, a day later, Doc was sitting in his favourite alehouse, chatting to an older man called Harold. Harold shared Doc's heartfelt views on the need for the government to get tough on football hooligans. Harold even suggested that if these thugs were all crucified, in public, outside the grounds of the clubs they supported, it would serve as a warning to other potential hooligans. Doc agreed wholeheartedly. At ten o'clock he said goodnight and walked home. It was a short journey, and a pleasant evening.

Phyllis was in bed when he got home. He entered the kitchen and made himself a cheese and pickle sandwich and a mug of tea. He sliced the bread thickly and used half a jar of pickle. Then he went into the living room and turned on the large black Sony TV that had fallen off the back of a Comet lorry. With his enormous feet resting on a pouffe, he surfed the channels as he ate his sandwich, eventually settling on a dull documentary about an opera singer. He kept the sound turned low for fear of waking Phyllis.

Then he heard it. A soft, melodious whistle.

Doc turned off the TV and listened. It seemed to be coming from directly outside the window. Grim-faced, he put his plate aside and went upstairs in the dark. He entered the boxroom, the room that had been his daughter's nursery, and approached an old, dusty doll's house. He opened the front of the doll's house and took his gun from its hiding place. It was a Browning 9mm. Doc kept it loaded at all times. He walked to the window and peered out. He could see nothing unusual. Just the dark lawn and the lights of neighbouring houses shining through the trees at the bottom of the garden.

Doc walked out onto the landing and listened at his bedroom door. Phyllis was snoring. He descended the stairs on tiptoe and waited by the front door. The whistling had ceased. He slipped the safety catch off the Browning. As softly as he could, he unlatched the front door and stepped outside, leaving the door ajar. He peered into the dark, stumbling over the flower beds under the living-room window. There was no one there, no one on the drive and no one, thankfully, hiding in the garage.

Amused by his own excessive caution, Doc re-entered the house and locked the door behind him. He tucked the gun into the belt of his trousers. The hall was pitch black. He flicked the light switch. Nothing. He turned the switch on and off several times. While he was engaged in this futile activity, he sensed movement in the darkness beside him. He turned towards the kitchen and saw a white disembodied face gliding silently down the hall towards him.

*

At eight next morning Heidi, who had been on night duty, picked up three pints of milk, the *Sun*, the *Sport* and a brown paper parcel from Malcolm Priest's porch. He opened the front door with a latch key. As he carried the milk and the parcel into the kitchen, Lucky the poodle, who slept in a basket under the table, peered up at him sorrowfully.

Glancing down at the poodle, Heidi said, without rancour: 'You horrible little rat, I'd like to stick a red hot poker up your shitty old arse.'

He deposited the milk in the fridge and placed the parcel on the table. The parcel was addressed to Mr Malcolm Priest, Avon Drive, Knutsford and had about three pounds' worth of postage on it. None of the stamps bore a postmark. Heidi made a mental note to mention this to the boss. The stamps could be used again. Priest loved to save money.

As he walked over to the kettle to brew some tea, he skidded in a puddle of cold dog piss, almost doing the splits. Old Mrs Priest entered the kitchen in time to bear witness to his misfortune. She was wearing a mauve quilted housecoat, buttoned up to the neck. It looked like a coffin, worn inside out. The dog leapt out of its basket and ran up to lick her hand.

While Mrs Priest petted the poodle, she admonished Heidi. 'What are you dancing about for?'

'I wasn't dancing, I just slipped,' Heidi explained

to the myopic old woman as he filled the kettle. His explanation failed to satisfy her. 'The dog's done a little tiddle, Mrs P. That's all. That's what I slipped in.'

'Who? My Lucky? Has my Lucky had an accident?' she crooned, as if the occurrence was in any way unusual. Heidi thought the old woman was even uglier than the dog. But their breath smelt about the same.

'No harm done,' said Heidi. 'I'll mop it up for you, shall I?'

Mrs Priest said nothing. She had taken it for granted that Heidi would do just that. She had more important business to attend to. It was her job to make breakfast for her son. She went to the fridge, took out a packet of lard and sliced half of it into a frying pan. While Heidi was clumsily filling a bucket in order to mop the floor, a bright shower of mail erupted through the front door.

After adding a splash of Dettol to the bucket of hot water, Heidi went to the door and returned with a Christmas-sized wad of letters, which he dumped on the table, next to the parcel. The usual collection of bills, writs, junk mail and job applications from prisoners in Strangeways.

Priest wandered in, dark circles around his eyes, his soft pink chest visible at the neck of his dressing gown. He'd been listening to the radio in bed.

'Nothing happens on Bank Holidays,' he croaked, voice still thick with sleep. 'Why is that? It's not a Bank Holiday everywhere in the world, is it?'

'Well, not in the, whadyacallit, the Amazon Rainforest, anyway,' said Heidi.

'Eh?'

'The Indians who, you know, live there don't need banks. They haven't got any money.'

'So what?' Priest demanded.

'So they should try going to the job centre, then, shouldn't they? Instead of chasing each other with blowpipes.'

Priest gazed at Heidi and shook his head. He was lost for words, which was just as well. His mother didn't like swearing.

It vaguely troubled Malcolm Priest that his mother lived with him and cooked his breakfast every morning. He wondered whether it made him appear soft. The Krays had loved their mum. But as far as he knew, they hadn't lived with her. Not as adults, anyway.

Heidi and Priest sat down to eat sausages, bacon and eggs glistening with yellowish fat. Priest's mother contented herself with two slices of buttered toast, which she shared with the poodle. 'No salt, missus?' said Priest suddenly. Mrs Priest leapt up dutifully and scouted round for the salt cellar, eventually finding it beside the bread bin and passing it to her ungrateful son. Priest shook the salt cellar until his plate and its contents were covered in a thin layer of frost.

The doorbell rang. Sighing, Heidi got up to answer it. It was Newey, signing on for the day shift. 'Want any brekker?' Priest asked him.

Newey pulled a pukey face and shook his head. He removed his coat and draped it over a chair.

'Open that for us, would you?' said Priest, nodding to the parcel. 'On second thoughts, take it outside and open it. You were in bomb disposal, weren't you?' Priest and Heidi cackled merrily at the prospect of Newey being blown apart.

Newey also expected the package to explode in his face, but did as he was told. Mrs Priest went for her morning bath, leaving the poodle to beg for scraps at the table. In the silence that followed, Priest noticed that the collar of Heidi's jacket was covered in white flecks. 'I see you've got dandruff,' said Priest.

'I've tried Head and Shoulders. I can't seem to get rid of it.'

'You know what you need to do?' said Priest, his mouth full of greasy sausage. 'Stop washing your hair.'

'Yeah?'

'Yeah. You wouldn't know it, but I get dandruff too. But I don't wash me hair and that sort of takes care of it.'

Heidi was interested. 'Really? And that gets rid of the dandruff?'

'No,' said Priest, quite serious. 'But the grease holds it in.'

Newey returned, carrying a shoebox and looking even less happy than usual.

'What's up with you?' said Priest.

Raising the lid, Newey held the shoebox out to Priest. The poodle, catching the scent, jumped onto a chair to rest its front paws on the table. Priest elbowed the dog out of the way. There was a white slug-like lump of flesh stuck to the bottom of the box. Roughly shaped like a diamond, it was caked in dried blood which now served as an adhesive. A circular pink stain showed through the bottom of the box. 'Bloody hell!' spluttered Priest. 'What the fuck is that?'

Heidi leaned over the table to look. 'Is it a dick?'

'Bloody small dick!' commented Priest.

'Look. It's glued down,' said Newey, holding the box upside down above Heidi's plate to prove his point. Heidi slapped his arm away angrily.

'Not over me fucking breakfast!'

'Might be a little lad's dick,' suggested Priest.

Heidi scoffed. 'What? With hairs on it?'

Newey coughed to secure their attention. 'If you'll excuse me, I think I know what this is. It's a human nose. I once scraped a nose just like that one off the pavement in Ulster.'

'Fucking hell,' said Heidi. 'That's disgusting, that is. Why's the IRA sending us noses?'

'It isn't the fucking IRA!' retorted Newey. Then, slightly less sure of himself, he turned to Priest. 'It isn't, is it?'

Priest was calm and thoughtful. It was at moments like this that his authority shone. 'No. What I'm thinking is, this looks more like a Mafia-type thing. Like that bit in *The Godfather* when someone's killed and his people are sent a fish. To let 'em know that this bloke "sleeps with the fishes". All I'm thinking is, maybe this nose is a similar kind of thing.'

Newey was sceptical. 'Saying what? "Don't be nosy"?'

Priest glared at him.

'But we don't know anyone from the Mafia,' pointed out Heidi.

Priest sneered. 'It's not the fucking Mafia! We're the only fucking Mafia round here.'

Priest peeled the cold, oily horn of flesh and gristle off the bottom of the box. He held the nose up between his thumb and forefinger and inspected it closely. Newey and Heidi edged away, worried that he was about to throw it at them. 'The point is,' said Priest, his voice low and measured, 'who'd be stupid enough to warn me? I'm Malcolm Priest. I'm the fucker who warns every other fucker.'

Priest looked down at Lucky the poodle. A glistening string of drool dangled from the dog's jaws. Casually, Priest relaxed his fingers and let the grisly trophy fall. Lucky snapped the nose out of the air and swallowed it in one.

Daylight came like a curse. And still Rawhead did not return. Billy decided that he'd had enough, that he was going home. Fuck the consequences. So what if the guy had spared his life? He shouldn't have been trying to take it in the first place. This cold, frightening man bore scant resemblance to the boy Billy had known and loved. He was a desensitized freak who killed people for money. Billy owed him nothing.

It was almost with a sense of elation that Billy hobbled out into the dawn and looked around him. He'd been unable to locate the clothes he'd been wearing on the night of the attack and was dressed in oversized garments borrowed from Rawhead.

Mist was rising from the earth. Birds twittered wildly in the trees around him. Two elderly horses grazed quietly in a far corner of the field. Billy lifted an iron gate and found himself on a wide dirt track, flanked by open fields on either side. Which way should he turn? Left or right? He chose left. Since reading *The Devil Rides Out* as a boy, he had always favoured the left-hand path. Perhaps that explained why, as its author would have said, he always suffered such 'infernally bad luck'.

Progress was slow because of the stiffness of his knee. When Billy had been walking for about six minutes, buildings appeared. He passed a farm. A dog started barking. A second dog joined in. To his left stretched a deep meadow, on fire with dandelions. The meadow was bisected by a narrow track. It was a scene from a children's storybook.

The trees on the horizon looked tantalizingly familiar. Suddenly Billy felt a rush of relief. He knew exactly where he was. He was in a part of Cheshire called Alderley Edge. Beyond the trees stood a pub called The Wizard, where he and Nikki had got drunk during their first weekend together.

Beside the pub lay a road that led down into Alderley village, where there were phones, a railway station, perhaps even taxis. Propelled by the prospect of freedom, Billy began to cross the meadow. The morning air tasted wonderfully sweet. Then he glanced to his left and saw a tall figure racing over the field towards him at incredible speed.

'Where did you think you were going?' Rawhead's head glistened with sweat. His calm, pale eyes searched Billy's face. It was almost as if he pitied Billy for being so foolish.

They were now standing on the Edge, a stone precipice overlooking the Cheshire plain. Below them lay the woods and a sickening, back-breaking drop. Billy had walked there without offering resistance or argument, acting as if Rawhead had joined him for an early morning stroll. 'I've told you. I was just exercising my leg.'

Rawhead swung him round by the shoulder, forcing eye contact. 'You're lying.'

Billy sighed. 'OK. I'm lying. Know why? 'Cause I want my life back. It may be a fucking shitty life, but it's still mine. I've struggled for years to attain my present level of obscurity. I can't just walk away from everything I've worked in vain for.'

Rawhead considered this in silence for more than thirty seconds. Eventually he said, 'Would you give me a year?'

'What do you mean?'

'A year. Will you go into hiding for one year? At the end of that year, you'll be able to carry on where you left off.'

'What about Priest?'

'I'll take care of Priest. But it's going to take time. He's got lots of people working for him. I'm on my own. So that's why I'm asking you. One year.'

Oblivious to the sacrifice that the killer was offering to make for him, Billy wavered. 'I don't know, Steve.'

Rawhead sighed. 'Billy, you'd better decide now.'

Billy swallowed hard. 'Are you threatening me?'

'I'm giving you a choice. I trusted you, didn't I? And what did you do? You walked away. Knowing that my life's on the line as well as yours.'

'Except they don't know who you are.'

'Not yet, they don't. But if they find you, they'll do everything they can to find me. So I'm asking you this, as someone who only ever wanted the best for you and wants it still. Give me your word, *now*, that you'll let me hide you, away from everyone and everything you know, for twelve months from today.'

Billy considered playing along. But he couldn't be bothered. 'Oh, fuck off!'

Effortlessly, Rawhead picked him up by the arm-pits, stepped to the brink of the precipice and held him over the edge.

With his feet suspended in thin air, Billy lost all desire to be flippant. 'OK,' he said. 'OK.'

'You trust me?'

Billy could only nod.

Rawhead left Billy hanging in space, as if waiting for him to say, 'I find it easy to trust people who dangle me over cliffs.' But Billy, his mouth dry, was clean out of punchlines. 'Steve, I promise. I'll do whatever you want.'

'Will you stop calling me Steve?'

'Yep.'

'One year?'

'One year. I absolutely promise you.'

And all the while, Billy was thinking: 'I'm promising nothing, you insane arsehole. I'll run a fucking mile from you, first chance I get.'

6

It is true, we shall be monsters, cut off from all the world;
but on that account we shall be more attached to one another.

Frankenstein, Mary Shelley

It was a sunny day. Priest was sitting in his garden. His mother had gone into hospital for a hip operation. He had been left at home, guarding the poodle. Priest was enjoying a cigar on the patio beside his favourite stink, a big, hard brunette called Fiona who wrote her own poems and recited them to him after sex. She was browsing through a copy of *Marie Claire*. The cover proclaimed: 'Women who eat their own children'.

Her lewd, tired tits were bursting out of a silk kimono. The Beast arrived, haggard and solemn in the morning light, his huge shoulders sagging under the pressure of recent events. Priest turned casually to the prostitute and said, 'Fuck off, you slag.'

Fiona looked at Priest as if she could have happily disembowelled him. But she made no comment as she snatched up her magazine and flounced away.

The Beast hardly glanced at the woman or her breasts, he'd seen all three of them too many times.

'There's plenty of toast left,' said Priest.

'No, ta,' said the Beast.

'No stomach for it, eh?'

The Beast attempted a pleasantry. 'Too much stomach, actually.' He patted his paunch, sinking into the chair that Fiona had vacated. It was unpleasantly warm.

'OK,' said Priest. 'I didn't trouble you yesterday because I knew you'd be upset about the Doc.'

'I was more upset about what happened to his fucking nose,' said the Beast bitterly.

'Aye,' said Priest. 'Pity about that. If I'd known it was the Doc's nose, I'd have shown it a bit more respect. I didn't even know Doc was dead, 'til I got a call from a mate in the CID.'

'How did he die?' said the Beast.

'You don't want to know.'

'Tell me.'

'His heart cut out,' said Priest.

'He had a heart attack?'

'I mean someone took a knife and *cut his fucking heart out*.'

The Beast's face crumpled. 'Jesus Christ, no.'

'It wasn't you, then?'

'You fucking *what*?'

'Calm down. I wasn't accusing you. But you were the last to see him, so I need to know exactly what happened after you left here on Saturday. In fucking detail.'

The Beast delivered a faithful account. When he described Billy being beaten up by Doc, Priest stopped him. 'Say that again?'

'Before we handed him over. The Doc saddened him.'

'Deeply saddened?'

'Yeah. Smashed in his face.'

'Did you join in?'

'No.'

'Did you try and stop it?'

'No.'

'Why the fuck not?'

'I didn't see the point, Malcolm. The fella was reap meat. What difference did it make if he died with a full set of teeth or not?'

Normally, Priest would have shouted, but he could see the Beast was upset. 'Well, the point, as I've tried to explain to you brain-damaged fucking bastards a thousand times, is that I don't want my own people with blood on their hands. Or on their clothes. Haven't you heard of forensic fucking science?'

The Beast nodded dumbly. It was like being back at school. One day, the Beast was sure of it, Priest would get his cane out and order him to bend over.

'I suppose you think I was wrong to give the order?' said Priest.

This made the Beast flinch. It was as if Priest had read his mind. 'No.'

'You lying ginger tosser.'

'No, not at all. I mean, I didn't personally have anything against the lad. I'm sure you had your reasons for boxing him.'

'Oh, *thank you*.'

'I just don't know what they were. I mean, I'm presuming it was 'cause he was asking questions about Bryan. But reaping him for asking questions about a guy we haven't reaped yet wouldn't make a lot of sense.' (Priest subjected the Beast to a steady glare.) 'I mean, we will reap Bryan when we catch up with him, won't we? We just don't know where he is.'

'Have you quite fucking finished?'

'Yep.'

'Good. Well, listen and learn. I decide who lives or dies, not you.'

The Beast nodded. 'Yes, boss.'

'What do you think this is? A fucking democracy?'

'I don't know.'

'You don't know what a democracy is, do you? You fucking idiot.'

The Beast squirmed. 'You don't get what I'm saying, though. I'm not saying you have to answer to me. Course you don't. All I'm saying is, I've known worse people than Billy Dye.'

Priest's nostrils flared. 'Like who?'

'Well, car clampers, for instance. Taxi drivers. And what about sales reps? I could wring their fucking necks. The way they hog the fast lane of the motorway in their shitty Cavaliers and Mondeos, cutting up everyone on the road for the sake of a bastard commission . . .' The Beast stopped, realizing he was rambling.

Priest took a deep breath, trying to calm down. He suffered from high blood pressure and the Beast wasn't helping. 'Just tell me why the Doc laid into Dye.'

'Oh, the kid was sticking it to him in the pub.'

'What about?'

'I can't remember. You know what a sarcastic bleeder he was.'

'And what happened then? After the pub? I want it all clear in me mind.'

The Beast told the story, including the two warning shots fired by Rawhead and the journey back to Priest's house. '. . . Then Doc got into his motor and said, "See you Monday."'

Priest spat cigar juice onto the patio. 'You certainly know how to tell a story.'

The rebuke was wasted on the Beast. 'Then he just drove off, same as always.'

Priest pondered for a few moments. 'So who boxed the Doc?'

The Beast said, 'The only person I can think of is Billy Dye.'

Malcolm Priest snorted with derision at the very idea. 'Yeah. And God exists!'

'Just a thought.'

'Are you seriously suggesting that a little fucking pen-pusher who had just had the living shit kicked out of him burned the best reaper we've got? 'Cause that's the only way he'd have got away with his life. Have you ever met this Rawhead fella?'

'No.'

'I have. He's big and he looks fucking evil, even in that stupid fucking hood. You wouldn't like to take him on and even I'd think twice. So Billy Dye had no chance. No fucking chance.'

'He may be dead,' mused the Beast. 'But that don't mean he can't hurt you.'

'Yeah? How?' Priest was grinning, obviously tickled by the idea that anyone could hurt him.

The Beast stood his ground. 'Dye might have been scum, but he was *respectable* scum. He had family. People who'll miss him. They'll go to his house and find he's not there, so they'll call the law. And when the law finds out he was mixed up with you, what's the first thing they're going to think?'

'That if I go to prison, they'll have to pay for their own fucking holidays.'

Rawhead boiled a kettle of water and washed. Then he cooked a huge breakfast for himself and Billy.

After the meal Billy lay reading on the bed while Rawhead climbed into a sleeping bag and slept on the floor. Perhaps he knew what was going through Billy's mind, because he slept with his head against the door. He slept like he did everything else: silently and with no superfluous movement.

After about an hour, Billy got bored. He leaned over the bed, bringing his face close to Rawhead's face. As he studied the strong, sullen features, Rawhead opened his eyes. In less than a second, he had pointed a gun at Billy's right eye.

Billy almost fell off the bed in surprise. 'I was just looking.'

'Don't.' Rawhead closed his eyes and fell asleep again, still gripping the gun.

Billy took *In a Glass Darkly* down from its shelf and began to read. Rain drummed on the roof. When he grew tired of the book, he gazed out of the nearest window. Despite the weather, a man was standing at the gate, face turned towards the caravan. His features were indistinct but he gave the impression of being overweight and in his fifties. He was wearing a Barbour jacket and some kind of black hat which covered his ears. His attitude was relaxed: leaning forward, elbows resting on the iron gate. Two minutes passed and he didn't move.

Billy was distracted by a soft slap. *In a Glass Darkly* had fallen off the bed. Because the book was a valuable first edition, he was unable to leave it lying on the floor. Returning the precious volume to its shelf took no more than a few seconds. But by the time Billy turned back to the window, the onlooker had gone.

Rawhead awoke in the middle of the afternoon, rinsed his face and made coffee. As they drank, Billy told him about the man at the gate. Rawhead questioned Billy thoroughly, forcing him to repeat his description of the stranger three times. 'Doesn't sound like anyone I've seen around. It's probably nothing. But we can't risk it. I've got to move you, Billy. Tomorrow I'll take you to your new home.'

Billy said he wasn't going anywhere until he'd visited his house in Albert Road to pick up a few things. Rawhead thought this was a bad idea. 'Why bother?'

'Clothes. Shoes. A few books. The disks I've saved my work on.'

'No. It's too risky. They'll be watching the house.'

'Come on. You can't expect me to leave my entire life behind.'

'You can start a new life.'

'Why the fuck should I?'

After a brooding silence, Rawhead sighed. 'All right. But we go there at first light. OK? And you do exactly what I say.'

During the long evening, Billy asked Rawhead about his real mother. 'You always wanted to meet her. Did you ever find her?'

Rawhead gave a slight nod.

'Yeah? What was she like?'

'She was a nasty old slag, Billy. I mean, literally. She was an alcoholic prostitute who dropped her knickers for the tramps at King's Cross.'

'I'm sorry.'

'Wasn't quite what I had in mind. Know what I mean? I was hoping for someone a bit more like Julie Andrews.'

Rawhead fell silent. Billy waited and waited for him to speak again, but he'd withdrawn to his dark inner sanctuary. Once again, Billy studied the savage face, now in profile. Billy decided that what made Rawhead so striking was not his presence but his absence. A quality of infinite remoteness, as if he had somehow crossed the barrier between this world and the next and had no further interest in earthly affairs.

'You didn't see her again?'

No answer. Billy was about to give up on the conversation when Rawhead turned to him and said, 'Well, I'll tell you the truth.' He gave a short, bitter laugh. 'She stank so bad I could scarcely get within ten yards of her.'

'What about Philip and Pam?'

'Oh, they had a bit of bad luck. Pam got Alzheimer's when she was about fifty-two. And when her mind was gone, he started abusing her.'

Billy found this hard to imagine. 'Who? Philip? I don't believe it. I thought he loved her.'

'So did I.'

'Did he hit her?'

'No, he just used to humiliate her.'

'How?'

'Oh, in odd little ways. For instance, did you know Nana Kenyon?'

'Don't think so.'

'Pam's mum. My nana. Anyway, Nana died and I went to the funeral. This'd be about five years ago, when Pam was pretty far gone. And Phil had dressed her up in a bright red coat with gold buttons, when everyone else was wearing black. By this stage, her mind was practically destroyed. But she still had these periods of lucidity, when for a few fleeting seconds she'd know exactly what was going on.

'So there we were, in the funeral car and, just for a moment, Pam's herself again. And she looks round, and sees that everybody's wearing black. And she can't understand why she's dressed in red. And he's just sitting there, smiling to himself.'

'That's horrible.'

'Yeah. She died soon after that.'

'What about Philip?'

'He died, too.'

Early the next morning, Rawhead drove Billy to Levenshulme in his van, a Mercedes Sprinter. On the way, Billy quizzed Rawhead about his personal life.

'So you've got no family? No friends?'

'That's right.'

'You're alone, then.'

The barbarous face, expressionless and calm, turned to Billy. 'You can't place your trust in people. People will always let you down. The centre of your life has got to be here.' He thumped his breast for emphasis. 'You've got to be at peace with yourself.'

'How can you be at peace with yourself,' asked Billy reasonably, 'when you go round killing people?'

'Billy, it's the only thing that's ever given me a sense of fulfilment. Murder's my creative outlet.'

Billy shook his head. 'Murder isn't creative.'

Cold fire flickered in the unblinking eyes. 'It is the way I do it.'

Billy lived in a crumbling three-storey Edwardian villa. They cruised past the house twice, looking for signs of movement. There were none. Rawhead parked the van and waited outside, keeping watch, while Billy went in to pick up a few belongings. He fumbled with his keys and opened the front door cautiously. Morning light flooded the dingy hall.

There was a pile of letters and free newspapers lying on the floor. But thankfully, no dog turds. He carried the post into the kitchen and turned on the light. Among the mail was a letter from Nikki. He recognized the handwriting. The envelope had a Congleton postmark. He shoved the letter into his jacket pocket and climbed the stairs.

On the first floor, he turned and walked into the living room, casting a wistful eye over his computer and his books. Floppy disks were scattered over his desk. There was nothing unusual about this. Billy was untidy. Rawhead had told him to fill one case. Billy felt a lump in his throat as he looked at his own published works, sitting proudly on the top shelf of his black Habitat bookcase. Wherever he was going, those books were going with him.

He walked into the bedroom and dragged a dusty suitcase down from its place on top of the wardrobe. Then he opened the case and piled in his favourite clothes. When the case was full, he realized that he hadn't packed his leather jacket. He was going to need a second bag. He didn't give a shit what Rawhead had said. Rawhead wasn't being asked to walk away from everything he'd ever known. Billy took a neat black flight bag from the bottom of the wardrobe and laid the jacket inside it. He'd just get his most crucial books and disks from the living room and then it would be time to leave.

He picked up both bags and walked out onto the landing. It was there that he bumped into Newey, who was descending the stairs from the top floor. 'Fucking hell!' said Newey, who thought he was seeing a ghost. The two men stared at each other, numb with shock. Then Billy, seeing an opportunity, rammed Newey's legs with the heavy suitcase. Newey grunted, lost his balance and rolled downstairs. Billy flung the case after him.

Halfway down, Newey hit his head on the banister rail and stopped bouncing. Billy's case spilled open, covering Newey with clothes. Billy, already out of ideas, remained on the landing, looking down. He didn't know what to do or where to go. So he just stood there.

Newey, now realizing that Billy was not a phantom but could easily be turned into one, reached into his jacket and yanked out a Heckler & Koch automatic.

Newey had wanted to shoot Billy ever since their first meeting. Now he had the chance. In his eagerness, he fired twice without taking aim. The thunderous double echo burned in Billy's ears. Two bullets slammed into the wall above his head.

A hunk of plaster broke free from the wall and clattered to the floor. Newey, still sprawled on his back, tried again. The shot went wide, hitting the bag Billy was holding and blowing it out of his hand. Newey grabbed hold of the banister and pulled himself up.

Billy still hadn't moved.

During his soldiering days, Newey had seen enough men freeze under fire to know that Billy posed no threat. With a care that was almost mocking, he raised himself on to one knee and aimed his weapon at Billy's crotch. Might as well enjoy himself.

It was then that Billy saw something moving on the ground floor. Newey, alerted by the direction of Billy's gaze, turned his head to see Rawhead standing at the foot of the stairs. He was wearing his executioner's hood and his long dark coat and his gun was levelled at Newey's back.

Rawhead held a gun as most people would hold a pen: calmly and unexcitedly, without a hint of drama. His weapon, a beautiful revolver with a blue finish, looked exactly like a six-shooter from a cowboy film. The ludicrously phallic barrel was at least seven inches long.

At the sight of Rawhead and his large gun, Newey visibly lost heart. All the confidence and aggression drained out of him and he lowered his right hand despondently, as if the rapid-firing weapon it held was no more dangerous than a water pistol. 'Don't shoot,' he said, his throat hoarse and dry.

The three men remained immobile for several seconds, Billy looking down at Newey and Rawhead, Newey and Rawhead staring at each other.

Rawhead ascended the lowest stair. 'Put the gun on the floor. Do it slowly.' His voice was chillingly calm. As Newey obeyed, Rawhead's eyes took in his neatly pressed grey trousers and navy blue blazer, with the badge of the Royal Fusiliers on the breast pocket. 'You look very smart,' he said.

'This is just a job to me. It's not worth getting killed for. Know what I mean?' said Newey.

'I know what you mean,' said Rawhead, taking off his hood.

7

*Certain houses, like certain persons, manage somehow
to proclaim at once their character for evil.*
'The Empty House', Algernon Blackwood

Rawhead escorted Newey out to the van at gunpoint
and drove him away, leaving Billy alone in the
house. Billy poured himself a glass of Scotch and
gulped it down neat. He half expected the neighbours to come round to complain about the noise.
But his neighbours were all junkheads. The useless
bastards probably couldn't tell the difference between
a gunshot and a knock at the door.

Billy's clothes, hair and body were drenched in
sweat, so he took a cool shower. Ordinarily, he
would have shaved. But he was shaking too much to
make such an undertaking practical. While he dried
himself, he examined his face in the mirror. The
bruises around his eyes were fading. Rawhead had
done a fine job of redirecting his broken nose. When
the swelling went down, he'd have a nose like Marlon Brando.

His eyes didn't look like Brando's, though. At the moment, he had eyes like Janet Leigh in *Psycho*, just after she's been stabbed to death by Tony Perkins. Rawhead had given Billy Newey's handgun and told him to use it on anyone who entered the house unannounced. The gun had 'Heckler & Koch' stamped on its breech. Billy kept the gun on the side of the bath while he showered, just in case he was caught out like Janet Leigh.

He was shocked and scared. He was also confused. Had he successfully carried out his plan to escape from Rawhead, he would now be dead. No question. The zeal with which Newey had tried to slaughter him corroborated everything Rawhead had said. Malcolm Priest didn't forgive and forget. That was why, instead of running away or calling the police, Billy dressed and made himself some tea and toast. Then he sat down and waited for the man who had saved his life.

Rawhead returned alone, shortly after nine. Billy watched him park, then carried his bags to the van. Rawhead sent him back into the house to fetch Newey's gun, which he'd left on the arm of the sofa. Rawhead was calm and in control.

'What did you do to him?' said Billy.

'I took him to McDonald's and bought him a Happy Meal,' said Rawhead impatiently. 'What do you think I did?'

'Oh, Christ,' said Billy.

'What's the matter now?'

'You fucking *executed* him,' said Billy. 'If you'd shot him while he was shooting at me, that'd have been different. But driving him away at gunpoint and then doing it . . .'

'What?'

'What do you mean, "What?"? Can't you see how cold-blooded that is?'

'Billy, the guy was about to kill you. What are you complaining about?'

'Don't you see anything bad about what you've done? You drove this guy to a lonely spot and you *put a bullet in him.*'

'No.' Aware that he had Billy's full attention, Rawhead smiled and said, 'The bullet went right through him.'

'You think it's funny?'

'Don't you?'

'I think it's *evil.*'

'Well, Bill, in case you hadn't noticed, it's an evil world. Any idea what that guy was up to? He'd come to wipe your computer and take away your tapes but he also came for this.' Rawhead dropped a narrow leather-bound volume into his companion's lap. It was Billy's address book. 'A complete list of names and addresses of anyone likely to ask awkward questions about you.'

They were heading for Stockport, crawling through heavy traffic in brilliant sunshine. Stockport

Road had never looked so ugly. Rawhead slipped a pair of Ray-Bans out of his coat and put them on.

'And now you've killed him,' said Billy. 'How do you feel? Better? Worse? What?'

'Honestly?'

'Yeah.'

'I feel irritated.'

'*Irritated?*'

'Yeah. I'd forgotten what a self-righteous arsehole you can be. It may have escaped your attention, but I didn't want to go to your poxy house in the first place. But you insisted, didn't you? If it wasn't for you, that guy'd still be alive. And now I've got a question for you. What's in those bags that's worth a man's life?'

The journey lasted three and a half hours, without a break. They took the M1 south, then the A14 to Kimbolton. Then they drove through miles of flat, featureless farmland until they came to a village called Dudloe. The village was as drab as its name. It had a school, a pub called the Ploughboy, a church and a chapel, but no shops. According to Rawhead, the post office had been closed down after a local scandal; the sub-postmistress had been sent to prison for opening other people's mail.

The church of St Michael dated back to the late seventeenth century and had an impressive spire that dominated the skyline, towering over the fields for miles around. Rawhead, to Billy's astonishment, lived in the old vicarage, next to the church and the densely populated churchyard.

The vicarage was a Victorian Gothic monstrosity with turrets, towers and steeply sloping gables. Ivy and Virginia creeper covered the grey stone walls. Stone-mullioned windows glared out at the world with genteel malice. Billy felt a real sense of doom. Rawhead's home looked bad enough by daylight. After dark, it would be terrifying.

The house was surrounded by an acre of unkempt lawn, where lime trees and wild flowers grew in profusion. 'Jesus,' said Billy, standing on the drive, 'when you said you'd got money put by, I didn't think you meant this kind of money. Where does the vicar live?'

Rawhead grinned. 'In the new vicarage next door. The one that looks like a council house.'

'Does he talk to you?'

'He has to. I'm a churchwarden.'

'A what?'

'A churchwarden.'

Billy gawped. 'Do you believe in God?'

'No, I just like having a key to the church.'

They mounted the steps of a ludicrously ornate porch that seemed to have been stolen from the Albert Memorial. Golden serpents coiled about its pillars. Tiny skulls and grotesque beasts leered from under the rim of its canopy. Rawhead unlocked the double front doors. Each contained a window of leaded glass in which a dark figure with black, outspread wings terrorized a small figure in a Quaker hat. 'Scenes from *The Pilgrim's Progress*,' explained Rawhead. 'Not the kind of book I'd care to read myself.'

In the hall, a white marble Madonna and Child provided an unsettling touch of piety. The house was virtually derelict. It hadn't been properly cleaned or decorated for years. There was no heating. The floors were mainly uncarpeted. Only four of the rooms were adequately furnished: the library, the kitchen, the dining room and the living room (which Rawhead insisted on calling the parlour).

Upstairs, there were five bedrooms, three of which were kept locked. Rawhead's bedroom contained a bed and a wardrobe. The so-called 'guest room' on the north side of the house, where Billy was to sleep, was empty apart from a bed. Green velvet curtains at the French windows were dark with grease. The glass itself was cracked. Cold wind blew through gaps in the rotten frame.

The window opened onto a hideous north-facing balcony that cowered miserably under the church spire. The only view was of the cemetery. The shadow of the spire ensured that neither balcony nor room ever saw the sun. Billy couldn't imagine staying here for one night, let alone a year.

'God Almighty, this place is straight out of a Hammer Horror,' said Billy.

Rawhead seemed pleased. 'Of course. Why do you think I bought it?'

'You don't expect me to sleep here?'

'Why not?'

'I'd fucking shit myself.'

'But you write horror stories. Don't tell me you're afraid of the dark.'

'It's not the dark that scares me. It's what's *in* the dark.'

'Billy, the dead aren't going to hurt you. It's the living you need to worry about. The dead just want you to be happy.'

'You believe in spirits?'

'Of course. We're surrounded by spirits, every hour of the day.'

'How can you kill people and think that?'

'Because it's only the living that fear death. The dead have no problem with death. It's like that line from *The Bride of Frankenstein*, "Hate living, love dead." The dead don't reproach me for killing, as long as I do it well. They see death as a release and a blessing.'

Billy shivered. 'You honestly believe that?'

'Billy, I *know* it.'

*

That evening, they went to the Ploughboy for supper. The pub was almost empty. To Billy's relief no one made any reference to his injured face. The locals seemed to know and like Rawhead, whom they addressed as 'Roger'. 'How's it going, Rodge?' Billy saw another side to Rawhead: the skilled, charming actor, flirting harmlessly with the fat, flint-eyed landlady and buying pints for the old men sitting at the bar.

'This is Monty,' said Rawhead, slapping Billy's shoulder. 'He'll be looking after the house for me while I'm away on my travels.'

'Monty?' said Dennis, an old man who had served at El Alamein. 'Now there's a name to be proud of . . .'

Billy complained about this when he and Rawhead were sitting down to microwaved lasagne. 'Fucking "Monty"!'

'Well, you can hardly use your real name.'

'I know. But "Monty"? Sounds like a porn star from the nineteen-fucking-seventies. And not even a big-dicked porn star.'

'I was actually thinking of Montague Rhodes James,' said Rawhead, 'a pot-bellied scholar from the eighteen hundreds. So no offence intended.'

The bullet that had pierced Billy's flight bag had also ventilated his leather jacket. There were two heat-scorched holes in the right sleeve where the bullet had passed through. Rawhead pointed the holes out to Billy while they were eating. 'Looks like your friend left you something to remember him by.'

'He was no friend of mine, Roger,' said Billy. 'By the way, can you explain something to me, Rodge?'

'What?'

'Why's it all right for them to call you Roger, but not all right for me to call you Steve?'

'Because my name's Rawhead.'

'Roger Rawhead? That's the stupidest fucking name I've ever heard.'

It wasn't funny, but Billy's old friend threw back his head and laughed. At that moment, Billy remembered that Newey was lying dead in a hole somewhere. The thought made him feel sadder than hell.

The trek back to the vicarage took about twenty minutes. Billy had to rest every few minutes because of his injured knee. They walked in silence, Rawhead having reverted to his habitual mood of majestic gloom. There were no street lamps. The lane was submerged in deep country darkness. Something snuffled and twitched behind a hedge as they passed. The sky was black, its stars digitally bright. As they neared the church, Billy's knee started to throb.

'How am I going to get around this dump?'

'What do you mean?'

'I mean, what's the local bus service like?'

'Pretty regular.'

'How regular?'

'Once a week.'

Rawhead let Billy swear and rant, then mentioned that he had a motorbike that Billy was free to use.

'I bet it's a fucking moped,' complained Billy.

As Billy had anticipated, the vicarage looked even less inviting by night. A cool wind was blowing over the fields, making the lime trees dance. As Rawhead unlocked the front doors, Billy glanced over to the shabby house next door and caught a glimpse of a pale face at the dark attic window. He waved and the face melted back into the darkness.

'Someone was watching us,' said Billy.

'The vicar,' said Rawhead, not bothering to look. 'The nastiest, most ungodly bastard on Satan's earth.'

'He spies on you?'

'He probably spies on God.'

'But you're a churchwarden.'

'Doesn't mean he likes me.'

They entered the house and walked through the dining room to the kitchen. Rawhead turned on the light. The stone floor was the colour of old bones. At the far end of the room, a narrow flight of steps led down to another locked door. 'I suppose this is where you keep all the bodies?' joked Billy.

'I keep my work where it belongs,' Rawhead said with a smile. He took two bottles of Beck's from the fridge and handed one to Billy. Then he went out and returned with a Remington shotgun and a big box of cartridges. 'Know how to use one of these?'

Billy laughed and shook his head. Deadly serious, Rawhead showed him how to pump and load the shotgun, then encouraged Billy to do the same. He showed Billy how to rest the stock against his shoulder to lessen the recoil. Billy pretended to shoot the electric toaster, then, as a joke, turned the sights on Rawhead. Instantly, Rawhead grabbed the barrel and twisted the shotgun out of Billy's hands. '*Never* do that. Never aim a gun at anyone unless you're going to use it.'

'Like I said, a true humanitarian,' said Billy.

A large fly was sitting on the blank wall beside them. Rawhead punched it flat with his fist. Then he went upstairs to sweep Billy's room and put fresh linen on the bed.

In the parlour, Rawhead kept an impressive collection of old horror films on video. Billy knew it was impressive, because he had virtually the same collection at home. Absolute classics like *Dead of Night*, *The Innocents*, *The Haunting*, *The Bride of Frankenstein*, and Murnau's *Nosferatu* starring Max Schreck as a vampire with a skull like a hairless rat. There was *The Devil Rides Out*, Hammer's most effective stab at the occult, and Billy's personal favourite, Jacques Tourneur's *Night of the Demon* (known as *Curse of the Demon* in the US). The film turned out to be Rawhead's favourite, too. It was a spirited if flawed adaptation of an M. R. James story called 'Casting the Runes'.

When they were on their second Beck's, Rawhead and Billy sat down to watch the film together, ridiculing Dana Andrews, the film's star, who appeared to have been carved out of wood. But they had nothing but admiration for the movie's highlights, like the children's party at which Karswell, played by the wonderfully wicked Niall MacGinnis, summons up a wind storm, and the sequence when the wooden star is pursued through the trees by an invisible demon.

'They should have read M. R. James a little more closely,' enthused Rawhead. 'Maybe they wouldn't have made the mistake of showing the demon at the start of the film.'

'Particularly as the demon looks like the Tasmanian Devil,' agreed Billy.

'Suggested terrors work best,' said Rawhead. 'I despise all those comic-book films like *The Evil Dead*. The highlight of *The Exorcist* is the dream sequence where the priest sees his old mother walking into the subway. We sense all his pain and guilt because she's too far away, he can't reach her. The green vomit and the head swivelling round, that's just cheap shit. But a man who feels he's abandoned his sweet old mother . . . that's true darkness.'

Billy nodded with too much enthusiasm and spilt

beer on his jeans. 'The dream sequence is the best, no contest. But you know which bit comes a close second? The scene where the girl levitates, and her eyeballs have rolled back in their sockets. There's a lovely shot of her taken from the ceiling, as she drifts up to the camera, all silent and staring.'

'That's a great moment,' acknowledged Rawhead.

'Fucking hell! Do you realize what happened? We practically had a conversation.'

Rawhead granted Billy a cautious nod.

'Steve, I want to go home.'

'I know.' Rawhead winked. 'Bear with me, Bill. We'll work something out.'

Then he caught Billy off balance by asking why his books weren't more successful. 'Well, it could be that they're no good,' said Billy, 'but I don't happen to believe that. I think part of the trouble has been Blake Terry.'

'Who?'

'My editor.'

'What's wrong with him?'

'He does a shite job of promoting my books, then blames me for the fact that no one fucking buys 'em.'

'I think you're exaggerating, Bill.'

'No, I'm absolutely fucking not! Last time I complained about it, the bastard told me to "hold my tongue". As if I was ten years old.'

'You need a new editor.'

'I'm not going to find one without an agent. And my agent thinks I'm crap, too.'

'Have you got one of these books on you?'

In a fit of drunken generosity, Billy dashed upstairs to his new bedroom and grabbed a copy of his latest book, *Necropolis*. On his return to the living room he presented the book to Rawhead, who accepted it in silence.

'You don't have to read it,' said Billy.

'No, I will,' said Rawhead, his eyes fierce and intense. 'I'll take it away with me.'

Billy's attention returned to the TV screen. The film was reaching its climax. Niall MacGinnis was about to be mauled by a demon on a railway line. 'You know, it was films like this that inspired me to be a writer,' declared Billy.

'They inspired me to be a monster,' said Rawhead.

'Yeah? You wouldn't even have known about all this shit if I hadn't introduced you to it.'

Rawhead nodded. 'That's right. You showed me the way to go, Billy. I may be a monster. But you created me.'

In the night, Billy awoke to find Rawhead standing by his bed. He was fully dressed, motionless and silent, staring down at Billy in the dark.

'What is it?' Billy mumbled, tongue stiff from sleep.

'Go to sleep,' answered Rawhead softly.

After Billy's most peaceful night in decades, he awoke refreshed in a house from a nightmare. Although the sun was shining, the old vicarage was filled with shadows and brooding silence. There was no sign of Rawhead, and the Sprinter van was missing from the drive. On the kitchen table lay a map of the area and a shoebox filled with drugs, all helpfully labelled. There were keys for the house, the church and the bike Rawhead had mentioned.

Billy found the bike in a ramshackle wooden outhouse that served as a garage. It turned out to be a 1999 Harley Davidson, an XL 1200 Sportster in black, with a matching helmet resting on the seat. Billy took the Harley for a test drive around the twisting country roads, at first driving conservatively, but speeding up when country yokels in cars tried to overtake him. Every fifth vehicle seemed to be a decaying pickup truck driven at ninety miles an hour by a thirteen-year-old farmboy with a fixed homicidal stare.

After visiting the supermarket and riding past the river in Bedford, Billy found he had exhausted the area's beauty spots. Deflated, he returned to the Ploughboy. The same few old men were seated at the bar, their backs to a room full of empty chairs and tables. Billy ordered a toasted cheese sandwich and a pint of cold Guinness.

Today the landlady, perhaps assuming that he was going to be a regular, was marginally more cordial. 'That'll wet your whistle,' she smiled, passing Billy his pint.

Dennis the war veteran said, 'On your own, Monty?'

At first, Billy didn't respond, not recognizing the stupid name Rawhead had saddled him with. When he saw Dennis nodding at him, he could think of nothing to say in return, so he nodded back.

'Roger off on his travels again?'

Billy confirmed this.

'A nice fella, that Roger,' said Dennis. His wizened cronies mumbled their agreement. 'When he's here – which ain't that often, I admit – but when he's here, he does a lot for the old folk in this village.'

'Does he?' said Billy, unable to conceal his scepticism.

'He does,' asserted Dennis. 'I know he looks a bit wild, but that lad's heart's in the right place.'

'A rough diamond,' chipped in the landlady, who seemed to have a cliché for every occasion.

'He keeps an eye on me,' continued Dennis. 'I got burgled, you see. So Roger promised to keep a lookout. And blow me if I didn't look out of the window late one night to see old Rodge standing in the front garden, watching the house. He was standing guard, you see. I don't mind admitting that I slept easier in my bed after that.'

Billy returned to the vicarage and its choking stillness. The silence screamed at him. He felt an unrest stirring inside him that might, if left unchecked, grow to panic. He may have been safe. But he was also lonely. Even if there had been a phone, he couldn't have called anyone; he was supposed to be dead.

Remembering the complimentary box of drugs, Billy considered taking an E to lift his spirits. But he feared the comedown, knowing it would coincide with the onset of night and the fresh anxieties the darkness would bring. Billy saw how easy it would be to slip into a life of squalid inertia, hardly washing, spending most of his time sleeping and watching horror videos. With drugs to speed his decline, Billy could imagine himself doing rash and foolish things, like phoning Malcolm Priest at home to announce, 'I'm still here, you fat bastard.'

He went for a walk around the locked church, watching the spire dragging the clouds behind it, his feet unsteady as he remembered that he was standing on a ball spinning through space. Four gargoyles leered out from the battlements, their faces turned to each point of the compass. Above the arched doorway in the west wall was lodged a deeply engraved stone tablet. It read:

In Memory of the mighty Hand Of the Great God and Our Savour – Jefus Chrift, Who prefurved the Life of William Dickins, April 17th 1718 when he was Pointing the Steepol and Fell From the Rige of the Middel Window in the Spiar Over the South-Weft Pinackel Yet when he See he was Faling Crid out Wots the Matter Lord Have Mercy Upon me Chrift Have Mercy Upon me Lord Jefus Chrift Help me he Dropt Upon the Batelment and their Broak his Leg Died Novr 29th 1759 Aged 73 Years

Locally, the event recorded by the tablet was known as the 'Dudloe Miracle'. Billy thought the most miraculous aspect of William Dickins's escape was the amount he managed to say between falling and the moment of impact.

Billy entered the porch. On a noticeboard beside the main door, a list of the churchwardens was pinned. Billy scrutinized the list until he found 'Roger Gawdy, The Old Vicarage, Church Lane'. He smiled, recognizing the provenance of the bogus surname: Gawdy was the name of a murderous spectre in M. R. James's 'The Mezzotint'.

He unlocked the door to the church with a huge rusty brown key that seemed positively medieval and stepped into the cool musty nave. Like the vicarage, the church was dark and unwholesome.

The stained-glass windows seemed only to be stained with dirt and age. Damp seeped up through the stone floors.

Near the altar stood a macabre bronze sculpture of St Michael wrestling with the devil. The devil was strangely emaciated, more like a famine victim than a fiend. To the right of the pulpit was a peculiar throne, which for some reason had been set aside for the exclusive use of the Bishop of St Albans. Hoping he was committing a blasphemy, Billy sat in the Bishop's throne and ate half a packet of Rolos from his pocket.

After locking the church, he wandered idly among the graves. Many of the headstones were cracked and broken beyond repair. Opposite the porch stood a stone sarcophagus in a railed enclosure. The lid of the tomb lay slightly askew, exposing the blackness within. Had he wanted to, Billy could have reached into the gap and shaken hands with the occupant.

There was one recent plot, covered with a mound of decaying flowers. The soil under the flowers was moist and dark. The inscription on the tablet read: 'Joseph Hartop, Aged 87, Bell Captain for 39 years'. He peered at the label on a large bouquet. Its label was damp, the ink smudged. The message read: 'To Grandad, thanks for all the fun we had together. Love James.'

A blackbird alighted on a nearby grave, its plumage contrasting starkly with the neat white headstone. The church clock struck three. Startled by the sound, the bird crashed, shrieking, under the boughs of a yew tree.

Billy took a bottle of whisky and a glass into Rawhead's library, where he spent the evening. He was so astonished by the treasures there, that for a few hours he almost forgot how terrible his life was. Every classic writer of supernatural literature was represented, from Mary Shelley to Stephen King.

There was a bound first edition of *Dracula*, dated 1893, its pages reeking of lavender and age. Billy found an awesome first edition of etchings from *Paradise Lost* by the artist Gustave Doré. The book contained the image of the angel he'd first seen in Rawhead's caravan: Satan hurtling down to hell after his eviction from heaven.

As Billy had expected, there was a first edition of *The Devil Rides Out* by Dennis Wheatley. As teenagers, both boys had loved this novel, blissfully unaware of its snobbery or its staggering ignorance of occultism.

The M. R. James section contained all the author's collections of ghost stories, as well as a reminder of his scholarly vocation: *The Apocryphal New Testament*. Glancing through this, Billy noticed that a section from The Acts of Thomas had been underlined in pencil. Surprised that his friend the bibliophile should deface a book in this way, Billy studied the lines carefully. They read: 'Again he took me, and showed me a cave exceedingly dark, breathing out a great stench, and many souls were looking out . . .'

That night, Billy found it hard to sleep. He left the landing light on and his door ajar so that the room would never be wholly dark. His king-sized bed was soft and comfortable. But several times, just as he was drifting off to sleep, a floorboard out in the passage would creak, shocking him into alertness.

Finally Billy went down to the kitchen, trying not to look at the stark blackness outside the uncurtained window. He snatched the shotgun and the box of cartridges off the kitchen table and took them upstairs with him. He returned to bed with the loaded weapon lying beside him like a cold and unaccommodating bride. Odd clicks and sighs sounded in the darkness as he descended into slumber. He closed his eyes, telling himself that such noises were commonplace in an old house.

Then he heard a scream.

It seemed to have come from downstairs. He sat up in bed, listening. He heard sobbing and a torrent of garbled words, as if someone was pleading for their life. This was followed by a harsh crack, like the sound of an axe descending. Sickened and scared, Billy picked up the shotgun. He got out of bed and opened his bedroom door.

He stood on the landing and peered over the banister. It was dark downstairs. The landing light cast his head and shoulders onto the opposite wall, advertising his presence to anyone below. Now he could hear footsteps and a slow, dragging sound. With exaggerated stealth, Billy went downstairs and stood in the hall, beside the effigy of Mary.

Billy waited there a long time without hearing or seeing anything unusual. Eventually, he walked into the dining room and turned on the light. There was no one there. Nothing had been disturbed. He walked through to the kitchen. In the light from the dining room, he could tell that the room was empty. Just to be certain, he turned on the light. There was no axe, no body.

Yet what was that smell? A pungent stench that reminded Billy of ammonia. While he was trying to locate the source of the odour, a slight movement caught his eye. He glanced up. At first, he thought that the tiles above his head were spattered with raisins. But as he stared, the raisins began to crawl. The ceiling was covered with flies.

8

I was out of spirits, and dreaded the approach of night.
'An Account of Some Strange Disturbances in Aungier Street',
Sheridan Le Fanu

Every year, throughout the summer months, Malcolm Priest held regular parties and barbecues on his
long, floodlit lawn. Loud seventies music shook the
surrounding houses as the gangster entertained
criminals, porn stars, footballers and their wives,
stars and producers from Granada TV studios and
the odd representative of the local aristocracy,
known laughably as 'the Cheshire Set'.

It was usual on these occasions for Lol Shepherd
to drive Priest's mother and her poodle to her
favourite hotel in Blackpool, so that neither she nor
the dog would have to suffer the noise or see the
glittering whores that Priest bussed in for the benefit
of his guests. Tonight Mrs Priest, still weak after her
hip operation, was recuperating in a private nursing
home.

It was Priest's first party of the year, an impromptu

affair to mark a very special occasion: that afternoon Priest had seen Manchester City beat Tranmere Rovers by two goals to nil. Whenever his team won, Priest was elated, just as he became foul-tempered and miserable beyond belief when they lost. Like most sports fans, Priest believed his personal fortunes to be inextricably linked to those of his favourite athletes. As today's win virtually guaranteed City's promotion to the Premier League at the end of the season, Priest had every reason to believe that his future was assured.

By nine o'clock, the house and the gardens were packed. Priest wasn't actually interested in meeting anyone. He could play the role of the affable villain to perfection, but his heart was closed to all but a select few. Yet there was never a shortage of people eager to meet Malcolm Priest. It gave them a thrill to know him, to be seen with him. Whatever his sins, no one could have accused Priest of being boring.

That afternoon, on a whim, Priest had erected a flagpole on his front lawn and hoisted the cross of St George. Malcolm Priest was an Englishman. Not a Briton – he despised Wales, Scotland and whichever part of Ireland was alleged to belong to the United Kingdom. Priest was a patriot – he preferred to screw the English over and above any other race on earth.

Shortly before midnight, Malcolm Priest and Boswell the PR man found themselves engaged in an impromptu debate with a Granada TV producer. The producer, Derek Tidy, had once arranged a visit to the set of *Coronation Street* for Priest's mother. Tidy had silver hair, a brick-red complexion and that distinctive sheen that people develop when they need never worry about money again.

Beside Tidy stood an attractive, extremely personal assistant. Thinking to impress the young woman, Tidy asked Priest how many major crimes he'd committed recently. Boswell, who knew what was coming, took a deep breath.

'Crime?' responded Priest. 'I'll tell you about crime. Do you know what kind of money an Avon lady earns?'

The producer shook his head nervously. The young PA tugged at his arm, as if trying to person-ally assist him into the safety of another dimension.

'My daughter worked for 'em for a while,' said Priest, 'so I know what I'm talking about. Before you can represent these wankers, you have to buy your own catalogues. *Buy* the fucking things! The goods are sold on approval, so customers have the chance to send stuff back. If they do, the company repre-sentative has to pay the return postage out of their own fucking pocket.

'The Avon lady (or fella, I'm not prejudiced) gets twenty-five per cent commission on the first hundred pounds taken, and twenty-five per cent of any fur-ther takings. If they make under a hundred, they earn about four quid. Four fucking quid! And they have the cheek to call *me* a criminal? Eh? Eh?'

Priest jabbed Tidy in the chest with his forefinger, confident that the point he'd made was flawless and unanswerable.

The producer, unable to tell whether Priest had made a point or not, bared his teeth like a frightened chimpanzee. Thinking to defuse the situation, Boswell touched Priest on the shoulder. 'Malc—'

'Hand,' said Priest, indicating the offending appendage.

'Malcolm, I'm sure Derek didn't mean anyth—'

'Hand!' snapped Priest.

Helplessly, Boswell removed his hand.

Priest pinched Tidy's cheek and twisted it. 'That favour you owe me, Derek. I'll be calling it in soon.'

Tears of self-pity brimmed in Tidy's eyes. Priest released his cheek, leaving a livid red thumbprint. Tidy's reprieve came in the nervy form of Lol Shepherd, who arrived to whisper a message in Priest's ear. Without another word, Priest walked away.

He wove his way slowly through the crowded house to the room that served as his office, where Chef was waiting. Chef, immaculately dressed, was sitting at the desk, filing a broken fingernail. His brown, heavy-lidded eyes looked up as Priest entered. Chef looked no more lugubrious than usual. It was impossible to tell whether the news he had for Priest was good or bad.

Without waiting to be asked, Chef said, 'I found this in the wall.' He placed a misshapen bullet on the desk before him.

'What fucking wall?' said Priest.

'At Dye's house. As you know, Newey carried a nine millimetre.' He prodded the bullet with the tip of his forefinger. 'That's from a nine millimetre.'

'So? Every two-bit shitehawk in Manny carries a nine millimetre,' objected Priest. Unruffled, Chef looked into his eyes. Priest said, 'How come you're telling me this now?'

'Only found out today. I went back there this afternoon for a good nose round.'

'Why didn't the Beast and Heidi notice that? The dozy cunts.'

'Not really their fault, Malcolm,' explained Chef calmly. 'Billy Dye lived in a slum. I'm not kidding. There are so many holes in his walls, you'd think the whole house had been shot by a firing squad.'

'And Newey's still missing?'

'That's right.'

'If he's on a bender or off with a slag, I'll fucking kill him.'

Chef's eyes closed momentarily as he shook his head. 'I think he's dead.'

'Oh, Christ,' said Priest, sinking into a chair. 'What the fuck's going on?'

'His fiancée's threatening to call the law. She thinks we might have topped him.'

'And once again, there's a connection with that big-mouthed little bastard of a writer,' seethed Priest.

'It looks that way.'

'What about Rawhead?'

'I've phoned Rawhead. He reaped the reap, like he was supposed to. No question, Malcolm, the guy's sound.'

'He wears a fucking bag on his head. We've paid a fortune to a twat with a bag on his head!'

'He keeps his word and he's kept it for seven years.'

'He shot at Doc and the Beast.'

Chef shook his head again. 'No, he didn't. They'd be dead if he had. He fired a couple of warning shots because they were out of order. Which, given that they were jeopardizing his carefully laid plans and placing him in danger, he was perfectly within his rights to do.'

'You should hear yourself sometimes,' scoffed Priest. 'You talk like a fucking vicar.' Priest was striding up and down the room. 'I want to see Dye's body.'

'Mal—'

'I want to see the fucking corpse! I paid for it, didn't I? Haven't you heard of consumer rights?'

Without knowing it, Chef belonged to an elite club that had only four members. The fellows of this club shared one quality in common, a characteristic that set them apart from the rest of humanity in one crucial respect: they knew Malcolm Priest, but were not afraid of him. The other members were Priest's son, his granddaughter Judith and Rawhead.

Chef shook his head firmly.

Priest was insistent. 'I want to see the fucking maggots crawling in and out of his sneering bastard face.'

'Malcolm, calm down. That isn't the way things are done. You know that.'

Priest poured himself a Scotch and drank it quickly, staring at the wall.

'There probably won't be a body now,' said Chef. 'There certainly won't be a face. And the head and the body won't be in the same place, if they're any place at all. But, Malcolm, being serious, now – I can't believe a guy who took out half of Moss Side in a single night is going to slip up over a journalist.'

'But what if he did?'

'How?'

'What if Dye legged it?'

Chef exhaled wearily.

Priest, choosing to accept his lieutenant's sigh as an admission of defeat, enlarged upon his theme. 'I'll tell you a little story. My old fella once rescued a woman from the canal in Salford. The silly cow was trying to drown herself. Dad jumps in and saves her. Only thing was, the silly old bugger couldn't swim. Still, he got her safely to shore, though. Himself an' all.'

'I don't see what you're getting at.'

'In a crisis, people find strength, don't they? Strength they didn't know they fucking had. Normally, Billy Dye was a lazy bastard who never took exercise. But who knows? Being shot at might have turned him into an Olympic sprinter.'

'Mal, even if you're right, I don't know what we can do about it.'

'Would you agree that it's better to be safe than sorry?'

Chef gave a weary nod.

Priest said, 'I think it's time to bring on the Doll.'

After his enforced retirement from the prison service, the Doll had bought a garage on Stockport Road. The name on his tax returns was Ashley Bloomer. Behind his back, his employees called him the Doll on account of his large staring eyes, his oddly delicate little mouth, his head of tight chestnut brown curls and his peculiarly tranquil smile. To his face they called him nothing at all. Hardly anyone had ever called him Ashley or Ash, not even as a child.

The Doll didn't smell. He just looked as if he did. When he was a boy at junior school, the 'Bloomer tick' had been a popular playground pursuit. The child who had been touched or 'ticked' was 'on', in theory becoming as foul-smelling and unpleasant as Bloomer was believed to be, until the torch-bearer touched another child and passed the curse on. Sometimes Bloomer himself, preferring infamy to obscurity, initiated the game of tick himself by picking a boy at random and sitting on his face.

Now that he was forty-one, no one spoke of the Bloomer tick. People no longer ran when they saw him coming. They just *felt* like running. A man so sadistic that even the Home Office had disowned him. Mechanics, trading insults freely, were reluctant to joke with the Doll. He was brutally strong, with forearms like clubs and a short, thick neck on which his small, sculpted head looked oddly out of place.

Anyone could see that there was something wrong with Bloomer. It showed in his mad eyes, his fixed smile. He appeared to shine, not with health or happiness, but with vindictiveness. If the Doll had ever been prosecuted for his repulsive crimes, millions of people seeing his image on television would have asked, 'Look at that face. How could they not have known?'

Years before, a swaggering salesman, showing off to two of Bloomer's apprentices, had dared to greet the Doll with the words, 'Hello, smiler.' The Doll had followed the joker into the gents. A few minutes later, the Doll walked out alone. The salesman was found lying on the lavatory floor. The walls, mirrors, ceiling were spattered with his blood. The salesman recovered, but was too afraid to press charges.

Business at the garage never thrived. It just about

ticked over. Although he was rarely at work, the Doll's presence hung over the premises like a cloud of locusts. Although business was seldom good, the Doll appeared to prosper. He wore good clothes and changed his car every two years.

He lived in a detached suburban house on a family estate in Poynton, with his wife Terri and their two children. Terri was deaf. She had lost her hearing as a child, after an attack of mumps. She was not stupid; but a woman capable of gazing into that cold, staring face and saying 'I do' could hardly be described as perceptive.

They had been together for twelve years. During that time, Terri had never known the Doll to read a book or a newspaper, listen to music or watch a television programme. He showed no interest in the world around him. This didn't trouble her. She, too, had always felt disconnected from the world. He had never hit her or the children. Surely that counted for something?

Nor did she ever seriously question where he went late at night, or where the money came from to pay for their new carpets, their supermarket wine and their regular holidays. Bloomer claimed to be lucky on the horses. Terri was willing to believe him. More accurately, she was unwilling to disbelieve him.

The Doll had come to Malcolm Priest's attention while he was still a prison warder. He was always willing to maim convicts that had transgressed against the Priesthood, or to turn a blind eye when a stabbing had been arranged. Bloomer had no conscience. For money he would do anything to anyone. If Rawhead was Priest's executioner, the Doll was his chief torturer. He took pleasure in his work: one man had his teeth smashed out with a hammer; a female cleaner who had stolen from the till at Priest's club had her breasts beaten with a baseball bat. Sure, it was business. But to Bloomer, it was also fun.

Like everyone in the criminal fraternity, the Doll had heard of Rawhead. So when the Doll learned that Rawhead's loyalty was in doubt, he was secretly delighted. This was the break he'd been waiting for. The chance to move up from mutilation to murder.

Chef met the Doll early one evening in the car park at Hazel Grove railway station. The Doll, immaculately dressed as always, arrived in a brand new Audi. He wore a pinstripe suit with a black tie. His shirt was white silk. The hands that extended from its cuffs were strong and matted with black hair.

The Doll sat beside Chef in the back of a pink Rolls-Royce. A nervous man the Doll didn't know occupied the driver's seat. He wore glasses. His face was long and forlorn. The Doll asked if the driver was trustworthy. Chef answered that Lol was a member of the Priesthood, meaning that the Doll was not, and should watch his mouth.

Chef spoke softly, smoking a rare cigarette and elegantly flicking the ash into a silver ashtray. Only occasionally did he direct his soulful brown eyes at the Doll. Those eyes reminded the Doll of a portrait he'd seen on a coffin lid in a Manchester museum. Some Egyptian boy in a white smock, preserved thousands of years ago so that parties of schoolkids could walk past him, sniggering, on their way to the gift shop. Served him right for being Egyptian and looking like a queer.

'You realize what you're being asked to do?' enquired Chef carefully.

The Doll caught the driver sneaking a glance at him in the rear-view mirror. He smiled. The driver quickly averted his eyes, as if caught peering down a female magistrate's cleavage. 'I think so,' said the Doll, still smiling.

The Doll's voice was a dry, leisurely sneer. Chef looked into his strange, staring face and had to repress a shudder. 'You think that's something to smile about?'

'That depends what you're planning to pay me.'

'Ten thousand to prove that the writer's dead.'

The Doll grinned. 'Not enough. Nowhere near. Not if the big fella's involved.'

'He might not be.'

'Yeah. But what if he is? It's me who's taking the chances. Not you. That bastard might find out where I live. What then? Nobody knows where he fucking lives, do they? Nobody knows what he looks like, either. Without that hood, he could walk up to me in the street, in the pub, anywhere. I wouldn't see him coming.'

'He'd be pointing a .44 Magnum at you. That should narrow it down.'

'Fuck you.'

Chef turned his face away, fighting to control his temper. He'd burned men alive for less than this and although he hardly smoked, he still carried a bottle of lighter fluid everywhere he went. But Priest respected the Doll, and Chef tried to respect Priest. So Chef let it go. 'Eleven grand, plus expenses. Give me all your receipts.'

'And what if it is Rawhead? What then?'

'Then we'll renegotiate your fee.'

'What if I'm the next one to go missing?'

Chef frowned to show he'd missed the point of the question.

'I'll need some guarantee that you'll pay compensation to my family. 'Cause if the guy's as good as they say, I'll be taking one hell of a fucking risk.'

'If *you're* as good as they say,' answered Chef smoothly, 'it shouldn't be a problem.'

The Doll refused to be flattered. 'I'm not being greedy. If you were asking me to cripple another teenager, it'd be different.'

'We're not just petty criminals, you know,' said Chef. 'We're the Priesthood. If you get boxed,

Malcolm'll look after your family, just like he looks after everyone who's loyal to him. You need have no worries on that score.

'And while we're on the subject of safety, that reminds me. I've brought you a little present. Lol?' The driver lifted a neat leather case from the front seat and passed it to Chef. Unhurriedly, Chef unfastened the case and opened it. Inside lay a gleaming machine pistol and two boxes of magazines. 'See this? It's a PP-93. Fires continuous or single shot, depending on what's required. It's Russian, but don't let that put you off. The magazines hold thirty.'

The Doll was unimpressed. 'I prefer knives.'

Not bothering to respond, Chef assembled the weapon and passed it to the Doll. The Doll was surprised. 'It's light.'

'Yep. You can fire it with one hand.' A family saloon, filled to capacity, drew up alongside. A teenage girl, showing off to her friends, pressed her face against a window and stuck her tongue out at Chef. 'Now, for God's sake, put it away.'

Moodily, the Doll replaced the PP-93 in its case. 'Where do I start?'

Chef passed him a cheap memo pad with a photograph inside it. The photo showed a long-haired man in his thirties, trying to look intelligent for the camera. 'Who's this scruffy wanker?'

'That's the writer. His name's Billy Dye,' said Chef.

'Die?' echoed the Doll. He gave a humourless laugh. 'As in "cease to breathe"?'

'D-y-e,' spelled Chef. 'As in colouring agent. His address is in the notebook. Plus the addresses of one or two people who might have heard from him. I don't care how you do it, but I want you to prove to me that he's dead.'

The Doll fixed Chef with his steady, malignant eyes. 'What if he isn't?'

'Then I want you to kill him. And I want you to cut his head off and bring it to me.'

The Doll set to work immediately researching Billy Dye: asking neighbours, showing the photograph in bars and betting shops. At first the Doll was unwilling to believe that Billy only had one friend. Most people, himself included, had drinking acquaintances who at least *pretended* to be friends. But Billy Dye turned out to be a genuine social outcast. When the Doll broke into Billy's house, he found only three messages on the answer machine. One was from a posh woman called Rosie, who sounded as if she'd got a peg on her nose. 'I'm not ringing about anything in particular, just wanted a chat.'

The second caller, a man in his thirties, gave no name. The Doll guessed this was the policeman. 'Dye, you bastard. That's not an instruction, by the way. Where are you, you unsociable cunt?'

The last message was from a woman who didn't give her name. She sounded about twenty-five. 'Billy, it's me. Why haven't you answered my letter? Call me. We really need to talk.'

The Doll dialled 1471 and wrote down the phone number. He recognized the code. It was Congleton, in Cheshire. The Doll had pleasant memories of Congleton. He'd once visited the town to throw acid in a woman's face. Out of curiosity, he dialled the number and waited. It rang and rang. No one answered.

Throughout the day, the old vicarage was silent – a silence so profound that it could not be masked by the TV, the stereo or Billy's feeble attempts to hold conversations with himself. Rain spattered the windows, the wind howled in the telephone wires. The flies that came from nowhere buzzed close to Billy's face, goading him to murderous onslaughts with a rolled-up newspaper. Three or four times a day he heard the clatter of hooves as horses passed in the lane. Always, underneath these sounds, lay a stillness as deep as death.

At night, the building came alive. From the timbers of the old house came vague and incoherent threats. Its pipes tapped, its floorboards murmured. Billy heard doors opening and closing. On the third night, just as he was falling asleep, he heard another scream. It was distant this time, like someone wailing at the end of a long tunnel. As before, Billy grabbed the shotgun and crept down to the kitchen. There were no flies. But he thought he heard footsteps. They seemed to be coming from under the ground.

He descended to the cellar door and listened. No footsteps. But as he pressed his ear to the door, there was a loud cry. The noise was barely human, somewhere between a snarl and a whimper.

Billy was now very frightened. He turned on the stereo and played 'Don't Fear the Reaper' by Blue Oyster Cult at thunderous volume, over and over again. He got drunk and leaned out of his bedroom window, watching the gravestones grinning under the church. The air was heavy with rain and the stench of smoke. On an impulse, Billy screamed and called God a bastard, in the hope that his neighbour the vicar would hear and take offence. He intended the outburst to be a grand gesture of rebellious despair. But his voice emerged as a wasp-cry, a schoolboy irrelevance in the drizzling dark.

Finally, he sat on the stairs with the shotgun across his lap. At first light, sober and weary, he went downstairs, turned off the stereo and pressed his ear to the cellar door. Nothing. Exhausted, he climbed into bed and fell asleep.

*

That afternoon, Billy took the Remington out into a cornfield behind the graveyard and shot a scarecrow. Unlike its counterparts in children's picture books, this scarecrow had no head. It was just two broom handles, incompetently bound together to form a cross, with an old raincoat draped over it. To Billy, the inept effigy was a perfect symbol of Bedfordshire, its people and its customs. He slotted a fat cartridge into the shotgun and took aim from about two yards away.

Billy had never fired a gun before, not even an air rifle. Gingerly, he squeezed the trigger. The gun boomed. Billy staggered slightly, unsteadied by the weapon's kick. The cross snapped in two and the scarecrow's coat flew into the air, travelling several feet before it dropped, smoking, into the corn. The blast of the Remington was far louder than he had expected. The shot echoed wildly, bouncing from earth to sky and back again. So painfully loud that Billy's ears ached.

Yet, to his amazement and dismay, firing the gun lit a small fire in the pit of his stomach. The fact that firearms caused misery throughout the world every day made no difference. The shotgun made him feel empowered and alive. Billy lowered the weapon and waited. It seemed inevitable that such a shattering explosion should bring people running. But no one came. Curious, he walked over the field to Church

Lane and looked both ways. There was no one in sight.

Billy searched through Rawhead's drawers and cupboards but found nothing to indicate that his friend had a past. There were no photographs, pornographic or otherwise. Bizarrely, the only item of interest was an application form for the Greater Manchester Police. The form was blank, so Billy filled it in, supplying his real name and his address in Albert Road. Under the section headed 'achievements', Billy wrote, 'I once had six wanks in a single day.' Question 7 read, 'Why do you wish to join the Police Service?' Billy's answer was, 'I'm fat, lazy and stupid, so might as well get paid for it.' Once he'd completed the form, Billy posted it, first class.

After dark, Billy went to the pub. With the exception of two teenagers, he was the only customer. The landlady confided that business was so bad she was considering suicide. To give her something to live for, Billy got drunk. After telling the landlady what a marvellous woman she was, and how attractive she was for her age, Billy drove the Harley back to the vicarage on the wrong side of the road. Sick with apprehension, he entered the dismal house.

He was greeted by the familiar smell of putre-faction.

He walked into the kitchen and descended the steps to the cellar. He stood by the cellar door and listened. Not a sound. He climbed back up the steps and noticed something tiny, wriggling under the kitchen table. Bending down to look, he found two live maggots. He wrapped them up in a sheet of kitchen towel and flushed them down the lavatory.

The church clock struck twelve. Billy took the Remington off the kitchen table and made sure it was loaded. Then he went to bed and sat up with the gun cradled in his arms, waiting for the screaming to start.

The next day was Billy's birthday. He was thirty-three years old. By that age, Alexander had conquered the world, Jesus had completed his ministry and John Lennon had written his best songs. Billy Dye had written four books, none of which had sold more than a few hundred copies.

As a birthday treat to himself, Billy had arranged to inspect the M. R. James papers held at King's College in Cambridge. By bike, the university was only thirty minutes away. He left the Harley on King's Parade and made his way through the main gates to the library. The librarian was an unwelcoming woman in glasses. She had a face like a disappointed haddock. Everything seemed to be too

much trouble for her. Billy had to interrogate her just
to find out where to hang his coat.

Fortunately, the archivist was as fair as the librarian was foul. She asked Billy for some form of identi-
fication and a letter of introduction. Billy showed her
his passport and a letter he'd written for himself on
headed paper stolen from the BBC. The letter
described Billy as the finest documentary maker of
his day and was purportedly signed by the director-
general of the BBC.

Billy chose a desk overlooking the courtyard and
the college chapel. He filled in a request slip and
passed it to the archivist. She went into another room
and returned shortly with the desired item: a complete manuscript of 'Lost Hearts', Billy's favourite
ghost story. Eight pages of foolscap were covered in
an unattractive and frequently illegible hand. Billy
waited to feel the thrill he'd experienced on seeing
original drafts of poems by Keats and Shelley, but
his emotions remained curiously dormant.

He kept telling himself that this was the actual
handwriting of the master, that these were the very
words that had fired his imagination. No emotional
response was forthcoming. He wasn't disappointed.
He didn't feel anything. He stared and stared at the
cold script and concluded that he needed a very long
holiday.

*

With great reluctance, he returned to the vicarage. He parked the bike at the side of the house and glanced up at his room. He was startled to see a pale face at the window. As he stared, the face drew back into the shadows.

Billy entered the house, shocked anew by its palpable hostility.

He stood at the foot of the stairs. 'Steve? Is that you?' He ran up to his bedroom. There was no one there. Systematically, he checked the other rooms, listened at all the locked doors and was forced to conclude that the face existed only in his disturbed mind. He was quite alone.

There were two more flies in the living room. Billy chased them with a rolled-up magazine, splatting one on the window frame and the second on the pane itself. Disheartened, but not wishing to surrender to despair, Billy decided to tidy the house.

He took off his leather jacket and hung it on a peg. Something fell to the floor from one of the pockets. It was the letter from Nikki. He had forgotten all about it. He stopped what he was doing, took the crumpled envelope into the living room and opened it.

The letter was six pages long. Billy read it slowly, and what he read astounded him. When Nikki had left in December, she had taken a secret with her. She had been expecting Billy's child. She was now seven months pregnant. Nikki wrote that because of Billy's moodiness, his unwillingness to go anywhere and his perpetual fury at the world and everyone in it, she had found living with him increasingly hard. In spite of this, she still loved him. And she was having his child. Would he consider starting again? If not, she understood. After all, it was she who had walked out on him.

Billy stared at the last page, the page containing his favourite lines. 'I tried to stop loving you. But I can't. Even when you're being miserable, I still like you more than anyone I've ever met.'

Billy appreciated this sentiment. Nikki had neatly summed up the way he felt about himself. Miserable or not, he liked himself more than anyone he'd ever met. He was overcome by emotion. Nikki loved him. Enough to have his child. Suddenly nothing else mattered. His mobile phone had vanished, probably with Rawhead's help. There were no phone lines in the house. But there was a call box in the village, outside the Ploughboy. He rode the Harley down the winding fairy-tale main road that led into the village. Trembling slightly, trying not to think about the stupidity of what he was about to do in case reason prevailed, he arrived at the phone box just as two cackling teenage girls were leaving.

The girls had left the phone box reeking of cheap scent and kiddies' sweets. Billy inserted a pound coin and dialled the number at the top of the letter. There was a pause, followed by the engaged tone. He tried again, got the same result.

Billy swore and cursed his luck. What now? On an impulse, he dialled Tony's number. It rang a few times, then Billy heard a young girl's voice. It was Steff, Tony's eldest daughter. 'Yeah?'

'Hiya. Is Tony there?'

Eschewing social niceties, Steff, who was no older than nine, clunked the phone down. With irritation in her voice, she shouted, 'Dad!'

There was a pause. Billy could hear a TV in the background, and a door banging. Tony picked up the phone. 'Hiya?'

'It's me,' said Billy.

'Bill? Fucking hell! I thought you'd emigrated!'

'You're not far off the mark, mate.'

'Where have you been? I've been phoning you for fucking weeks.'

'I'm in trouble.'

'What kind of trouble?'

'Malcolm Priest trouble.'

Tony groaned. 'Oh, you deranged bastard. I told you, didn't I? I *told* you not to go near that fat sack of shit.'

They hadn't spoken since January, when Tony had phoned to wish Billy a Happy New Year. He knew nothing of Priest's unholy commission and the grief it had led to. 'How are you, anyway?' said Billy, making conversation.

'Fine,' answered Tony curtly. 'But I can tell you're not. What's wrong with your voice? You sound bloody awful.'

'I feel it,' said Billy, his voice cracking. 'It's my birthday.' Then, to his surprise and embarrassment, he began to snivel.

'Oh, for fuck's sake!' protested Tony. 'I'll send you a card tomorrow. Don't start crying on me. I don't need pain and misery. I get that at home, every day of the week. What's wrong with you, anyway?'

Billy told him about the letter from Nikki.

'Pregnant, eh? Didn't think you had it in you.'

'I just tried to ring Nikki but I can't get through. I'm scared that Malcolm Priest has got hold of her.'

'Why would he bother?'

'He's taken out a contract on me.'

'You're joking.'

'Do I sound as if I'm joking?'

'For fuck's sake! I told you, didn't I? Didn't I tell you this'd happen?'

'I take it Nik hasn't been in touch?'

'Billy, she pretty much hated my guts. She wasn't that keen on you. Why the fuck would she get in touch with either of us? But your Carole phoned.'

'What did she want?'

'Oh, she was worried because you'd forgotten one

of your nephew's birthdays. And apparently, you never forget their birthdays. And she went round to your house and got no answer. '

'Ah, shit. Shit!' Billy sniffed loudly. 'I just want to go home.'

'I thought you *were* home.'

'No. I'm in a phone box in the middle of Bedfordshire.'

'Bedfordshire? Where the fuck's that?'

'Fucking nowhere! '

'Well, come home then.'

'I can't. I've gone into hiding.'

Tony sighed laboriously. 'My God, it gets better.'

There was an uneasy silence. Billy wiped his nose on his sleeve. 'Maybe I could come and stay with you.'

With indecent haste, Tony said, 'No! *No way!*'

'I thought you were a mate!'

'I am. Unfortunately, I'm also a coward.'

'Thanks. Fucking great.'

'Look, Billy. Let's be realistic. You're probably going to get shot. Do you want to get me shot as well?'

'At this precise moment, it doesn't seem like a bad idea.'

'I take it they haven't found you yet?' asked Tony.

'They've found me twice.'

'Eh?'

'Twice. I got away, both times.'

'Who did they send? An old biddy with a rolling pin?'

'It's a long, complicated story. I'll tell you when I see you.'

'Well, at least you've still got your health, Billy. Although, admittedly, you're not likely to stay healthy for much longer.'

'Tony?'

'Yeah?'

'Get stuffed.'

'Oh, don't be like that. You know I wouldn't want anything bad to happen to you. You must know that.'

'Yeah.'

'It's just difficult, Billy. I've got a family to think of.'

'And do you?'

'Do I what?'

'Think of them.'

'I think of them all the time, you cheeky bastard.'

'Just asking.'

'I'll try and think of some way to help you, Bill. In the meantime, hang on. You're still alive. Maybe you'll stay alive if you don't do anything stupid. No. Let me qualify that: if you don't do anything more stupid than the fucking insanely stupid things you've already done.'

'Tony, would it do me any good to go to the police?'

'No.'

'Why? There are decent police officers.'

'Where? Billy, what are you talking about? We couldn't solve a murder if it was committed at the police station, with all of us watching. Know why? 'Cause only useless bastards join the police. If they can't get in the police, they join the fucking army. If I had any talent, I'd jack the job in tomorrow.'

'I could still get police protection.'

'Protection?' scoffed Tony. 'At the very most, you'd get one uniformed bobby standing outside your house. If he saw Priest coming down the road, he'd hide. Or more likely, he'd hold his fucking hand out. Try living in the real world, Billy. Malcolm Priest owns the police.'

'He doesn't own you.'

'No, but he could. If he played his cards right.'

'Tony. Don't joke.'

'Who's joking?'

'Listen. I need to see you. I've got to talk to someone. Tony, I'm going out of my fucking mind here.'

'All right. I'll come to see you. But no more crying. OK? You've got to promise me. 'Cause if anyone sees us together and you're crying, they're going to think we're a couple of gays who've just split up.'

*

For two nights running, the Doll crouched in the long grass at the bottom of Tony's garden, watching the house through a pair of opera glasses. On the second night, he saw Tony on the phone, smoking and sitting on a table by the open French window. All the lights in the house were on and the windows were uncurtained. It was that kind of house. The bottom of the garden backed onto a school playing field.

The Doll had squeezed through a gap in the hedge. Tony had never bothered to mend the gap because it provided a useful short cut for his daughters when they were late for school. Before the phone rang, the Doll had been about to give up for the night.

Unlike his wife, the Doll couldn't lip-read. Nor had he heard a word of Tony's conversation, just the distant murmur of Tony's quiet, throaty voice. But when the call was over, he heard the harsh voice of a woman, bellowing a question from another room. And the Doll heard, was *sure* he heard, Tony shout, 'Only Bill!' in reply.

As soon as he returned to the caravan, Rawhead knew something was wrong. He unlocked the door and was hit by a wall of icy cold air. He searched for the source of the draught, found nothing and was troubled. It was a mild night. There was no reason for the caravan to be cold.

To Rawhead, who depended on his senses for his survival, the chill was a warning, a sign that something in his dark, self-contained kingdom had begun to decay.

In his heart, he knew why. A murderer cannot show pity. Rawhead had always prided himself on his hardness, his refusal to baulk at unjustifiable acts of violence. In sparing Billy, he believed he had offended his guiding spirit, the nameless daemon that had driven him to murder and slowly isolated him from all other human beings. Billy had been the ultimate test of his faith. He had failed that test, because he was bound to Billy in a way that he couldn't begin to explain or comprehend.

But if letting Billy Dye live had been a mistake, the killing of Doc had been an act of wanton insanity. He knew that now. The third death, the killing of Newey, had been a natural disaster brought about by the previous two misdeeds. In a matter of days, a single act of charity had upset the delicate balance of Rawhead's world.

That night at the vicarage, Rawhead had tried to kill Billy while he slept. The idea came to him while he was checking the doors and windows before bed. He realized that hiding Billy away for a year, or even a day, was not practical. Billy couldn't be trusted. Unlike Rawhead, who had deliberately chosen his life of loneliness, the writer was not self-contained. Although the world didn't need Billy, Billy needed the world. How long before he sold his story to a Sunday newspaper? He couldn't keep his mouth shut for twelve seconds, let alone twelve months.

So Rawhead had climbed the stairs to Billy's room, entered noiselessly and held the Ruger Blackhawk revolver to his old friend's head. It seemed the right thing to do. They'd had their happy reunion. They'd laughed and got drunk and recovered something of their former rapport. Now it was time to say good-bye. No fear, no malice, just a single shot and one beautiful, unique spirit would be set free forever.

But Rawhead hadn't been able to do it. Standing there, watching Billy's chest rise and fall, Rawhead's mouth went dry and his finger froze on the trigger.

The prospect of Billy's absence, and of how Raw-head would feel about himself having created that absence, effectively paralysed him. So Rawhead had let the gun fall to his side. It was then that Billy had awoken to see him standing by the bed.

It wasn't that Rawhead felt love for Billy, or even affection. Such emotions were quite beyond him. Imprisonment, betrayal and death had murdered his heart. What Billy awoke in him was a desire to protect. The thought of Billy Dye in danger made Rawhead tense, set his teeth on edge, charged him with an unfamiliar sense of urgency. *Billy was part of him.*

Equally, Rawhead knew that Billy carried chaos in his wake. He had read the signs. Since St George's day, Rawhead had seen monsters in the clouds and skulls grinning through the trees. He knew that a bloodbath was coming and accepted the fact with grim fortitude. It wasn't a question of 'if', but of 'when'.

Many years before, misguided loyalty to Billy Dye had prompted Rawhead to stab a boy at a disco. Their friendship had already led him to a life of crime. It was about to launch him into a full-scale war.

9

Who is this who is coming?

'Oh, Whistle, and I'll Come to You, My Lad', M. R. James

'Screams?' said Tony. 'What kind of screams?'

'Like some poor fucker being tortured.'

'You're joking. Every night?'

'No. Not last night,' said Billy. 'I didn't hear a thing. Last night, I just stayed awake *waiting* for the screams.'

'Jesus,' said Tony. 'No wonder you look ill.'

They were sitting by the river in Bedford. Tony had arrived in a police car, wearing full uniform. He hadn't been able to get time off work. But, like the dedicated officer he was, he turned up anyway. They sat on a bench, sharing a spliff. It felt strange to be smoking dope, in public, with a uniformed policeman. No one but Billy appeared to notice. The few people who were around studiously looked the other way, as if they were afraid of being strip-searched.

'Won't they miss you?' asked Billy.

'Who?' said Tony.

'Your employers. The Cheshire Constabulary.'

'Well, sure, they'll try to contact me, and they'll get no answer on the radio. But that's nothing unusual. The Cheshire pigs have got no money. We're not like Manchester – sponsored by Malcolm Priest. Our radios are completely obsolete. They've got a range of about two hundred yards. And that's only if it's sunny.

'But we couldn't afford new radios this year because our boss spent a third of our annual budget on putting nice new toilets in the police station. Presumably so his officers have somewhere to sit while they're weeping over the boredom and emptiness of their fucking lives.'

It was a Sunday afternoon. The slow river glittered in the sun. A Salvation Army band was making a depressing day even more depressing by playing 'Onward, Christian Soldiers'. Billy told Tony that he and Nikki had once stayed in the former home of Sabine Baring-Gould, the hymn's composer.

Tony squinted. 'So what?' His tone vaguely hostile.

'Well, it was a nice place to stay. An old country manor. This guy was a vicar but he was also a writer, wrote loads of books. So his house had a lovely warmth.'

'You mean it had central heating?'

'No! I mean it had a good aura.'

'A what?'

'Sorry. Forgot you were illiterate.'

'Billy, why are you telling me about a vicar's house?' said Tony. 'Unless that's the house you're living in?'

'No. The vicar's house is in Devon. I'm staying in another house, a fucking haunted house in a village about seven miles from here. Which also happens to be an old vicarage.'

'You're living with a vicar?'

'No. The vicar doesn't live there any more.'

Tony started to laugh. 'What village?'

'I can't tell you.'

'Priest's really after you?'

''Course he's after me. How do you think I got this fucking nose?'

'You could have walked into a wall. This could all be a very sad person's fantasy you've invented to make yourself seem more interesting.' Billy wasn't amused. After a pause, Tony said, 'He isn't after me as well, is he?'

'Why do you say that?'

'Oh, the other night. One of my daughters came running into our bedroom. Fucking frantic, she was. Said she'd heard someone trying the handle on the back door.'

Billy shrugged. 'She may have imagined it.'

'Let's fucking hope so. I'll be a bit annoyed if my entire family's wiped out.'

'Gangsters don't tend to kill families. It's an unwritten code. If they go round killing wives and children, that leaves their own wives and children vulnerable. So they don't do it.'

'Oh, right. That's a relief.' Tony snorted smoke through his nostrils. 'So it'll only be me who fucking snuffs it.'

Billy shrugged. Tony spread his arms over the back of the bench and let his head fall back. 'What happened, Bill? How did you and fat Mal come to fall out of love?'

Billy related everything that had happened in the past few weeks. Tony listened, gradually growing more serious and silent as the story unfolded. Finally, he said, 'Well, let's try not to worry. I'm sure it'll all work out in the end.'

'Is that all you've got to say?'

'What do you want me to say? You're not the only one with problems. I've been kicked out of the fucking drug squad.'

'What for?'

'Oh, nothing personal. You're only allowed to be on the job for a year. On account of the fact that working with drugs always turns police officers into junkies. So here's me with a coke addiction and nowhere to steal my fucking stash from. As if that isn't bad enough, I've got to wear this stupid fucking uniform.'

'Do you wear a hat?'

'I'm supposed to, like. But I've hidden it at the bottom of the wardrobe.'

'So you haven't got any advice for me?'

Tony hesitated, then slipped his CS gas spray out of his jacket. He passed the spray to Billy. 'Here. You'd better have this.'

'What do you expect me to do with this?'

'Use it like an aerosol. If you aim it at someone's face, they won't be able to see to shoot you.'

With an ungrateful shrug, Billy slipped the spray into a side pocket of his combat trousers and buttoned it. 'I said *advice*. A bit of objective guidance from a well-disposed observer.'

'Ah. Right.' Tony offered him the last of the spliff. Billy shook his head. 'My advice is that you're up to your neck in shite.'

'That's not advice, either. That's stating the fucking obvious.'

'My *advice* is, stick with this Rawhead. Sounds like he can do a lot more for you than I can.'

Billy was stunned. 'You what? He was sent to kill me.'

'Yeah. But he let you off, didn't he? He sounds like a reasonable bloke. For a murderer. How are you for money?'

'Enough to last me for another two months.'

'I can't lend you any.'

'Would you do something for me?' asked Billy.

'Depends what it is.'

Billy gave Tony a scrap of paper with an address scrawled on it. 'Would you go and see Nikki? Tell her I love her. Say I'll be in touch with her as soon as I can.'

'Won't that blow your cover?'

'Just give her the message, will you? She's on her own. I don't want her to think I don't care about her.'

Tony sighed. 'OK. But it seems a funny way of going into hiding, Bill. First you call me. Then you tell me to go and see Nikki. Why don't you place an ad in the *Manchester Evening News* and have done with it?'

Billy sighed.

'Don't look at me like that,' said Tony.

'Like what?'

'As if I'm a giant dog turd.'

'I'll try not to.'

On his way home, Billy crashed the Harley. It wasn't his fault. A farmer drove a tractor directly into his path, the bike smashed into the side of the tractor and erupted into flames. Billy jumped off before impact, ending up in an oozing ditch, bruised and covered in mud, but otherwise unhurt. The farmer, a youngish man with a red face, a side parting and no teeth, helped him out of the ditch.

'Sorry and all that.'

'You blind fucking knobhead,' said Billy, looking at the burning bike.

'Oi. No need for that,' said the farmer. 'The speed you beatniks drive your bikes, it's a wonder there aren't more accidents on this road.'

'Beatniks?' said Billy, thinking he must have misheard. 'Did you say *beatniks*?'

'Yeah. You make me tired. And when the police arrive, I'll make bloody sure they know it was your fault. '

'No. It was your grandfather's fault,' said Billy, walking off. 'If he hadn't shagged your mother, you wouldn't have been born.'

Billy started walking. By the time the farmer had worked out what Billy had said, he was too far away to hit.

'I'll bloody have you!' the farmer shouted.

'Will that be before or after you have your sister?' yelled Billy.

The farmer started up the tractor and drove after him. Billy was forced to hide behind a hedge until he'd passed. Then he started on the three-mile walk to the vicarage, wondering how he was going to break it to Rawhead that he'd written off the bike.

Back at the vicarage, Billy filled a kettle to make himself a cup of tea. While the water was boiling, someone rapped on the front door. Billy had no intention of answering it, but he was not especially nervous. It could have been the gasman, the postman, a salesman, someone selling raffle tickets. There was no reason to suppose the worst.

He tipped boiling water onto an Earl Grey tea bag – Rawhead was too proud to stock Lady Grey – and placed two digestive biscuits on a plate. Then the light in the room darkened. Billy glanced up and was startled to see a face at the window, looking in. The face belonged to a smiling policeman. He was about fifty, innocuous and bespectacled, with sparse grey hair. His head didn't match the black, threatening uniform he was wearing. It was as if Mr Pickwick had joined the Gestapo. The constable pointed at himself and Billy to indicate he wanted a word.

Billy cursed as he unbolted the door, suspecting that the police officer had come to investigate the road accident. The constable extended his hand, which was dry to the point of crustiness. Billy shook it, still uncertain how to proceed.

'Constable Andrews.' The policeman smiled. 'I'm the community policeman for Dudloe, Pilton and Amhurst. You must be Monty? Roger's pal?'

Billy nodded sullenly.

'Call me Andy. Everyone does: "Handy Andy".' The officer chuckled self-deprecatingly. 'I suppose it beats being called "Randy Andy". Or "Bandy Andy".'

'Or Andy Pandy,' sneered Billy.

'Anyway,' said Andy with an ingratiating smile.

'Anyway what?'

'I wonder if I could come in for a minute? Nothing serious – just a chat.'

With ill grace, Billy opened the door wide and admitted the constable, now convinced that the tractor driver had rumbled him. Andy, with excessive eagerness, accepted Billy's offer of tea and biscuits, then settled his large, shiny-trousered arse on the living-room sofa. Billy took a seat by the window, on the opposite side of the room.

After a few lines of obligatory chit-chat, Andy came to the point.

'Well, it's a bit delicate really, Monty, and I don't like having to do this. Don't like it at all – for reasons that I'll explain later – but the long and the short of it is, we've had a complaint.'

In keeping with police tradition, Andy paused to give Billy time to confess.

'A complaint?'

Andy nodded, smiling. 'The vicar, no less, has made a complaint. He claims – I repeat, *claims* – that he's heard you shouting out rude things in the middle of the night.'

Billy fought to conceal his overwhelming relief. 'Rude things?'

'That's right. Your neighbour, Reverend Phipps – sorry, *Canon* Phipps – he says you call out obscene things. He says he's even heard you take the name of the Lord in vain.'

Billy tried to conceal his relief. 'It can't have been me.'

'Well, now. I'm only telling you what he told me.'

'You don't understand,' stressed Billy. 'I would never blaspheme. Under any circumstances. Jesus Christ our Saviour is the most important man in my life.'

Andy looked pleasantly surprised. 'Really? You a churchgoer, then?'

'Not at the moment. But never a day goes by when I don't think of how Jesus died on the Cross. Because, let's be honest, Andy, he died to save us all. Pretty fantastic of him, really.'

The constable was completely taken in. 'Yes, he carried a cross. His own cross. Think about that.'

'I'm thinking,' enthused Billy. 'Must have weighed a ton, mustn't it?'

A fly landed on Andy's face. He brushed it away. 'Well, then. I must apologize. The vicar's obviously made a mistake. And I shall tell him so, mark my words.'

As he shuffled out, Andy struggled to explain, as tactfully as he could, that the vicar was well known for his hatred of humanity. His indifference to the sick and needy was legendary. He refused to marry people who didn't attend his church and had even criticized parishioners for placing too many flowers on the graves of their loved ones, feeling that it made the churchyard look untidy.

In fact, Canon Phipps was disliked by everyone apart from his wife and the Bishop of St Albans.

At the door, Andy assured Billy that if he ever wanted a good time on a Sunday, he could do worse than visit the constable's own place of worship, the Baptist Church in Bedford.

As Andy walked to his car, Billy shouted, 'God be with you.'

Tony had a low opinion of himself; he was a good judge of character. But he was not entirely insensitive and when he arrived home, late that night, Billy's plight was very much on his mind. Billy had looked haggard. He wasn't enjoying life, and had little reason to.

It would have been tactless to mention the incident to Billy, but two years ago, Tony had been called out to an accident. A man had fallen in front of a train on the Buxton line. The train had sliced him in two and torn off one of his arms. Before he died, the victim told Tony that Malcolm Priest's men had thrown him off the bridge, into the path of the train.

If Tony had been able to help Billy without endangering himself, he would have. No question. But he suspected that Billy was beyond help. Malcolm Priest was going to kill him, and that was that. It was sad, but it was a sad world. There was fuck all that Tony could do about it.

The single light in Tony's hallway told him that his wife had gone to bed. This was good news. Anticipating a pleasant hour of drug abuse before bedtime, he removed the plastic sachet containing the last of his coke supply from the dashboard of his Vauxhall Cavalier. Then he locked the car and ambled up the drive.

Before he reached the door, someone spoke his name. 'Tony?' The voice was male, its tone light and friendly. A man of medium height, his face in shadow, stepped into his path. Before Tony had time to think and respond, he felt cold metal against his face. He heard a sharp crack, felt fire against his cheek. A violent jolt passed through his body, leaving him gagging and trembling on the ground. Realizing he'd been assaulted with a stun gun, a strange thought passed through Tony's head. He reflected that electrocution wasn't too bad, that appendicitis was worse. He was vaguely conscious of two men standing over him, and the faint sound of laughter. Then he passed out.

Tony tried to open his eyes, and bright light burned the back of his skull. Something tugged sharply at his wrist. A taste like the smell of dodgem cars filled his mouth. His face still burned from the electrocution. He heard a clunking sound near his head and the pressure on his wrist intensified. When his eyes opened he saw that he was on his belly, face down on a dirt floor. His wrists and ankles were bound to metal pitons by lengths of thin cord. The clunk-clunk in his ear had been the sound of the final piton being hammered down.

He was in some kind of wooden outhouse. There were nails and cigarette butts in the dirt. Bags of cement were stacked high against one wall. The wielder of the hammer knelt down and held his face close to Tony's. He had wide, bulging eyes that didn't blink. He was wearing a white linen shirt and a black silk tie. The tie was tied with a neat Windsor knot. 'Hello, Tony. You're probably wondering what this is all about.'

Tony was too dizzy and confused to talk. He could feel cold air on his buttocks. With a shock, he realized that his trousers were down to his knees. What was going on?

The staring man continued. 'I've got quite a reputation in Manchester and the surrounding area. They call me the Doll, and not because of my sweet nature.'

Someone laughed appreciatively. There was at least one other man in the room.

'Maybe you've heard of me?' pressed the Doll.

'No,' said Tony.

The Doll opened his mouth and yelled in Tony's

face. It was like the roar of a demented beast. Tony shut his eyes, expecting a blow. The Doll immediately relaxed, gratified to have provoked a reaction.

'Would you mind telling me what this is about?' said Tony.

'What's this about, Tone? This is about you having phone calls from little bastards who are meant to be dead.'

'I don't know what you're fucking on about.'

'Billy? I heard you use his name. Are you going to tell me you know anyone else called Billy?'

'Ah. You're thinking of Bill Eden.' Tony's mouth had gone completely dry. 'Detective Constable Eden. He wanted to borrow a porn video off me.'

'Yeah? I thought maybe it was Billy Dye who was calling you.'

'Billy Dye? No. Isn't he in prison? Haven't heard from him in yonks.'

'Oh, you've disappointed me now,' said the Doll. 'I was hoping we wouldn't have to get rough, Tony.'

The Doll nodded to someone out of eyeshot. The man who had laughed stepped into view. He was about forty, big and stupid-looking, heavy arms and shoulders protruding from a stained T-shirt. He had no hair. His pink scalp glistened. He was leaning on something bulky and metallic, something heavy enough to knot the tendons in his extensively tattooed forearms.

Tony, still dazed from the electrocution, took a few moments to identify the object as a pneumatic drill.

'This is Conrad,' said the Doll. 'He's been drilling motorways since he was eighteen. If you don't talk to me nicely, like a grown-up, he's going to drill your arse for you. Isn't that right?'

'Oh, yes indeed,' answered Conrad with a nod.

Tony felt sick with fear. Without hesitation, he told the Doll everything he knew about Billy and Rawhead. Except he had misremembered Rawhead's name, referring to him as 'Rawhide'. All that he left out was Billy's new address, because he didn't know it.

'I swear, I swear to God,' pleaded Tony. 'He wouldn't tell me where he lives.'

'Really?' said the Doll mockingly. 'I thought he was your friend.'

'Never! The guy's a complete cunt!' blustered Tony. 'Billy Dye's never been my friend, he's just a boring wanker who buys dope off me!'

'What did he want to see you about?'

'He's getting stir-crazy. Nikki's pregnant.'

'Who?'

'Nikki. His ex-bird. She's up the duff. He wants to get back with her.'

'Yeah? Is it his kid?'

'Dunno. Doubt it.'

'Is that why they split up?'

'No. She left him at Christmas. She thinks he's boring. I don't blame her. He *is* boring. I've never liked him.'

'So you keep saying.'

'No really! I hate the fucking bastard! If you gave me a fucking gun, I'd shoot him myself!'

'Then tell us where he's hiding.'

'It's in a vicar's house in a village in Bedfordshire. That's all I know. I swear on my children's lives.' (The Doll nodded to Conrad, who carried the drill over to Tony and rested the cold, heavy-duty bit against his exposed sphincter.) 'Please God, I'm telling the truth! I swear!'

The Doll believed Tony, but wasn't about to let this stand in the way of his enjoyment. 'This might hurt a little bit,' he laughed, backing away so that the blood wouldn't splash his clothes.

The drilling lasted for a couple of seconds, ending abruptly when the bit struck bone. When the drill fell silent, Tony was still screaming.

The Doll stood back to inspect the damage. The Doll and Conrad chuckled. 'Dear me,' observed the Doll, shaking his head.

He knelt down and looked at Tony's sweating, plum-coloured face. 'Give me the address, Tony.'

'I don't know it,' sobbed the victim.

The Doll glanced at Conrad, who shrugged. Perhaps, after all, the policeman was telling the truth. With a resigned sigh, the Doll stepped over to a bench and picked up a butcher's knife. Then he walked back to Tony, grabbed his hair, yanked his head back and cut his throat wide open.

Conrad was startled. 'Fuck! Fuck?'

The Doll's eyes gleamed coldly. 'What?'

'What've you done?'

The Doll leered, his face and arms spattered with arterial blood. 'I give up. What *have* I done?'

'You burned him. You burned a fucking copper!'

'Well spotted.'

'Fuck.' Conrad threw down the drill and started pacing up and down, rubbing the stubble on his jaw. 'Fuck!'

'What're you getting so sensitive about?' demanded the Doll, annoyed by the big man's attack of conscience. 'He'd have bled to death because of what *you* did to him. I just put him out of his misery.'

Acting like a disturbed child, Conrad squeezed his own face between his strong fingers. The Doll looked at him. Conrad was the Doll's older brother. He was slow-witted, a bit too emotional. He'd spent most of his life in prison or out of work. The Doll had always looked out for him.

'I didn't think you was going to burn him,' said Conrad, emphasizing every syllable to get his point across.

The Doll placed his hand under Conrad's chin, forcing eye contact. 'Wake up, big brother. That's what I do now. I burn people. In fact, no. I work for

the Priesthood, right? I don't burn 'em, I *box* 'em.
I've waited a long time for this. Don't you understand? This Rawhead fucker's out. He's fucking
dead. I'm moving up, Con. I'm gonna be Malcolm
Priest's blue-eyed boy. You and me, we're going to
be *fucking loaded*.'

While he was incinerating Tony's clothes, the Doll
found Nikki's address in Tony's pocket. He went
home and slept for three hours. After a light breakfast, he drove to a middle-class housing estate in
Congleton, Cheshire. While neighbours took themselves to work and their children to school, the Doll
rang the doorbell of a pleasant detached house,
hoping to meet and question Billy Dye's ex-
girlfriend.

There was no answer, no sign of life. The Doll
drew back, standing on the lawn to watch the windows. The curtains to the bedrooms were closed. A
passage barred by a gate led to the back of the house.
The Doll tugged at the gate, found that it was locked.
He sensed that someone was watching him and
glanced round to see a man hovering beside a shit-
brown Volvo.

The man was about the Doll's age, tallish with
dark greasy hair, combed into a side parting. His
suit was shit-brown, like the Volvo. He looked like a
bank manager. Uncowed by the Doll's stare, he

waited a second. Then, jangling his car keys, he crossed the neat lawn to where the Doll was standing.

'Can I help you at all?' The question was pitched perfectly between politeness and hostility. The speaker was coming across like some kind of hard man, despite his pot belly and sagging shoulders. The Doll changed his mind about the man's occupation. A tax inspector. No doubt about it.

'I don't know,' said the Doll, matching the taxman's tone. 'Can you?'

The answering stare was not accommodating.

'I'm a friend of Nikki's,' explained the Doll. 'Is she home, do you know?'

The taxman relaxed marginally, yet was still far from happy. Now he's wondering if I'm the father of her bastard-to-be, thought the Doll.

'They're away.'

The Doll sighed, affecting disappointment and frustration. 'That's bad. I really needed to see her.'

The man half nodded, more interested in removing the Doll from his neighbour's property than hearing about his personal problems.

'Do you have the right time?' asked the Doll. The taxman didn't answer, not willing to waste any more words on someone to whom he had taken a dislike. The Doll took the hint and strolled casually over to his Range Rover. As he opened the car door, he had one last try. 'Any idea when she'll be back?'

The taxman was crossing the road to his crappy Volvo. He gave the Doll another piercing look, then shook his head curtly.

'Thanks for your help,' said the Doll. As he climbed behind the wheel, he smiled directly at the taxman. It was a mocking smile that carried a direct threat.

The taxman just stood there, his purpose blatantly clear. He was committing the Doll and his registration plate to memory. A good citizen. It was irritating. But the Doll forced himself to smile and take it, even though he could have taken the man apart with one hand tied behind his back.

The Doll reversed onto someone's drive, turned and drove away. In his mirror, he could see the taxman. The bastard was still standing by his car staring after him. One dark night, thought the Doll, the taxman might walk out of his house and catch a knife through the middle of his back. He could picture the scene. The taxman wouldn't look so haughty then. He'd be writhing on the ground, squealing. 'Remember me?' the Doll would say, standing over the dying taxman with a blade at the ready. 'I'm the guy you wouldn't give the time to.'

'Schoolmates?' echoed Priest incredulously. 'You mean two of my men are dead and Dye's alive because him and Rawhead used to play fucking conkers in the playground?'

'Looks like it,' said the Doll indifferently.

'Reminds me of Hardy,' remarked Chef, instantly wishing he'd kept his mouth shut.

'Who the fuck's Hardy?' demanded Priest.

'Oh, just someone who was, you know, big on coincidence,' murmured Chef.

'We're talking about Hardy out of Laurel and Hardy, are we?'

Chef wriggled in his seat. 'No, Thomas Hardy, the writer. I studied him at O level.'

Priest bristled. 'What subject?'

'English, of course.'

'Did you pass your exam?'

'Would I be here if I did?'

'Shut your fucking mouth. If you didn't pass, you've got the same qualifications as me and him.' Priest nodded at the Doll. 'Fucking zero. So don't pretend you're better than us. All right?'

Chef didn't answer.

'Fucking Laurel and Hardy!' scoffed Priest. 'We're trying to have a serious conversation here.'

The Doll smiled, knowing this display of power was for his benefit. Chef flicked a tiny ball of fluff from his sharply creased trousers, apparently impervious to Priest's rudeness.

It was the morning after Tony's murder. Priest,

Chef and the Doll were holding an emergency meeting at Diva. The club, like Priest's restaurant, had initially been an attempt to launch a legitimate business. But on the opening night, two outsiders caught dealing were disfigured on the dance floor as a warning to others. By the second night, customers were able to order the drug of their choice at the bar. In this sense, Diva was no different to any private members' club in London.

It was the first time that the Doll had come face to face with Malcolm Priest. Suffused with quiet triumph, he sat in a cramped office and told them all he'd learned. It was a bright summer's day. All three men were sweating in the heat. When the Doll had finished talking, Priest and Chef fell into a thoughtful silence.

'The Jesus? He's taken care of?' asked Priest after a while.

'Sorry?' said the Doll, not understanding.

'Jesus,' explained Chef. 'It's another word for a constable.'

By way of illustration, Priest stretched his arms wide like Christ on the cross. 'They've always got their fucking hands out.'

'Had to kill him,' said the Doll with authority. 'He would have tipped off Dye.'

'Correct.' Priest nodded with satisfaction. 'In your shoes, I would have done exactly the fucking same.

Only next time, *ask*. Remember. No one dies unless I say so.'

'I'm sorry . . . I didn't—'

'Doesn't matter.' Priest shook his head so vigorously that his jowls wobbled. 'Just don't make a habit of it. We can't have too many coppers going missing. Even the police, thick as they are, can't fail to notice that.'

The Doll could see Priest was impressed. After many years of routine face-carving, his time to shine had finally arrived. Priest, as always, filled the room with his presence. Without speaking, he pushed a cheque across the table. The Doll looked at it and grinned. 'Twenty grand?'

Priest lit a slim panatella. 'I heard you weren't happy with the feed on offer. I like them that work for me to be happy.'

Chef nodded in agreement, as if paying the Doll well had been his intention all along.

The Doll folded the cheque carefully and slipped it into his wallet. 'Oh, before I forget: I know where Billy Dye's ex-girlfriend lives. Do you want me to talk to her?'

Priest shook his head. 'Nah. He's not hiding there, is he? Forget it.'

The Doll looked disappointed.

'The more people you involve, the messier it gets,' advised Chef. 'Let's keep it nice and simple.

We want you to go after Billy Dye. Don't we, Malcolm?'

'We most certainly fucking do,' agreed Priest.

'But first,' said Chef, 'we'd like you to take a pop at Rawhead.'

The Doll whistled. 'What's it worth?'

'To me?' said Priest. 'Wait and see.'

'I could kill anyone,' said the Doll. 'How would you know it was Rawhead?'

Priest smiled unpleasantly. 'We're assuming you don't want to cross Malcolm Priest. We're assuming you don't want to spend the rest of your fucking life looking over your shoulder. Because, believe me, my friend, I don't forgive. And I don't fucking forget.'

The Doll smiled.

'What're you fucking smiling for?' said Priest. He turned to Chef. 'This cunt never stops grinning.'

'I'm happy,' said the Doll.

'Fucking hell.' Priest snorted, as if even temporary happiness was the most preposterous state imaginable.

Soon they were all smiling. Priest sat back in his chair, marvelling at this man who had found happiness. He laughed and shook his head. 'Fucking *happy*. Now I've heard fucking everything.'

His mood altered abruptly. 'Anyway, enough of this shit. Chef's got a plan.' Priest sucked on his cigar and held it in front of his face to watch it burn.

'There's a fella I don't like. He's a producer at Granada Studios. A big fat silver-haired puff.'

The Doll nodded, smiling his doll-like smile.

'His name's Derek Tidy,' continued Chef. 'He owes us one. If I tell him to look after you for a night, he'll do it, no question.'

'I don't get you,' said the Doll.

Priest tilted his head towards Chef without shifting his eyes from the Doll.

'Chef here is going to phone Rawhead, tell him to box Tidy, give him a specific time and place. Now, here's the clever bit: *when Rawhead turns up to do the hit, you'll be waiting.*'

'Nice one,' said the Doll. 'How important is this TV cunt?'

'Not important at all.'

'What if he gets in the line of fire?'

'Good riddance,' said Priest and laughed.

'In fact,' said Chef, 'we couldn't help thinking you'd be best waiting until Rawhead had boxed Tidy before you made your move.'

'Yeah.' The Doll nodded appreciatively. 'I like it.'

Priest blew a smoke ring. 'Way we see it, Rawhead must have a guilty conscience. He'll be on edge, half expecting to be crossed. But if he kills Tidy with no trouble, he'll think he's in the clear. He'll be nice and relaxed. It's then that you hammer him.' Priest fashioned a make-believe gun with his fingers and pointed at the Doll. 'Bam! One in the back. Bam! Another in the fucking head. Sound good?'

The Doll acknowledged that it did. He cleared his throat before saying, 'I've got this friend, a guy who helps me out. He's reliable. He helped me to net the, er, "Jesus". I was thinking, maybe I'll use him on this job.'

Priest held out his hands, indicating he wished to hear no more. 'I don't want to know. That's up to you. Get the right result, I don't care if you hire the seven fucking dwarfs. All I'll say, if this friend fucks up, I'll kill the pair of you. '

The Doll nodded. 'Oh yeah . . . one more thing. Sorry if this sounds cheeky, yeah? But could you sell me a gun?'

Priest looked baffled. 'I thought we'd given you a piece.' He scrutinized Chef. 'What happened to that Russian job?'

'He gave it to me,' the Doll interrupted. 'I meant a gun for my mate. The guy who helps me out.'

'You mean, your brother,' said Priest, with a sapient smirk.

The Doll feigned amazement. 'How did you know that?'

'Because he's Malcolm Priest,' announced Chef.

Priest nodded to Chef. 'Guns? We've got loads of fucking guns, haven't we? Get him sorted.'

Chef nodded sagely.

The Doll got up to leave. Priest took his hand and

clasped it in both of his. 'But, listen. I'm being straight with you, now. This Rawhead cunt has hurt me. He's hurt my pride and he's hurt my business.' To the Doll's amazement, Priest's eyes filled with tears. 'Him and Dye – I want them both to suffer. I want their heads on a fucking plate. Their bollocks, too. Comprendez? When the job's done, call me. And remember,' Priest stared unflinchingly into those cold, primordial eyes, 'what you do for me, you do for Manchester.'

10

The Angel of Death was sent against us tonight,
but he failed to get us, and he will never return
empty-handed to his dark kingdom.
The Devil Rides Out, Dennis Wheatley

After his meeting with Malcolm Priest, the Doll went along to Conrad's tiny terraced house in Longsight clutching a brown paper parcel. When Conrad answered the door, he was wearing a string vest. He'd once worked as an ice-cream man, wearing that same vest, looking just as sweaty and unshaven. Then he wondered why people didn't buy his ice cream.

'Look at the fucking state of you,' said the Doll.

Conrad opened the door wide. The Doll walked in, ducking his head to pass beneath his brother's reeking armpit. The air was stale from chips and cigarettes. The Doll, used to exerting authority over his brother, set the parcel down on the kitchen table and unwrapped it to reveal a sawn-off shotgun. 'Two barrels. Two massive holes in whoever you aim it at.'

'Ash,' said Conrad mournfully, 'I'm not sure about this.'

The Doll pinched his cheek. 'You don't need to be sure. Just do what I tell you.'

'I couldn't sleep last night. Thinking about . . . you know.'

'Shut up.'

'All that blood. It wasn't even red. It was black. Like oil.'

'Fucking button it!' snapped the Doll, reaching for his wallet. He took out twenty crisp fifty-pound notes and pressed them into Conrad's hand.

'What's this?' asked Conrad, his eyes dull and beaten.

'It's yours. Your share. Are you still telling me you're not interested?'

Conrad looked at the Doll, then gazed down at the money, more money than he'd ever seen.

'Look around you, you clown,' spat the Doll. 'Look at this shithole you live in. There's your Maureen works full-time in that fucking biscuit factory and she doesn't bring enough home to buy shoes for your kids, let alone take 'em on holiday. I'm giving you a chance, Con. A chance to better yourself. Can you seriously look me in the eyes and tell me you'll not take it?'

'What do I have to do?'

The Doll explained the set-up, nice and slowly, so that Conrad would understand. '. . . So this guy's going to shoot someone. Then, when he's done the job and he feels safe, I'm going to burn him. Unless I call for help, you don't even have to show your face. It's money for fuck all. Minimum risk. This cunt won't even know what's hit him.'

Conrad hung his head. 'It's still murder. I never minded breaking teeth, it never fucking bothered me. But I don't know about anything else. I just don't know.'

'You soft sod.'

The big man shrugged. 'Yeah. Maybe I am.'

The Doll, who rarely touched anyone with affection, laid his hand on Conrad's shoulder. 'Well, look. This is what we'll do. You come along with me one last time. If you don't like it, I won't ask you again. How does that sound?'

The call came early that evening, while Rawhead was reading *Necropolis* by William Dye. The paperback original had been produced at minimal cost. The pages were thin and the cover illustration, a grinning skull-face peering over a log, looked like the work of a sixth-former who was about to fail his art A level. Rawhead felt sorry for Billy. He loved the book, and only wished Billy's publishers shared his sentiments.

Some writers, no matter how good they are, can't speak to us. Something about the way they see the world, think, string sentences together, alienates us as surely as the ramblings of a madman on a bus. But Rawhead shared Billy Dye's view of the world without reservation. The story he told went straight to Rawhead's heart. It was about dead people who love killing for its own sake. Rawhead was on the final page when the phone rang. He was reluctant to stop reading, but knew that only one person ever rang him. 'Yeah?'

'Hi,' said the caller. The voice was deep, emotionally disengaged.

'Evening,' said Rawhead. 'What've you got?'

'Another bag of rubbish that needs taking to the tip.'

Within a space of about three and a half years, Rawhead had personally despatched twenty-seven people on behalf of the Priesthood. During that time, he had grown accustomed to Chef's austere instructions, always delivered in the same flat, emotionless tone.

Chef sounded the same as usual. The job was nothing special. The man's name was Tidy. He lived in a large detached house in Anglesey Drive, Poynton. The spacious back garden overlooked the dark waters of Poynton Lake, known locally as Poynton Pool. Chef promised that at midnight Tidy would be found alone, at the rear of the house, in a room with a large picture window, sipping iced gin and watching the lights shimmering over the water.

Repressing his inner doubts, Rawhead drove to Anglesey Drive at the end of a swelteringly hot day. It was only 10.44 in the evening when he cruised past Tidy's house in his Mercedes van. Sprinklers were at work on the generous lawns. Many of the houses had names that reflected the pretensions of their owners. There was a Fisherman's Rest and a Toes-in-the-water. Tidy's eight-bedroomed house was called Summer Deep. A Jaguar and a Range Rover were parked on the drive. A sign on a nearby lamp post proclaimed that the house was in a Neighbourhood Watch area. This made Rawhead smile.

He turned right onto South Park Drive and left the van in an empty car park. Then he climbed over a stile and crossed the park that bordered the lake and the comfortable houses. In the daylight, locals walked their dogs in this field and anglers kept vigil by the water. Now, in the scented dark, sheep and bats were Rawhead's only companions. Bands of winking light bled into the water from the windows on the far shore. Rawhead walked to the water's edge. It was easy to pick out Tidy's house, with its black and white mock-Tudor façade.

A long, immaculate lawn, flanked by two neatly clipped rows of conifers, sloped down to the lake from the house. A golden rectangle defined the picture window that Chef had mentioned. The windows around it were dark. The lawn dipped steeply towards the bank, where a wooden summer house, shaped vaguely like a bandstand, faced out towards the lake. There was a rotting jetty at the water's edge. The jetty was a mere seven hundred yards from where Rawhead was standing.

He took a sniperscope from his jacket and attached a night-vision eyepiece. He focused on Derek Tidy's house and glimpsed a man standing at the picture window, looking out. Rawhead's whole body tensed. Tidy had been described to him as short and flabby, with copious white hair. The man at the window was slightly under six feet, with a white face and a head of dark curls. He was motionless, but something about his brooding demeanour suggested an extraordinary appetite for violence. The stranger was visible for a few seconds, then he was gone.

Rawhead knew the members of the Priesthood by sight. This man was not of their number. Rawhead had heard about someone who carried out the little jobs, the maimings and the beatings that he had often been offered but always turned down. Someone they called the Doll. Could this be the same man? If so, he was unlikely to be alone. Rawhead had heard that the Doll worked with a partner who held his victims down while he tortured them.

A bat flitted close to Rawhead's scalp, missing him by a fraction of an inch. Rawhead didn't react. He watched the house in silence for four long minutes, but the man with the white face failed to reappear. Rawhead lowered the scope. Above his head, a thin black cloud briefly assumed the likeness of an enormous scythe. Rawhead smiled in grim recognition, knowing that death was waiting for him across the water.

'I'm tired. So bloody tired,' said Tidy. 'A couple of hours I was told. Two hours have passed and I want you to go. Look here, do you actually *understand English*? I want you to leave.'

It was a quarter past one and Derek Tidy's nerves were showing. Malcolm Priest's two friends had shown up just after ten. When they'd surveyed the house and garden, the tall bald man had taken an expensive bottle of malt out to the summer house and stayed there. The smaller one, the man with the terrifying face, had ordered Tidy to wait in the living room with the picture window open and to ask no questions. Then he had positioned himself behind a long curtain.

It had been a tense evening. Tidy, with six Bloody Marys inside him, was feeling courageous. He snatched the curtain aside and confronted the Doll. 'I mean, have you any idea how ridiculous you look?'

It was not a good time to antagonize the Doll. His golden opportunity had turned into a fiasco. He knew that a man like Rawhead would not be late and felt sure that he had seen through Chef's ruse and chosen to stay away. After working himself into an adrenaline-fuelled fever, the Doll now felt flat and humiliated.

Tidy continued his tirade. 'I mean, what are you hiding behind a fucking curtain for, anyway? What do you think this is? *Dial M for Murder?*'

The Doll stared at Tidy with poisonous hatred and took two paces forward, forcing Tidy back into the centre of the room. 'Sit down and shut up,' said the Doll, pushing Tidy onto the Liberty sofa.

'Don't tell me what to do,' snapped Tidy, slurring slightly. Then he noticed the weapon that the Doll was holding loosely at his side. Tidy exploded with indignation. 'What's that? Is that a gun? What the fuck gives you the right to bring a gun into my house?'

The Doll, bored of the conversation, slapped Tidy across the face. Tidy staggered, spilling tomato juice on the carpet. He was astonished. 'What was that for?' he whined, a red handprint appearing on his left cheek, tears welling in his eyes.

The Doll gave Tidy a swift blow to the side of the head, knocking him to the floor. 'The same as that.'

Tidy landed heavily, moaning and holding his ear.

There was a dull crash from the direction of the garden. The Doll froze, remembering Conrad. Suddenly, ignoring everything he'd learned, the Doll rushed out onto the lawn, gun at the ready. He threw himself down, scanning the shadows for any sign of movement. Everything was still. The stars above were heartbreakingly beautiful.

From where he lay, the Doll could see most of the garden. Nothing stirred. The pale dome of the summer house was starkly framed against the sky and the dark shoreline. Behind, still in the house, Tidy swore colourfully. The Doll waited for a moment, listening intently. He thought he heard a groan. It seemed to come from the direction of the summer house.

He got to his feet and started running. He circled the lawn until he was between the lake and the summer house, then knelt on one knee at the foot of its wooden steps. The door was slightly ajar. With the PP-93 resting on his knee, he took careful aim at the door and waited. For a few moments, all he could hear was his own breath.

There was a moan, followed by a few unsteady steps. Then the door swung wide open. Here at the water's edge, visibility was poor. The figure that staggered through the doorway was a mere shadow, but even in the dark it was easy to see that the shadow wore a pale hood. The Doll opened fire, sending one shot into his target's chest. The hooded man grunted in surprise but refused to fall. The Doll fired again, this time directly at the hood. The victim sank to his knees and toppled down the steps, head towards the Doll's feet.

The Doll was so thrilled he was trembling. He

couldn't believe how easy it had been. Excitedly, he snatched off the hood to reveal the face of Manchester's most efficient killer. Instead, he found himself looking down at the dead, staring face of Conrad. The bullet to Conrad's head had entered his left eye, leaving a fierce red orifice. The Doll inspected the hood, saw that it had no eyeholes. It was just a cotton bag, pierced twice by the bullet that had passed through Conrad's head.

To his credit, the Doll didn't lose his nerve. He searched the summer house and the garden, resisting the urge to fire blindly and indiscriminately into the dark. Only when he was convinced he was alone did he return to Conrad's body. His own brother. The sadistic ingenuity of it made the Doll reel. This monster, this terrible, relentless executioner, had tricked him into fratricide. Rawhead had sent the Doll a clear message. The message said 'You're Nothing.'

A cool breeze from the lake played around the Doll's face and neck. He stared down at Conrad's ruined face, knowing that Priest didn't tolerate failure. Quietly, unhurriedly, the Doll removed his jacket and laid it over Conrad's head and shoulders.

Numb with shock, he re-entered the house. Tidy was cowering by the window, peering out into the dark. At the sight of the Doll, he flinched. The Doll approached the drinks cabinet and poured a liberal measure of cognac into a whisky glass. Then he noticed that Tidy was staring at the blood on his hands and shirt.

'What's happened?' said Tidy. 'Are you hurt?'

The Doll behaved as if Tidy hadn't spoken. He swallowed the brandy in one and sank into a chair. Placing the PP-93 on the arm of the chair, he threw back his head and closed his eyes. Watching this, Tidy began to sweat. The blood on the man's clothes and his pallor told Tidy that something dreadful had taken place.

Too timid to venture outside, Tidy started to move away, thinking to call the police while he had the chance. He crept across the room in virtual silence, until one of his knees cracked near the door, giving him away. Instantly, the Doll opened his eyes. He picked up the machine pistol, sprang out of the chair and followed Tidy into the kitchen.

While Rawhead and the Doll were otherwise engaged, Malcolm Priest and his men were playing Trivial Pursuit.

All that day, Malcolm Priest had been in a foul mood. He knew it had been unwise to hire a man with a secret identity. He only had himself to blame. But Priest never blamed himself for anything. Instead, he laid the full responsibility for his present misfortunes on Chef. That evening alone, Priest had openly referred to his right-hand man as 'greasy Joe', 'dysentery-breath' and 'he who wanks'.

Chef was philosophical about the verbal abuse. He understood that the underlying reason for the boss's anger was insecurity. If Priest's trusted Reaper could defect on a whim, what was to stop his entire crew from doing the same?

In an attempt to take the boss's mind off the planned hit on Rawhead, Chef had arranged a diversion. Priest loved quizzes almost as much as he liked eating, so Chef organized a barbecue and quiz evening, reasoning that the boys might as well enjoy themselves while they were waiting for the phone to ring. He ordered Filthy, head chef from the Moroccan, to fry burgers and sausages on the patio, while in the living room two teams of gangsters demonstrated their extensive lack of general knowledge. Chef joined forces with Heidi and the Beast to do battle with Priest, Lol Shepherd and Dogman.

Dogman was Priest's newly appointed head of security. Previously Priest had shown no interest in security, believing that his own fearsome reputation was all the security he needed. Now Priest's property was under armed surveillance twenty-four hours a day.

Heidi suspected Priest of rigging the game by memorizing the answers, a suspicion that was confirmed when Priest won the game with a question about the eating disorder bulimia. As a cackling Priest shared out his winnings, he remarked on his good fortune. 'It was just that I knew the phrase. It's one of them phrases you either know or you don't.'

'What does it mean again?' queried Lol.

Heidi, grinning down into his beer glass, said, 'It's a disease that fat bastards get.'

Priest was out of his seat before Heidi had finished speaking. Heidi, realizing his error, looked up and choked back a nervous laugh. Moving quickly for a man of his girth, Priest hurled the Trivial Pursuit board across the room and dragged Heidi to his feet. 'Yeah? Anything you want to say to me?'

Grabbing Heidi by the balls, Priest thrust him against the wall. Heidi screamed. The other gangsters gathered round. Priest's thick stumpy fingers gripped Heidi's heavy scrotum like steel pincers. 'I didn't mean you! I didn't mean you!' Heidi pleaded.

'Yeah? Who else is fat in this fucking room?'

'He wasn't talking about you, boss,' said the Beast, desperately trying to defuse the situation. 'You're not fat, you're just big boned.'

'I'm fucking *fat*!' roared Priest. Then to Heidi: 'What am I?'

'Fat!' screamed Heidi.

Incensed anew, Priest butted Heidi in the teeth. 'Who are you calling fat, you fucking wanker? I'll cut your dick into tiny little pieces and feed 'em to you. D'you hear me?'

Priest tightened his grip. Heidi howled. His contorted face reddened and tears filled his eyes. Tentatively, Lol reached for Priest's arm. 'Steady on, Malcolm. You might do him permanent damage.'

Chef knocked Lol's hand away, shaking his head to indicate that this was the worst thing he could possibly do. 'Malcolm, he didn't say anything,' repeated Shepherd.

Without shifting his tiny eyes from Heidi's sweating, empurpled face, Priest said, 'You: shut your face and go walk the fucking dog.'

Disconsolately, Lol obeyed.

In an impressive feat of strength, Priest raised his right arm so that Heidi's feet left the ground and his head scraped against the wallpaper.

Filthy appeared at the open window to announce that the food was ready. Priest was hungry, so he released Heidi. Gasping, Heidi slid down the wall. As Priest walked out he said, 'Not worth the fucking effort . . .'

Filthy and the Beast helped Heidi up and smoothed down the creases in his suit.

Chef's mobile began to play the national anthem. He answered it hastily, anxious for Priest not to be aware of the call. If the Doll had failed, Chef wanted to break the news to Priest gently. He wandered off into the empty hall. 'Yeah?' Chef heard a steady hiss on the end of the line. 'Hello?'

'I wonder if you'd like to apologize to me?' The caller was instantly recognizable as Rawhead.

Chef was too startled to answer. His scalp began to tingle. He waited, breathing noisily into the phone, until Rawhead spoke again. 'For trying to kill me. That wasn't very polite. I think I deserve an apology.' The voice sounded tired and bored.

'What did you expect? Flowers and chocolates?'

There was a long silence.

'Would you mind answering one question?' said Chef. 'Would you mind telling me why?'

'Why what?'

'Why throw up everything for, let's be honest, someone who's a second-rate writer and a tenth-rate human being. The guy's got a huge ego, he acts like he's this great artist, and you know what? I've never seen a single one of his books in any shop.'

'Is that why you took out a contract on him?' For the first time, Chef heard amusement in Rawhead's voice.

Chef suddenly had an idea. 'You can laugh, my friend. But I promise you this. If you were to bring us Billy Dye, deliver him alive or dead, Malcolm Priest would wipe your slate clean.'

'Sure.'

'I mean it.'

'Yeah. I bet he'd give me my old job back, too.'

'No, we're not lunatics. But we'd let you walk away. In exchange for Dye. That's the deal.'

'Why's Billy so important to you?'

Chef pretended he hadn't heard. 'Think I don't know how good you are? You're the best there is. The fact that you're talking to me now only goes to prove that. So, if there's some way to negotiate a peace between us, let's do it.'

'Answer my question.'

'Which question?'

'What's Billy supposed to have done?'

'We don't like his attitude.'

'Sorry?'

'He's got an attitude problem. He shows no respect.'

'So what?' It made Rawhead smirk, the way this guy talked about respect, as if he was a Mafia chieftain. He knew Chef's background. His family had managed a cheap and nasty coffee bar in Hazel Grove. Their idea of respect was brushing the pubic hairs off the chips before serving them to customers.

'Not just no respect to Malcolm. To anyone.'

'Yeah. But what did he *do*?'

'He made jokes about Malcolm behind his back. He acted like he was better than Malcolm, even though Malcolm was trying to help his career. '

'Did he *tell* Priest he was better than him?'

'He didn't need to. Malcolm could see it in his face.'

Rawhead snorted.

Chef was growing impatient. 'Yeah. Big joke. All of a sudden, you're asking for reasons. That's funny, 'cause reasons never bothered you before.' There was no reply. 'Now, I've made you a good offer, better than you deserve. Bring us Billy Dye, and we're quits.' The silence was prolonged. 'You still there?'

'Yeah.'

'Think it over. '

The line went dead. Chef turned off the mobile, scratched an itch above his eye, felt wetness on his fingertip. He dragged his hand across his brow, irritated to learn that he was bathed in sweat. He felt sick, knowing that the Doll had failed, was probably dead, and that he would have to break the news to Priest.

A lavatory flushed nearby. A door opened and Priest's mother emerged. She was wearing a thin cotton nightdress and leaning on a stick. Her shriv-elled face was caked in make-up. She looked like the oldest, most infirm prostitute in the world. Peering up at Chef with screwed-up eyes, she said, 'Oh. It's you, is it?'

'Afraid so, Mrs Priest.'

'You were spying on me through the keyhole. You dirty swine!'

'No. No!'

'Why have you gone red, then? Eh? Eh?'

He shook his head despairingly. She poked his arm with a bony forefinger.

'Where's Lucky? I say, where's my Lucky?'

'Gone for walkies, Mrs Priest.'

'I'll tell Malcolm about you. I say, I'll tell Malcolm. You liar!' she said, walking away. 'You're born liars, you Spaniards.'

Chef began to explain that he was actually half Greek, but she hobbled away, waving a dismissive hand at him. Chef thought the old woman had been acting strangely since her hip operation. Perhaps she'd suffered brain damage while she was under the anaesthetic. With a brain like hers, it was difficult to say.

He walked out to the patio. Immediately, Priest confronted him. Priest was eating an enormous hot dog. Grease dripped from his first chin to his second. 'Any news?'

Chef played dumb. 'Sorry?'

'You were on the fucking phone, you useless glob of monkey cum.'

'I gave the wife a bell.'

'Fuck off.'

'No, really. You don't know her. If I don't tell her when I'm coming home, she goes on strike and won't do any housework.'

Priest nodded, but his eyes were hard and calculating. He turned away to slop another layer of onion onto his hot dog while Chef helped himself to a blackened burger. Unable to locate the ketchup, Priest consulted Dogman. Dogman led him to a picnic table where there was a selection of homemade relishes. One of them was red. 'Maybe that's ketchup,' suggested Dogman. 'Try it. Or why not ask Filthy?'

Priest shook his head. 'I doubt he'd know.'

'Nice night,' commented Dogman, passing Chef a cold beer. 'Know anything about the stars?'

'I only know one constellation: the Plough,' replied Chef.

'Is that the one shaped like a sailor?'

'No,' sneered Chef. 'You're thinking of the constellation of Popeye.'

Dogman's radio crackled. One of the three men patrolling the perimeter fence was trying to contact him. Staring up in the general direction of Polaris, he said 'Yeah?' into the mouthpiece and was answered by a crackle of static. 'Jed?' With a shrug, he rammed the radio back into his jacket. 'The only trouble with technology is it doesn't fucking work.' Dogman cackled toothlessly.

'What you saw in there,' said Chef quietly. 'With Malcolm – it only happens from time to time. He's under a lot of pressure.'

The Beast, hand on Heidi's shoulder, was trying to persuade his embittered friend that there had been nothing personal behind Priest's spirited attack on his testicles.

'Forget it,' said Dogman nonchalantly.

In the far corner of his vision, Dogman glimpsed movement. A tall figure was crossing the floodlit lawn towards them. Dogman assumed it was Jed, coming to tell him what he couldn't relate over the radio. Returning his gaze to Chef, Dogman said, 'He's paying the bills. Long as he doesn't try any of that stuff on me or my boys, there'll be no argument.'

There was a loud boom. At first, Chef thought that someone had let off a particularly noisy firework. Then he looked at Dogman and knew that the head of security had been shot. Although he remained standing like a dazed sentry, Dogman had lost the top of his skull. His bloody cranium was now sitting on the barbecue, where it sizzled amiably. Without uttering a sound, Dogman toppled and fell.

Chef turned to see where the shot had come from. The gunman was now less than fifty yards away. He was wearing a white hood and a long black coat. There was a magnum in his right hand. He looked like a figure from a nightmare. More astonishing than his appearance was the assassin's relaxed and leisurely gait. He moved as if nothing on earth had ever posed a threat to him.

Rawhead fired again. The bullet hissed past Chef and hit Filthy, who was standing in front of Priest.

Filthy swayed slightly and grimaced as if he'd tasted one of his own omelettes. His left hand gripped his neck and blood spurted through his fingers.

Filthy's immediate reaction was angry denial. Yelling unintelligibly, he grabbed a steak knife. He charged forward, blood pulsing rhythmically from his neck, certain that this was not his day to die.

Chef, who had hastily pulled an automatic from his trouser belt, fired in Rawhead's general direction. The wind from the bullet brushed Rawhead's right temple. Before Rawhead could retaliate, Filthy lunged at him with the knife. Almost irritably, Rawhead shot Filthy in the chest and he fell, face down.

Malcolm Priest had thrown himself to the floor and was covering his head with his hands. Heidi and the Beast were already reaching for their guns. Barking orders at them, Chef threw himself protectively over Priest.

As the Beast took cover behind the barbecue, Heidi raised a snubnose revolver. A bullet brushed Rawhead's scalp. Rawhead aimed coolly at Heidi's forehead and was about to reply when Filthy, crawling on his knees, grabbed Rawhead's gun arm. The shot went wide. Heidi fell, but Rawhead couldn't tell whether he'd been hit or whether he'd merely slipped. He was certainly not dead, because he rolled sideways to join the Beast behind the barbecue.

Bleeding badly, clinging to Rawhead's arm, Filthy raised the knife in his right hand. He lifted the knife slowly, growing weak as his life gushed away. He was bellowing incoherently, bloody foam dribbling down his chin. Rawhead prised the knife out of Filthy's fingers. Then, with the dying man still gripping his gun arm, Rawhead lowered his revolver and fired into Filthy's open mouth.

Chef bundled Priest through the French windows and turned quickly, now holding a gun. Rawhead shot at him hurriedly, missing Chef and shattering the window by his head. Chef dived for cover. Rawhead kept firing until the gun was empty and the patio was covered in broken glass.

He started to run, circling the house in an anti-clockwise direction. When he was in view of the drive, he paused to reload the Ruger. He was slotting the sixth cartridge into its chamber when he heard panting. Around the corner hurtled a young guard who had heard the shots and was running to intervene. The two men collided, Rawhead remaining on his feet while the other grunted in surprise and crashed to the floor. Rawhead shot the guard in the back of the head before he had a chance to turn around.

The security gates at the front of the house were closed. But as Rawhead approached, walking briskly, the gates opened and Lol Shepherd entered with Lucky the poodle. Lol passed through the gates. The poodle squatted to release a small, rolling turd. Lol halted as he struggled to slip his pass card into his wallet. As usual, his hands were shaking and the task demanded all his concentration.

Lol didn't see Rawhead until he was two feet away. Sensing the assassin's overwhelming presence, Lol looked up and found himself staring at a hooded giant. Lucky drew back instinctively, snarling with fear. Lol glanced down to see the impressive gun with its Wild West barrel and his mouth fell wide open.

Without mercy or malice, Rawhead pointed the weapon at Lol's heart.

Trembling, Lol Shepherd closed his eyes. He saw the father who never came home, waving to him from the top deck of the ninety-two bus; Laurie, his bride, on their wedding night; the pub they'd managed on Lancashire Hill; Laurie in bed, dying of cancer at the age of thirty-three; himself driving the wedding car for Malcolm Priest's daughter; outside the church in Mobberley, Priest in a top hat and tails, shaking hands with Lol after offering him a job. The flood of poignant images ceased as the gun roared in his ears.

When Lol opened his eyes, the stranger was gone. Lol felt no pain, but he had heard that the shock of being shot sometimes numbs the victim to physical sensation. He ran frantic hands over his body, searching for the entry wound. But there was no blood. Nothing.

Lol could see Priest and the Beast running towards

him, shouting excitedly. If he could see and hear them, Lol reasoned, he must be alive. Weak with gratitude, he stooped to pick up Lucky's leash. Something resembling a scruffy red and white rug lay at his feet. Lol released a soft moan of dismay.

Rawhead had shot the dog.

11

I can see it building up in the west. There are some clouds
there and I saw one of them kind of rip apart.
There's a wind coming, all right.
'The Wind', Ray Bradbury

Eighty minutes after the attack, three taxis rolled
up at Priest's house, containing eight burly, stupid-
looking young men. The Beast met them at the gate,
paid off the cabbies and escorted the new arrivals
onto the premises. Shortly afterwards, a lone squad
car pulled up outside the house. One of the neighbours, an elderly widow who was too senile to
appreciate the possible consequences of her action,
had phoned the police to complain about the noise.

Priest and the Beast met the car at the gate and
explained that they'd been letting off fireworks in
honour of Martin Luther King Day. The two police
officers didn't know whether it was Martin Luther
King Day or not. Nor did Priest. But they knew
that Priest was a racist, and found the idea of him

celebrating a nigger's birthday very funny indeed. They apologized for disturbing Priest, who slipped them each a fifty-pound note for their trouble and wished them well.

When the police were out of the way, a black transit van left the house, followed by the three cars that Filthy, Chef and Dogman had arrived in. By first light, the keen young tools were in position around the perimeter of Priest's house. Many of them had shaved heads. All of them wore sunglasses and sported chunky gold chains and bracelets. They resembled a pack of rabid dogs with a rich and nasty owner. Which, in effect, is precisely what they were.

At ten fifteen, an ambulance arrived. After the Beast had greeted the paramedics at the gate and searched them, the ambulance was admitted to the drive. Shortly afterwards, a single stretcher emerged from the house. The stretcher contained Mrs Priest, who had collapsed on learning of Lucky's demise. Malcolm Priest, who hadn't been to bed, accompanied his mother in the ambulance.

Dogman and Filthy meant nothing to Priest. Doc had been close to retirement. No one had liked Newey. Priest had barely glanced at the young security guard, before or after his death. But by shooting the dog, Rawhead had delivered a direct blow to the heart of the Priest family. This was a crime that Malcolm Priest could not forgive. Losing good men is never easy. But the carnage that followed was caused by the death of a poodle.

Billy was woken by the sound of footsteps. He glanced at the radio alarm clock by the bed. It was four in the morning. He felt around the bed for the shotgun. Failing to locate it, he sat up sharply in bed. Immediately, there was an ominous clunk. The weapon, which had slipped to the edge of the mattress, now dropped heavily to the floor.

The mistake could have been fatal. Seconds later, the door opened and a dark shadow filled the doorway. Billy waited, dry-mouthed, until he heard a voice say, 'It's me.' The door had closed again before Billy recognized Rawhead's voice.

Billy was showered and dressed by nine. He went downstairs to find Rawhead sitting at the dining-room table, drinking coffee and eating toast. He looked ill and drained. His face was the colour of unbleached calico. He greeted Billy with an imperious nod, eyes cold and watchful. The Ruger Blackhawk revolver rested on the table. Billy tried to appear relaxed as he brewed himself a pot of tea. Then he filled a mug and sat down at the table.

With an effort, he smiled at Rawhead and said, 'This house is haunted. Isn't it?'

Rawhead shook his head.

'You don't think so?' Billy eyed him warily. 'Well,

how come I've been hearing footsteps and screams every fucking night?'

Ignoring Billy, Rawhead refilled his coffee cup.

'Yeah. I even thought I heard someone moving about in the cellar.'

Displaying complete disinterest in what Billy had to say, Rawhead sipped his coffee.

Billy could see he was pissed off about something. 'What's the matter with you?'

Rawhead looked into his eyes. 'Only this. Malcolm Priest knows I didn't kill you. He tried to set me up, so I paid a visit to his house and took out three of his men.'

Billy laughed, thinking he was joking. When Rawhead failed to join in, Billy asked him what had really happened. Rawhead explained. Billy was incredulous. 'You might have taken Priest. Then all this would have been over.' (Rawhead stopped eating and examined Billy coldly.) 'Know what you've done? You've just made Priest madder. Now he's going to try even harder to fucking kill me.'

'You selfish little prat.' Rawhead's eyes glittered with animosity. 'You only think of yourself, don't you?'

'No.'

'Do you know what I think? I think you called somebody. I think you waited until I'd gone, lasted a day and called somebody.'

'Rubbish,' said Billy. 'You're just trying to put the blame on me because you lost it.'

Rawhead stood up. 'If you weren't such a big-mouthed little prick, I wouldn't have lost anything.'

'Meaning what?'

'You've got a big mouth.'

'And you've got a little prick.'

Without further debate, Rawhead dragged Billy out of his seat and slapped him in the mouth, splitting his lip. In retaliation, Billy cracked Rawhead on the side of the head with his mug of tea. The mug shattered and hot tea splashed them both. Billy saw Rawhead reel slightly and took advantage of the moment to punch Rawhead in the jaw harder than he had ever hit anyone before.

A terrifying look appeared on Rawhead's face, but before he could hit back, Billy lunged at him, knocking him against the table. Both men toppled to the floor and for a few moments Billy found himself sitting astride Rawhead's chest. Billy's sense of triumph was short-lived. He hadn't had a real fight since his schooldays and he was trying to remember what to do next. As far as he could recall, it was something to do with raining ineffectual blows on your opponent's face and head until a prefect arrived to escort you to the head's office.

While Billy was reminiscing, Rawhead grabbed his left wrist and twisted it. Two seconds later, Billy was face down on the floor with his arm twisted tightly behind him and Rawhead's knee in the small of his back. 'You're enjoying this, aren't you?' said Billy, unwisely. 'You big fairy!'

'You called someone. Didn't you?' Rawhead tugged lightly at the captive wrist, knowing exactly how much pressure to apply in order to cause maximum pain without breaking Billy's arm.

Billy screamed. Then, unexpectedly, he burst into song. He sang the first verse of the Tom Jones classic, 'It's Not Unusual'.

Completely disarmed, Rawhead laughed and shook his head. Unable to continue, he released Billy and sat down again. 'Billy, there's no hope for you. None at all.'

Billy got to his feet, rubbing his aching shoulder. He could taste blood in his mouth. 'Fucking violence. That's all you understand.'

Rawhead nodded. 'Pretty good at it, though. Aren't I?'

Billy snatched the revolver off the table and pointed it at Rawhead, who looked unconcerned. 'I could kill you now,' said Billy.

'It's not in you, Bill,' said Rawhead confidently. 'You'd never kill unless you absolutely had to.'

There was a long silence. Billy replaced the weapon on the table. Then Rawhead asked Billy what had happened to the Harley. With a dry mouth, Billy told him. Rawhead shrugged. 'Don't worry about it.' He put his feet up on the table and began to roll a spliff. 'So who did you tell?'

Billy felt there was no point in continuing to lie. Rawhead knew him too well. Wearily, he explained about Nikki, how her letter had intensified his loneliness and led to the meeting with Tony. Rawhead's anger had evaporated, leaving calm resignation. In silence, he lit the spliff, inhaled deeply and passed it to Billy.

'You realize he's probably dead now? Your policeman friend.'

Billy turned cold. 'Jesus Christ, don't say that.'

'Part of your trouble, Bill, is that you don't understand what kind of people you're dealing with. You're cynical, but you're also naive. The evil of men like Malcolm Priest is beyond your comprehension. You'd never torture or kill your enemies. You'd feel it was enough to be sarcastic to them.'

'I've always fucked up, one way or another,' admitted Billy soberly. 'But I've never fucked up as much in my life as I have done in the last few months.'

Billy took a nervous blast at the spliff and passed it back to Rawhead. 'Well,' mused the killer reflectively, 'I don't know why I get mad at you. You've always been the same.'

'A fuck-up?'

'No. That's not what I mean. I mean you don't seem to respect any rules, not even your own. Something that happened at school sums you up. Remember our old gym teacher?'

'Barney Jones. He was a vindictive midget.'

'Yeah. But you were always pissing him off. The one sport you excelled at was cross-country running, but you refused to do your best because you hated Barney. Every sports day, he made you run and you deliberately walked to make sure you came last. I remember him screaming at you, accusing you of not having the balls to run five miles. And you just laughed at him.'

'What's your point?' said Billy.

'Well, people who don't respect rules will never find life easy. I knew a guy in London, an old East End hard man called Dennis Hill. He never married because he couldn't accept that marriage was real. He couldn't accept any ritual, any custom, that other people followed. Used to say, "When yer fink about it, it's all facking made-up." He felt the same about the laws of the land. "Facking made-up, my son." When he got sent down for his part in a robbery, the judge asked him if he had anything to say. Dennis said, "You've got no right to judge me, there's no such thing as a real judge. This isn't a real court. It's all facking pretend!" To which the judge replied, "In that case, I'm sentencing you to prison for twenty pretend years."'

Smiling at the memory, Rawhead turned to look at Billy. 'You may laugh, Bill. But that's what you're like. That's what's wrong with your life. People with your attitude might, in a few cases, be outrageously successful. Most likely they'll turn into angry misfits.'

'Or mass murderers,' retorted Billy.

They went for a walk over the fields. The air was heavy, the clouds black with rain. A storm was on the way. Rawhead took the Remington, carrying it over one shoulder. Billy asked him about the visit to Priest's house. 'Weren't you scared?'

'No. If you're scared, the bullets know. They come straight for you, as if you're a giant magnet. If you don't fear death, they fly past you, they can't hurt you.'

'You think bullets are alive?'

Rawhead turned his hard, tired face to Billy. 'Don't be a tit.'

Billy laughed.

With his high cheekbones and his fierce expression, Rawhead looked to Billy like a demon carved in stone. Rawhead sat down under a hedgerow. Billy sat beside him. On the grey horizon, the church spire pointed to a heaven full of pain. Thunder murmured in the west. The sky was streaked with approaching rain.

'If you're not afraid,' said Rawhead, eyes straight ahead, 'everyone can sense it. If you walk down a dark street without fear, people step aside to let you pass.'

'If you look like you, they do.'

'No, you're wrong. You know the seventeenth-century swordsman, Musashi Miyamoto?'

'No.'

'He wrote something that I've kind of taken to heart. "In a life or death situation, choose death."'

Billy yawned. 'That your motto, is it?'

'Suppose so.'

'You couldn't just choose a normal motto like "Life's what you make it" or "Treat others as you'd like to be treated"? It has to be: "Choose death."'

'Yeah, but think what it means. If you've chosen death, actually walked into a situation knowing that there's a good chance you're finished, but deciding you'll go down with all guns blazing, that gives you one hell of an edge. By choosing death, you're massively increasing your chances of survival. Do you see what I mean?'

Billy thought about it. A wind arrived from nowhere, whipping their clothes and hair as if to warn them of the coming storm. At last he shook his head.

'That's because you've never chosen death,' said Rawhead.

'No,' said Billy, 'it's because you're talking total bollocks. You don't have to choose death to survive. I'd rather run away any day than get fucking shot at.'

'Then you'll just get shot in the back.' Rawhead

DAVID BOWKER

laughed darkly. 'I've made some bad people very angry, and they won't stop until we're dead. They're coming for us, Billy. Don't doubt that. When they get here, I might need a little help.'

Billy's misery must have shown on his face, because Rawhead slapped him on the shoulder. 'What say we take half a tab apiece? It's the perfect time for it. A moment of calm and beauty, shared among friends.'

In Rawhead's outstretched palm lay a stamp-sized square of paper bearing a brightly coloured picture of a pirate ship on the ocean. Billy's heart sank. 'You're kidding me. I'm sitting in a field with a murderer, it's going to piss down, I'm dogged by loneliness and a growing sense of failure and any day now, I'm likely to die a violent, agonizing death. These are not the required conditions for the ingestion of hallucinogenic drugs. I'll have a panic attack. I'll be overwhelmed by feelings of inferiority.'

'You've never taken acid like this before.' Rawhead winked and tore the perforated line to bisect the tab. He swallowed one half and held the other out to Billy. 'You'll be fine. I promise you.'

'Last time I tripped, I ended up on my knees for four hours, staring at a fucking peanut on the carpet. I swear the peanut was making faces at me.'

Supposing that life couldn't get much worse, Billy swallowed the sugar paper. Then they started back to the house. The wind pursued them, carrying the sweet, metallic scent of rain. On the way, a huge black rook alighted on a fence and cawed loudly. It glared at them, its eyes black and defiant. Rawhead looked at Billy and smiled.

'If you were a deity, who would you be?'

'Pan probably. Lots of boozing and shagging, without hangovers or guilt. What about you?'

'Belial.'

'Who's B. Lyall?'

'*Belial*. Leader of the sons of darkness.' Rawhead swung the shotgun round and blasted the rook into space with a screech and a cloud of feathers. '"All his dominions are in darkness and his purpose is to bring about wickedness. All the spirits associated with him are but angels of destruction."'

Something else happened before they reached the vicarage. The acid took effect and Billy felt he'd divided neatly into two: one Billy was walking in the country with Rawhead; his inner self was soaring through unknown, uncharted regions, blissfully free. The sensation of flight was wonderful and unambiguous, yet outwardly he remained steady and sober.

They reached the vicarage as the sky turned black. As Billy hung his jacket in the hall, a fly buzzed close to his face.

'Steve, where do all the flies come from?'

'You want a biology lesson?'

'No, I mean the flies in this house. Every time I look, there are gnats and fucking flies.'

'It's the country, Bill. It's normal to have flies in the country.'

'What about the smell? Sometimes this place stinks worse than shit.'

'Bad drains. Don't let it bother you. '

With a tremendous boom, the clouds unleashed a deluge. Billy went to the parlour window to watch the storm. The rain descended vertically, pounding the roof and the trees and the graves beyond with unrelenting violence. To Billy, in his drugged state, it seemed as if the rain was spouting upwards from the very earth.

'Bill?' Rawhead was standing beside him, holding a steak knife. He was smiling. To Billy's eyes, Rawhead seemed transfigured, a boy again. Making no further attempt to be cool or aloof. 'Are you flying, Bill?'

Billy laughed. Lightly, Rawhead drew the steak knife over his right palm. Blood swelled from a small incision. Then he nodded to Billy, who held out his own right hand. Rawhead nicked the skin and they joined hands, mingling blood. Rawhead's eyes blazed with warmth. 'Now we're really brothers.'

Rawhead left the room. Billy stayed by the window, watching the rain. Minutes later, Rawhead returned. 'Billy, come with me. I've got a little surprise for you. Something amazing.'

Intrigued, Billy followed Rawhead across the hall and into the kitchen. There was a man sitting at the kitchen table.

He had his back to Billy, and his dark head lolled forward. Billy glanced at Rawhead, who urged him forward with a friendly nod. But something about the stranger's demeanour made Billy hold back.

Gently, Rawhead took Billy by the arm and steered him to the table. Then he grabbed the stranger by the hair and raised his head so that Billy could see his face. Billy began to shake. Rawhead's gift to him was a corpse. The killer laughed with grim satisfaction. The victim's face was geisha white. In his cheek and forehead were two circular holes, so clean that they might have been made by a drill.

The staring eyes were coated with a greyish film, like the eyes of a carcass in a butcher's window. A dark red bib of dried blood extended from his open mouth to the lap of his corduroy trousers. There was no mistaking the dead man's blank expression or the distinctive shape of his nose. It was Blake Terry, Billy's publisher.

Eyes shining, Rawhead grinned at Billy. 'Remember what he said to you, Bill?'

Gasping for breath, Billy looked at Rawhead, who nodded downward. Billy turned back to Terry, and noticed that his mouth looked unusually cavernous. He glanced down at the corpse's right hand. A spear of purple flesh protruded obscenely from the clenched fist. Blake Terry was holding his tongue.

In case Billy Dye came home unannounced, the Doll had arranged a nice surprise for him. On the night of Conrad's death, the Doll had driven to the empty house on Albert Road and had dumped his brother's body in the attic, among boxes of old punk records and dusty stacks of Marvel Comics.

The Doll told Maureen, Conrad's widow, that her husband had offended some bad people and gone into hiding. And that it might never be safe for him to return. The Doll thought he saw relief in the woman's weary face. In return for her silence and co-operation, the Doll promised to provide for Maureen and her children. She asked one question. 'Have you killed him?'

The Doll was able to answer truthfully. 'I would never harm Conrad or you or the children.'

All that remained was the delicate matter of Malcolm Priest. There had been absolute silence from the Priesthood. Three days after Conrad's death, the Doll phoned one of Priest's loan sharks to find out why he was getting no answer on Chef's mobile. Silver informed him that some men and a poodle had died and that Priest's mother was in a nursing home, her mind gone. The Doll was convinced that he would be blamed for the massacre.

Then the Doll did something unusual. Rather than running away or waiting for Priest to exact vengeance, he decided to go to Priest's house and apologize for his failure. That way, he reasoned, there was a slim chance that Priest would let him live.

The Doll phoned a florist and arranged for thirty pounds' worth of roses to be sent to Mrs Priest's bedside. Next he drafted a hasty will and left it with his solicitor. Then he waited a day, took a last, thoughtful look at his wife and his children, and drove to Knutsford. Heidi, a surgical dressing over his left eye, met him at the gate. The Doll said he wanted to see Priest. Heidi answered that, under the circumstances, he doubted Mr Priest would want to see anyone.

The Doll insisted. Heidi relayed the request to Priest and was obviously surprised and impressed when an audience was granted. When the Doll had been frisked and declared clean, he was escorted into the presence of Manchester's number one.

Priest was sitting in the living room with the curtains drawn. Although it was midday, he was still in his dressing gown. He was unshaven. His stubble grew in irregular, reddish brown patches. The room smelt of cigars and sweaty feet. An authentic World War Two Luger lay on the coffee table before him. The Doll had no doubt that it was loaded.

Priest looked up at the Doll with dead eyes. 'I'm fucking surprised to see you.'

'Yeah,' said the Doll, waiting for Priest to explode.

'Thought you were dead – was sure you were fucking dead. What happened?'

The Doll explained. 'So I never even saw him. He took my brother.'

'He what?'

'He shot my brother.' The Doll told the story, omitting to mention that he'd shot Conrad himself. He could see that Priest didn't give a fuck about Conrad and was more interested in the notion that Rawhead had spared the Doll.

'That means something,' said Priest. 'It fucking must do. He came in here, bold as a prick, and he takes a pot at me but he doesn't take you on? Where's the fucking logic in that?'

'Maybe he didn't know I was there.'

'Maybe. Or maybe you and him are in this together.'

The Doll looked sickened. 'What? And kill my own brother?'

'I wasn't serious,' said Priest.

There was a long silence. The Doll's mouth tasted of ashes. 'I suppose you blame me for . . . you know?'

'Normally, I'd have blamed Chef. He enlisted a

fucking head-the-ball and we've all had to pay for it. But, you know, when that bastard came calling, Chef proved his loyalty. I mean, *big-time*. I fell over, you see. Chef shielded me with his own body. I mean, it wouldn't have made no difference. The gun Rawhead was packing could have blown a hole through the fucking pair of us. But it's the thought that counts.'

The Doll waited. Priest obviously wanted to talk. The obese crimelord eased a wedge of dirt from under a thumbnail. Then, in a matter-of-fact voice, he said, 'Me mam died today.'

The Doll was shocked. 'I'm very sorry.'

Priest looked up at him. 'Yeah. Rawhead shot the dog, you know. That was what finished her off. By my way of thinking, that's a war crime. That dog was an innocent civilian. Your brother, my mam. We've both of us been hit where it fucking well hurts. She was a grand old girl.'

'I'm sure.'

'You say you've got some idea where Dye is hiding?'

'Rawhead's got a house. Somewhere near Bedford. An old, whadyacallit, parsonage.'

'You know where it is?'

'No, but I could find it.'

'Do that. Don't risk yourself. Just find the address and report back. This time, I'm sending the best I've got.'

The Doll's face dropped. 'But I thought you wanted *me* to take care of things. I thought that was why I'd been hired.'

'You're worth more to me than that, now.'

'You're putting me on the payroll?'

'We'll see.' Amused by the Doll's directness, Priest bared his teeth in a simian smile. The Doll realized that Manchester's number one wore dentures. 'We'll see. Be careful, now. Don't forget.'

'I won't forget.'

Priest nodded. He lit a cigar and lapsed into silence. The meeting was at an end. As the Doll reached the door, Priest whistled to him. 'Hey! Thanks for sending them flowers. Roses were her favourite.'

Swaggering slightly, the Doll returned to his Range Rover. It was always the little things, he reflected. In life, it was the little things that got you noticed. Or got you killed.

12

Twelve struck, and one and two and three, and still
we sat waiting silently for whatever might befall.

'The Adventure of the Speckled Band', Sir Arthur Conan Doyle

It was daylight when Billy opened his eyes. Rawhead was standing by his bed, holding a tray with a plate of toast, a glass of orange juice and a mug of tea. Billy had a feeling that something terrible had happened, something bad enough to make him wish he was still asleep.

'Got you some breakfast, Bill.' Billy sat up in bed. Rawhead placed the tray on his lap. Billy remembered seeing Blake Terry dead in the kitchen, then himself staggering around the house, screaming, pursued by Rawhead's laughter.

When he'd eaten, Billy dressed and went down to the kitchen. Rawhead was at the table, cleaning and oiling his shotgun.

'If I ask you a question, will you answer it honestly?'

'I'll try to.' Rawhead's answering smile was candid and unassuming.

'Did you kill my publisher?' asked Billy.

Rawhead gave a little shrug, sighed and shook his head. He sat down on the bed and watched Billy with bored, unblinking eyes. 'It was the acid, Bill.'

'I fucking saw him! He was sitting right there!'

'No. It was good stuff, incredibly pure, but for some reason you had a bad trip. Sorry, Bill. A long time ago I had a fight with the devil on the stairs of Stockport College. It was my first trip. My devil wasn't any more real than your dead body.'

'You're telling the truth?'

'It was all in your mind, Bill. I even had to give you a small shot of morphine.'

'*Morphine?*'

'You were losing it. You walked into the kitchen and just freaked.'

'But you said you were going to show me something. "Something amazing." I heard you say those exact words.'

'That's right, Billy,' explained Rawhead patiently. 'Do you want to know what it was?'

Billy nodded. Rawhead stood up and took the key to the church off its nail. 'Come with me.'

It was raining again. They walked out of the house and crossed the waterlogged lawn. The churchyard was separated from the garden by a tall beech hedge. Rawhead led the way through a narrow gap in the hedge and they hurried past the graves to the main door.

Rawhead unlocked the church door and, in the nave, used the same key to unlock the door to the belfry. From the belfry, a narrow spiral staircase climbed the tower. The steps were worn and slippery. Thunder rumbled, vibrating through the ancient stones.

They passed the five bells hanging in the tower. Rawhead reached into the bell chamber and patted one as he passed. And then they were at the top, under the spire.

'Where's the surprise?'

'The view, Billy. I wanted to show you the view.'

The perfumed wind whistled through the window slats. There was a hole in the floor. The five bells hung below his feet like great domed skulls. He walked to a window and surveyed the land below. He could see every church, cottage, road and field for miles around. In yesterday's storm, it would have looked amazing.

Rawhead and Billy drove to a nearby village for lunch. In the pub, Rawhead told Billy that he liked his book. 'The characters are great. Exactly how I imagine dead people to be. How come no one's tried to turn it into a film?'

'The BBC were interested,' said Billy. 'I went in to see this woman producer about it.'

'What was she like?'

'Upper-class background. Privileged little porker. Turned out she'd only read the first chapter. When I mentioned dead people, her mouth dropped open. "You mean to say that the dead *actually* come to life?" I said yes, and she looked worried. She said the head of drama hated anything supernatural. She said she'd have a think and ring me. A few days later she emailed me with a suggestion. If I could make all the dead people – and remember, this is a book with no living characters – if I could turn the dead people into living people, then maybe she could pitch the idea to her boss.'

Rawhead frowned. 'But the dead people *are* the idea.'

'Exactly. But I was desperate. So, like a tit, I did what she said. I wrote a new treatment and changed the corpses to living people. And she still wasn't happy. So I rang her up and told her she was fat.'

'Do you think that was helpful?'

'At least I didn't fucking shoot her – which is probably what you'd have done.'

'What was her name?' asked Rawhead casually.

Billy lowered his beer glass and looked at Rawhead warily. 'What does her name have to do with anything?'

Rawhead acted as if Billy hadn't spoken.

Before setting back, they stopped at the village shop to buy milk and bread. Billy looked at the newsstand and saw a single copy of the *Guardian* sitting on its own among the stacks of *Mirror*s, *Sun*s and *Mail*s. Billy hated the *Guardian*, but was so amazed to see a liberal newspaper on sale in the Bedfordshire countryside that he simply had to buy it.

On the journey back to the vicarage, Billy read while Rawhead drove. He was half hoping to find a paragraph about his disappearance. However, his books hadn't been sold to Hollywood and he hadn't fucked Madonna, so the British press treated his absence with the same indifference they had reserved for his presence.

After skipping through the *Guardian* once, Billy did what he always did. He skipped through it again, unable to believe how boring it was the first time. Then, on page five, he found a small paragraph of interest:

Police appeal for publisher's safe return

Circumstances surrounding the disappearance of publisher Blake Terry are not regarded as suspicious, a police spokesperson said last night. Mr Terry, 36, is editorial director at Bevis Lane. Mr Terry failed to return home from work last Monday. He is said to have been experiencing emotional problems. His estranged wife, the award-winning illustrator Rowena Sykes, says: 'Blake believes that he has no friends. In fact, he has many friends and a family that loves him dearly. We beg him to get in touch.'

It had taken the Doll three days. He was a meticulous man. He had toured the countryside around Bedford, visiting twenty-three churches. For two nights he slept in a bed and breakfast run by a resentful blonde woman, a single parent who talked to the Doll about her favourite TV shows while he ate his cooked breakfast. Then he went out to show Billy Dye's face to vicars and villagers, none of whom admitted to recognizing him.

It was raining as he drove into Dudloe. Although it was mid-afternoon, the black sky had plunged the countryside into premature twilight. The spire of St Michael's remained in view as he drove his Range Rover up a wide, winding highway. He turned off into Church Lane and parked on the grass verge outside the gate. A woman was passing with her dog. She sported a tweed skirt and a headscarf tied under her chin. The Doll asked her where the vicarage was. She pointed to the nearest house, said, 'Not there,' and laughed. 'It's the house next door.'

'Does someone called Ellis live there?' asked the Doll pleasantly.

'No.' She laughed again. 'It's where the vicar lives. Truly.'

He walked to the vicarage, hardly glancing at the house beside the churchyard. A thin wind blew rain into his eyes. There was no sign on the gate, nothing to indicate that a man of God lived here. The Doll knocked on the door, his hand on the automatic pistol in his trouser belt. Disappointingly, the door was answered by a plain middle-aged woman in brown stockings and a baggy cardigan. She was eating a sandwich. The Doll did his best to smile at her. The smile was not returned. 'Hello there? Is this the vicarage?'

'I hope so,' she said tartly.

The Doll showed her the photograph. 'I wonder if you could help me? This is my brother. He left his wife and family a few years ago, simply walked off and hasn't been in touch since. A lot of people are very worried about him. He's had mental problems and we think he may be living rough somewhere. You haven't seen him?'

She studied the snapshot and shook her head. 'No. No. But my husband might have. Wait there.'

She took the photograph into the house, leaving him standing in the rain. Typical Christian, thought the Doll. A few minutes later, a tall, grey man in a dog collar came to the door. He had nice, white hair with a side parting that showed a rosy pink scalp. But his face was as welcoming as a shovel. He handed the photograph to the Doll. 'Unless I'm very much mistaken, this fellow is living next door.'

'Next door?'

The vicar avoided eye contact. 'In the old vicarage. I'm fairly sure it's the same chap. And you say he's a mental defective?'

'Well . . .'

'Yes. That'd explain a lot. I've heard him shouting, you know.'

'Shouting?'

'Blasphemies. Frightful blasphemies. In the middle of the night. I've been meaning to mention it to Gawdy.'

'Who?'

'Mr Gawdy. He owns the house. As I understand it, this other person is his lodger.'

'Mr Gawdy. Would he be a tallish chap? Well built?'

'I suppose he merits that description.' The vicar paused, glancing sharply at the Doll over his spectacles. 'Why do you ask?'

'No reason.' The Doll waved the photograph. 'And we're definitely talking about the man in this picture?'

The vicar was tiring of the conversation. 'I think so. You've come to take him away, then?'

'That's the general idea.'

'Good,' said the vicar, closing the door.

The Doll didn't leave immediately. He walked through the churchyard and tried to get a look at the house where Billy Dye was hiding. But the old vicarage was shielded from view by a tall hedge. He had to fight a powerful urge to rush the place, now, in broad daylight. Then the glory would be all his. But so would the funeral. He was in the Priesthood. Malcolm gave the orders now.

The rain had eased and turned to drizzle. Birds prattled in the trees. There was a light on in the vicarage. A window was open on the ground floor. The Doll could hear music: something classical-sounding with strings. Had he known anything about film scores, he might have recognized Bernard Hermann's theme for *The Ghost and Mrs Muir*.

But the Doll wasn't interested in films or their soundtracks. He walked the length of the hedge, searching for a means of entry, before realizing he was not alone. An old man in a cagoule was kneeling before a grave with his back to the Doll. The inscription on the white headstone read:

Richard Hartop
1971–1992
Not dead, but sleeping

Fucking heavy sleeper, thought the Doll with a sneer. His task completed, the old man picked up his trowel and wandered off. The Doll watched him walk down the church path to the gate.

When the old man had gone, the Doll noticed something peculiar. The birds had stopped singing. He walked to the far corner of the cemetery, where the oldest graves languished in various stages of ruin.

The old vicarage loomed into view.

It was a more compact version of the buildings he'd seen in old American horror films: all turrets and towers and ominous windows. There was a high balcony at the near corner of the house, and on the balcony stood a figure. It was a tall man with razored hair and an impressive build. At this distance, the Doll could not see the face, but he knew that the man was staring directly at him.

The Doll felt his stomach muscles contract. Excitement and panic mingled inside him. He knew perfectly well who the stranger was, knew by his presence alone. This was the man who had killed his brother. Rawhead and the Doll gazed at each other for no more than six seconds. After this the Doll had the good sense to turn away.

He strode between the graves and passed through a gap in the hedge to join the bridle path that bordered the cornfield. Walking fast, eyes straight ahead, all the while feeling that murderous gaze burning into his back. Soon the vicarage was hidden by the trees and the Doll was hidden from Rawhead. The Doll took a deep breath. At that moment, the birds began to sing again.

Rawhead cooked a spaghetti bolognese for supper. The meat was organic. 'I thought you weren't scared of dying,' said Billy.

'I'm not scared of dying from a bullet. But I don't see why I should die because some greedy bastard farmer feeds his cattle their own shit.'

They sat down to eat at the kitchen table. Billy shoved the *Guardian* across the table, folded open at the Blake Terry article. 'Read that,' said Billy.

'Why?'

'It's about the guy I saw sitting where you're sitting now.'

'Oh, for God's sake. Let it drop, will you?'

'Steve, don't lie to me. My editor's missing. I didn't imagine that. It's in the *Guardian*. Page fucking five.'

Rawhead pushed the newspaper away. 'Why would I waste time on a bloody publisher?'

'Because he hasn't helped my career.'

Rawhead laughed and shook his head. 'If I was killing off all the people who haven't helped your career, you know what? You'd be the first one to go. You're the one who phones TV producers to tell 'em they're fat. I mean it, Billy. With your attitude, it's a wonder you've had any kind of career at all.'

Billy had to laugh. He knew this was the truth. He grabbed a can of beer. Rawhead asked him to put it back. 'You're forbidding me to drink my own beer?'

'No, I think we should have champagne.' Rawhead opened the fridge and produced a bottle of Bollinger. 'Let's celebrate.'

'What's the occasion?

Rawhead studied Billy's face. 'Priest's boys have found us.'

'You what?'

'I've seen someone. A guy they call the Doll. They're coming. They'll be here tonight.'

'You *fucking what*?'

Rawhead nodded calmly.

Billy exploded. 'What are we sitting here for?'

The cork popped. Rawhead filled two glasses. 'Relax.'

'You *want* them to come, don't you? You crazy bastard!'

'Sit down, Billy. I know what I'm doing. I'm pretty certain they don't.'

'They know how to blow our fucking heads off!'

'Maybe. Let's drink to staying alive.'

Unwillingly, Billy raised his glass and drank. The champagne was ice cold and delicious. 'Could I propose another toast?' asked Billy.

Rawhead nodded.

'To Nikki.'

'Who? The woman who left you?'

Billy nodded. 'I'd like you to drink to her.'

Rawhead put his glass down on the table. 'Why would I want to do that?'

At twenty-seven minutes past ten, in the porch outside the main entrance to the church, Rawhead handed Billy a torch, a mobile phone and a gun. The gun had belonged to Newey. Perhaps the same was true of the phone. Rawhead said there were three rounds in the breech. Billy complained, feeling it was unlucky to hold a weapon that had belonged to a murder victim. Rawhead agreed. 'But we're low on ammunition; my arms dealer has gone missing. Priest probably got to him. Every bullet I've got left has to count. That's why I want you to do something for me.'

'What?'

Rawhead smiled wolfishly. 'You're not going to like this.'

Billy said, 'Surprise me, why don't you?'

At ground level, two spotlights were trained on the church steeple. Rawhead picked up a half-brick and smashed them both, plunging the graveyard into darkness. Then he donned his hangman's hood and climbed over the fence that encompassed the vicar's meagre garden. A single light glowed at the top of the house. Rawhead wasn't troubled by this. The same light shone every night. The vicar was probably afraid of the dark. He deserved to be.

Rawhead walked round to the back of the house, crouching as he passed under a kitchen window that threw a broad band of light across the back lawn. He entered an ugly, functional porch that reeked of turpentine. In the porch stood a refrigerator. A cat brushed past his ankle in the dark and slipped out of the porch door. Rawhead opened the refrigerator door and took out an empty margarine tub. He peeled off the lid and took out the spare key that he knew would be there.

Taking care not to rattle the key in the lock, he opened the back door. He drew the Ruger and prodded the door with his toe. The door didn't open. Rawhead pushed it, felt something blocking the way. He pushed harder and squeezed through the gap. His way had been barred by a basket of dirty washing.

The door that led to the living room opened with a slight squeak. He waited patiently for about ten minutes, long enough for anyone who had heard the noise to stop listening and go back to sleep. Then he moved slowly and confidently through the hall, his path illuminated by a light on the landing above. At the foot of the stairs, Rawhead paused. The pig-like sound of snoring came from upstairs. Rawhead climbed a stair and waited, continuing in this fashion until he reached the first landing.

The snoring came from behind a door at the top of the stairs. It was slightly ajar. Rawhead pushed it open and waited. The snoring continued unabated. He stepped into the bedroom, which smelled of mothballs and unwashed socks. For a long time he waited, allowing his eyes to adjust to the semi-darkness.

He walked over to the bed. Predictably, it was the minister of the Lord who was making all the noise.

The vicar lay on his back with his mouth open. His wife was curled at the far corner of the bed with her back to him. Rawhead produced a small plastic freezer bag that held two hypodermics, each containing just enough morphine to drug a person until the following noon.

The vicar's left arm, clad in crumpled pyjamas, hung limply from the stale coverlet. Rawhead took the dry old wrist and, with businesslike efficiency, inserted a needle into the vein. The vicar gasped slightly, but did not wake. Rawhead rounded the bed and prepared to inject the vicar's wife. He raised the quilt and was about to take her arm when she opened her eyes and looked directly at him. She raised her head and released a strange inarticulate murmur.

Rawhead slammed his hand over her mouth and forced her head down into the pillow. She struggled lamely, bleating against the palm of his hand as he thrust the second hypodermic into her neck. He held her fast until she ceased struggling and her body relaxed. In the morning, her ordeal would seem like a dark, hazily remembered dream.

The vicar and his wife were an awful couple. Rawhead bitterly regretted that he couldn't kill them. But they were his neighbours, and their disappearance would only implicate him. Tonight, all that mattered was that they remained horizontal. After returning the empty syringes to their plastic bag, and placing the bag in his pocket, Rawhead tucked the couple in and left them to their unnatural sleep.

Billy entered the church, feeling its dampness envelop him. As he climbed the steeple, the great clock chimed half past ten. Its voice was so loud that Billy had to stop and cover his ears. His throat was tight and dry. He wished he'd remembered to bring a bottle of water.

Rawhead had appointed Billy his lookout. To assist him in this task, Rawhead had loaned him an infra-red sniperscope. It was a remarkable toy. By twisting it into focus, he found he could peer down into every shadow. The lens gave everything a bloody hue.

The sky grew darker as he kept his lonely vigil under the spire. Newey's Heckler & Koch was tucked in his trouser belt. Every now and then Billy patted the handle of the weapon to check that it was still there. From the southern window he could see the roof of Rawhead's house and the lane stretching to the winding highway. Occasionally a car would travel along the highway on its way to Bedford or Kimbolton. Each time Billy saw headlights approaching, he wondered if this was the vehicle that carried Priest's men. And each time the cars would drive past, making that lonely nee-ow sound that reminded Billy of childhood holidays.

The night was dry and overcast with a mild breeze. The time passed with torturous slowness and the parish clock chimed every quarter, sending dull vibrations through the boards beneath Billy's feet. Bats wheeled above and around his head. Glancing down, he thought he saw Rawhead at the gate to the churchyard. A tall, dark figure, his head slightly cocked to one side. He peered through the sniper-scope but there was no one there.

The clock struck twelve. One by one, the lights in the surrounding cottages winked out. Seen from this height, the world was a cosy place, a model village full of warmth and fascination: it was only when you stood outside the windows of the houses that you could hear the threats and recriminations.

The passing cars were now few and far between. Billy thought of Nikki and the child growing in her belly and was filled with longing for real life. Warmth and noise and light. He took a leak through the hole in the floorboards and heard his own piss tinkling over the sacred bells. He began to feel the cold and raised the collar of his jacket.

The church, like most churches, stank of hymn books and fear. The bell-ropes creaked softly beneath his feet. Sometimes Billy thought he heard footsteps on the stairs. Then he waited, clutching the gun, but no one ever came.

Billy saw an owl drop silently from an elm like a phantom. Seconds later, he heard the agonized screech of its prey. In the light of recent events, Billy's sympathies were entirely with the victim.

To keep warm, to stay awake, he kept circling the four windows, peering out over the dark fields. Billy's palm ached from the knife that had made him Rawhead's blood brother. The wound throbbed gently, a steady reminder that, whatever happened, each man would protect the other. Billy wasn't sure that he wanted to protect Rawhead. Whenever he thought about the man and what he'd done, he felt nausea in the pit of his stomach. But he was also keenly aware that without Rawhead, he had no chance whatsoever.

It was after two before he saw bright headlights approaching from the north. Billy prayed that the car would continue down the winding road towards Bedford. Instead, it turned into Church Lane, cruised slowly past the new vicarage, the old vicarage and the graveyard. Gradually picking up speed, the car drove on for another quarter of a mile and was gone.

His suspicions aroused, Billy raised the sniperscope, watching the bend where the road disappeared. Long minutes passed. Then the red haze seemed to shift and take form, and out of the darkness walked a figure, quickly followed by three more. Billy adjusted the zoom and homed in on the face of the leader. He couldn't be certain, but the length and weight of the jaw reminded him strongly of Chef. Shaking with adrenaline, Billy grabbed the mobile and dialled.

Rawhead answered. 'Yeah?'

'They're coming.'

'Meet you at the church door.'

Billy turned on his torch and descended the winding steps. He was halfway down the church tower before he remembered the sniperscope – he'd placed it on the floor while phoning Rawhead. He ran back to retrieve it. Then he hurried down to meet Rawhead in the church porch. The beam of his torch fell on Rawhead's white hood. 'You fucking idiot!' hissed Rawhead, snatching the torch and turning it off.

'Sorry.'

'How many?' Rawhead demanded.

'Four. I'm pretty sure it's four.'

'Which direction?'

Billy pointed.

'Where's the 'scope?'

Billy handed it over. Rawhead grabbed his shoulder and led him to the rear of the churchyard. Rawhead nodded towards the broad cornfield beyond. 'Go out there and wait. When it's clear, I'll signal with the torch. Three quick flashes. Then a five-second pause. Then three more flashes. Got it?'

Billy answered with a nod.

Rawhead gave him a shove. 'Now run!'

Billy didn't need telling again.

13

The dead and the living can never be one . . .
God has forbidden it!
'Schalken the Painter', Sheridan Le Fanu

Earlier that evening, a Chrysler Voyager containing Chef, Heidi and the Beast had arrived at the Doll's guest house. The people carrier was like a small bus, giving the absurd impression that the gangsters were off on a works outing. In keeping with this effect, the Beast was wearing a loud checked sports jacket.

To discuss tactics, they drove to a pub in Kimbolton. The pub, appropriately enough, was called the Manchester Arms. The Doll stuck to mineral water, while the others drank brandy. For a while the gangsters talked about football, beer – anything but the task ahead of them. Heidi happened to mention that an aunt of his was in intensive care after being mugged in broad daylight. 'It makes you wonder what the world's coming to.'

'The world's as bad as it's always been,' said Chef quietly.

'You're wrong, and I'll tell you why,' said the Beast. 'People nowadays have no respect. I'll give you an example. Twenty years ago, a fella who was queer would have kept it to himself. Now, all right, these people can't help 'emselves. And I feel sorry for 'em. But do they have to push it in our faces?'

There were general nods of agreement.

'What I mean is, these days the bastards are actually proud of being bent. They go on marches, shouting: "I'm gay! I'm gay!" They haven't even got the fucking decency to be ashamed of 'emselves. Well, it gets on my wick. In fact, it's bloody disgusting!'

Chef smiled. 'What would you rather see? A kid being hanged for stealing a loaf of bread? Or a bunch of hairdressers going for a walk?'

'What're you on about?'

'You said the world was getting worse. I think you should read a few history books.'

The Beast scowled.

The Doll told the others what he knew, omitting to mention that Rawhead had already spotted him. 'They're both there, Rawhead and Dye. Now there's only one problem: the neighbours. The vicar and his wife live next door. They'll need taking care of before we move in.'

Chef shook his head sombrely. 'No.'

'Are you fucking joking?' sneered the Doll. 'They'll hear the shots. They'll phone the police.'

'If we do our job right, there'll only be two shots.

We want to shoot Dye and Rawhead in their beds. No heroics. Fuck all that. Let's concentrate on staying alive.'

They raised their glasses to this.

'Beast, you'll go in first. Phone us when you've opened up the house. Then we all go in together.'

The Beast tutted.

'What's the matter now?' demanded Chef.

'Housebreaking?' grumbled the Beast. 'Where's the fucking class in that? It's the kind of thing idiots do.'

'You're right,' said Chef. 'We'll send Heidi instead.'

Now, as they loaded and checked their weapons on a manure-streaked country road in the darkness, no one was in the mood for conversation. The people carrier was out of sight around the corner, parked behind a barn. No light shone from the two houses near the church. Chef handed out weapons and flashlights. He'd brought along two M16 assault rifles, one of which he gave to Heidi.

'Any trouble, use that,' advised Chef. 'Here's a fresh magazine. It holds thirty rounds.'

The Doll took Heidi to a stile at the side of the road. He pointed out the bridle path. The path ran parallel to the hedge that enclosed the churchyard before passing the perimeter fences of both the old and new vicarages. Heidi climbed over the stile and stepped in a pile of cowshit. 'Fucking thick bastard farmer cunts!' he snarled, at no one in particular.

At a signal from Chef, Heidi nodded and ran off into the dark.

The other three went back to the people carrier and waited. Chef opened a packet of Liquorice Allsorts and offered them round. The Doll turned him down, feeling that it was beneath his dignity to eat sweets. Chef and the Beast entered into a mild disagreement about who should have the coconut ones.

'Going anywhere nice for your holidays?' said the Beast to Chef, making conversation.

'What is this?' said Chef. 'A barbershop? You'll be asking me if I'm interested in football next.'

'Well? Are you?'

'Am I what?'

'Interested in football?'

Chef was drily amused. 'No. I'm interested in silence. Understand? The beautiful peace that falls when arseholes stop talking.'

There was a long, tense period of waiting. The Doll swallowed loudly. In case anyone suspected him of nerves, he said, 'What's keeping that big dozy cunt?'

'Listen,' said the Beast loyally. 'If he gets us into

this fucking house, the lad's as clever as he needs to be.'

The other two grunted in assent.

The minutes ticked by. Light rain fell, tapping the roof of the car at irregular intervals. Chef's mobile phone failed to ring. It had been 2.14 when they had seen Heidi off. By 2.23 all conversation had died away. The three men shared a growing feeling of apprehension. 'Give him time. He's only been gone ten minutes,' announced Chef to no response. He glanced at his mobile to confirm that it was switched on.

By 2.49 Chef knew something was wrong. 'All right. One of us had better go and look for him.'

The Beast and the Doll said nothing.

'Who's it going to be?'

'Why can't we all go?' demanded the Doll.

Chef pulled a face. 'What are we? Big girls? Do we have to go round linking arms and dancing round our handbags? Rawhead'd love that. To pick all three of us off at once. A nice easy night's work for him.'

Chef's throat was parched. He opened a bottle of cheap lemonade and took a long swig. After passing the bottle around, he spoke again. 'OK. Beast, go and look for him. I think it's stopped raining.'

'It's not getting wet that worries me,' answered the Beast.

Chef leaned close as if explaining something to a

child. 'Listen. You'll be all right, as long as you're careful. Get as close as you can without putting yourself in danger.' He touched the Beast on the back of the head. 'If there's no sign of Heidi, come straight back. OK?'

The Beast nodded sombrely. 'Mr Priest isn't going to like it if we go back empty-handed.'

The spare M16 was propped against the front seat. Chef passed it to the Beast. 'Mr Priest isn't out here risking his fucking neck.'

'Yeah. Why is that, I wonder?' asked the Doll with a smirk.

The Beast left, slamming the door behind him. The remaining two men waited. Chef kept his eyes on the digital clock set in the dashboard as he took out his gun and loaded it. It was a new Smith & Wesson, an SW9P.

'What're you packing?' asked the Doll, leaning over from the seat behind.

Chef didn't answer. The Doll's overfamiliar manner was beginning to grate on him. While they waited, another brief shower of rain spattered the roof and the windscreen. The downpour ceased, giving way to yet more silence. The Doll began to tap his fingers on the seat. Chef told him to quit.

Chef wasn't much of a smoker. Normally it took him a week to go through a pack of ten. But he needed something to calm his nerves. He took out a fresh pack of Benson & Hedges, opened it with his thumbnail and offered one to the Doll. The Doll never smoked, but accepted anyway, grateful to have something to do. They lit up with the flame from Chef's gold-plated Zippo lighter. In seconds, the car was full of blue smoke. The Doll coughed. Chef rolled down his window, admitting fresh air and the smell of cowshit.

The Beast had been gone for twenty minutes. Chef knew he wasn't coming back. He turned his weary eyes to the Doll. 'OK. Whadya wanna do?'

'About what?'

The Doll stared at Chef without blinking. Chef thought, 'Look at this idiot. He thinks he's Michael Caine in *Get Carter*.' Patiently, Chef explained himself. 'Do you want to go in or not? I'm not going to force you.'

'I want Rawhead.'

'Do you?' sneered Chef. 'Me, I just want to bring Heidi and the Beast back alive. Then you know what I'm doing? I'm getting the bloody hell out of here.'

The Doll said nothing.

After checking that their torches worked and their weapons were primed, Chef and the Doll moved off into the dark. In the distance, a dog began to howl. Another dog, nearer this time, took up the chorus.

They approached the church by cutting through two fields. The fields were separated by a wide drainage ditch which they had to jump to clear. The Doll went first, reaching the far side with ease. Chef landed awkwardly and slithered down the bank, coating his exquisite suit in thick brown mud and dropping his handgun in the water at the foot of the ditch. He climbed down to retrieve the gun. The Doll had to haul him out.

'Will it fire OK now it's wet?' asked the Doll.

'Pull the fucking trigger and find out.'

Now they were opposite the vicarage. The parish clock struck the hour as they squatted behind a hedge in the dark and peered across the deserted road. The Doll complained that his feet were wet. Chef pointed out that his entire body was wet. They watched the house, feeling its menace, its Gothic skyline stark against the starless sky. Apart from the gentle rustling of the trees in the garden and the churchyard, there was absolutely no sound.

'Do you think he knows we're here?' said the Doll.

Then they heard the ominous sound of a bell. It was coming from the church. There was a brief pause. The bell rang again. The clear, mournful voice filled the darkness and carried far over the fields.

'There's your answer,' said Chef.

The Doll shook his head, not wanting to believe.

'Let's go,' urged Chef.

The bell rang on, its toll slow, measured and controlled.

The Doll turned to him sharply. 'What?'

'Move it. Unless you want to die.'

'Scared are you?' The Doll's voice was mocking.

Chef grabbed the Doll by the collar and shook him. 'Yes, I'm scared! And if you had an ounce of common sense, so would you be.'

For a moment the Doll quivered with rage, considering whether to punch Chef out. But he knew he would need all his strength for Rawhead. He broke away angrily. 'Fuck you! I don't need you!'

With that, the Doll ran across the road and vaulted over the church gate, accompanied by the mournful chime. Chef lingered, knowing the bell's significance. He was a Catholic boy. He knew a death knell when he heard one. And the Doll? The Doll didn't even know whose funeral it was.

The bell boomed in the spire. The Doll could feel the vibrations in his toes as he darted from grave to grave. Meagre light flickered in the long west window. He ran to the porch, torch in his left hand, gun in his right. The bell chimed for the last time.

Now he was facing the porch. Its door yawned wide, as did the door to the church itself. Two candles burned in a bracket on the far wall of the nave. Carefully, his pulse increasing, the Doll inched over the threshold and looked to his left.

The belfry door was wide open. He could see the bell-ropes, but the bell-ringer had gone. The Doll's finger tightened on the trigger. He scanned the nave.

Rows of empty pews were flanked by two aisles. A floorboard creaked. The Doll caught his breath.

The candlelight failed to penetrate the deepest recesses of the church. At first he could see nothing. There was a large ornate chair to the right of the altar. Someone was sitting in it. A large man in dark clothes, with a white hood on his head. His head sagged forward, as if he was dead or unconscious.

Rawhead had tricked the Doll before. He was unwilling to be caught out again. Holding his fire, he crept down the right-hand aisle, glancing quickly to left and right as he passed over the crossing. He walked past the altar, where a golden cross shone faintly. On his right, St Michael wrestled with the devil. A powerful odour filled the air. Dust and rotting fish.

The hooded figure occupied the Bishop's throne. Gun at the ready, the Doll drew nearer. The foul smell obviously emanated from the seated man. Shooting furtive glances in every direction, the Doll gave the body on the throne a quick dig with his left hand. It sagged sideways. The Doll yanked off the hood. It was sticky to the touch. Nauseated, he threw it down. He turned on his torch and shone it over the exposed face.

The hairless scalp was now as white as parchment and scored with brownish black weals. The hole over the left eye had widened, exposing a black socket.

Like a melting cake, the face had detached itself from the skull and shifted slightly to one side, so that what remained of the nose now lay a few centimetres to the right of the gaping nostrils. The single eye was coated with thick, reddish jelly. Yet the Doll knew who he was looking at. How could he fail to recognize his own brother?

The Doll couldn't believe it. It took an act of will to avert his gaze. Even then, Conrad's rotting face drifted before his eyes. Coughing and reeling, he staggered up the aisle. Rawhead had followed the Doll to Billy Dye's house, stolen his brother's corpse and then paraded it before him, like a running joke in a comedy revue. The bastard was *toying* with him. All the Doll's instincts told him that he should leave now, while he had the chance.

But as a boy, fighting in the street, he had never abandoned a fight, not even with his face smashed and his courage gone. Nor would he surrender now. Rawhead had humiliated him twice. Somehow the Doll would make him pay.

A shadow hurried over the transept from left to right. The Doll rushed forward and stumbled. He got to his knees in time to see a small door in the southern wall close quietly. He lurched towards the door and wrenched it open.

Sweet night air washed over him. He was on the south side of the churchyard, facing the hedge that ran between the graves and the vicarage. Blood welled up in his mouth. He'd bitten his tongue as he fell. Angrily, he spat a metallic-tasting gout onto the church wall. He found the gap in the hedge and stormed through it. Rawhead was walking past the shrubbery to the house.

'Come and fight like a man!' roared the Doll, spraying blood into the air.

Rawhead kept walking until he was hidden by the house. The Doll limped after him. By the time he reached the drive, Rawhead had disappeared from view. Light shone from the hall, casting a yellow arc into the darkness. The Doll climbed the porch steps and sidled into the entrance hall through the double front doors. He paused and listened. He heard nothing. Upstairs, all was quiet and dark.

Glancing to his left, he saw that the dining-room light was on. He walked through the dining room, into the kitchen. The naked bulb revealed smears of red on the bone-grey floor. The Doll hobbled to the cellar steps and looked down. A trail of tiny red droplets led down to the open door.

The Doll waited and listened. All he could hear was his own laboured breath. He felt something crawling on his face and plucked it off with his fingers. It was a large fly. A plump, sleepy bluebottle with violet wings. Shuddering, the Doll threw the insect to the ground and scraped his foot over it. The fly popped and burst, spilling a surprising amount of blood.

As he was looking down, the Doll noticed yet more gore. The right leg of his trousers was torn. His injured kneecap was bleeding. He was again reminded of the lost battles of his childhood. The Doll didn't want to fight. He wanted to go home. But he knew that he couldn't live with himself if he let Rawhead win.

As he descended the steps to the cellar, the stench he'd encountered in the church drifted up to meet him, borne on a damp gust of air. Combating the urge to run, the Doll crossed the threshold and looked around.

There was no light in the cellar. The Doll faltered, then realized that he'd tripped over a pair of human legs. The legs were still attached to their owner. With a boldness that he instantly regretted, the Doll shone his torch over the body's upturned face. It was the Beast. *Not dead, but sleeping.* His features wore an expression of mild indignation. His throat had been cut so savagely that the head was almost severed.

The Doll turned. The torch flung his shadow at the wall. The cellar was long and bare, apart from a few stacked boxes in a far corner. There was another doorway to the right of the entrance. This second door, made of sturdy oak, was slightly ajar.

Uncertainly, he walked to the door and opened it.

The smell was much stronger now. The beam of the flashlight revealed a long, low tunnel, propped up by wooden posts and beams. The gnarled timbers looked older than the house itself. The Doll reached out to touch the tunnel wall, felt damp earth against his hand. At the far end was a stone wall, with a curious ragged hole in its heart. The mouth of the hole lay deep in shadow. The Doll realized he was looking at a concealed passage that linked the vicarage with the church. He began to feel a little foolish, as if he'd accidentally wandered into a story by Enid Blyton.

Suppressing his mounting disquiet, the Doll began to edge forward, keeping his head low. The air was thick with flies. Large and bloated, they crawled over the walls, flew into his face. The stench of putridity was overpowering. With a peculiar lack of effort or discomfort, the Doll opened his mouth and emptied the contents of his stomach onto the floor. Apart from the buzzing of the flies, all was silent.

When he reached the end of the passage, he placed his gun down carefully on the floor. He leaned through the gap in the masonry and shone his torch into the chamber beyond. The stench hit him full in the face like a warm wind. He covered his mouth and nose with his forearm as he shone his flashlight into the darkness.

He was peering down into a long-abandoned crypt, its belly deep and narrow. The ceiling, which he was close enough to touch, was intricately vaulted and supported by a maze of stone pillars. On the opposite wall hung a delicate lapis lazuli plaque. The plaque was crawling with flies, but he could dimly make out a death's head and the inscription *lumine cassus* (robbed of light). The allusion was wasted on the Doll, who knew no Latin. Further along, half hidden by a pillar, the pale ghost of a long-vanished cross was visible.

He paused to catch his breath and leaned through the gap so that his belly rested on the masonry. Insects droned in his ears as he shone his torch down into the dark vault. The yellow beam cut through a blizzard of flies to illuminate a scene from hell. The Doll had expected at least three corpses, maybe half a dozen.

The vault was piled high with bodies. Not the dried and leathery mummies that are sometimes glimpsed in cracked and broken tombs – these people had all died within the last few years.

The bodies were piled one on top of the other, the recently slain uppermost. Some of them wore smart clothes with designer labels. The only woman he could see was dressed entirely in Chanel. She had no head. Her severed windpipe protruded horribly from her butchered neck. Beside her lay a man in a military-style blazer. His eyes were ink-black clots of blood. His dejected face glowed with greenish putrescence.

Across his legs, head twisted horribly, sprawled Heidi. He had no face, only a jagged skeleton smile

that shone through a veil of blood. But the Doll knew
it was Heidi. He recognized the bad haircut.

The Doll retched savagely, but his belly was
empty.

As he was struggling to control his nausea, two
large hands appeared over his shoulders and
snatched the torch out of his grasp. Then a pair of
powerful arms joined around his waist and tipped
him head-first into the pit.

The Doll landed in the stinking mass of bodies. As
he fell, his right hand punched through a decaying
ribcage, showering him with slime and stomach
juices. He struggled to stand upright. Instead, he
sank deeper into a filthy sea of carrion.

The light in the wall faded, became a pale radi-
ance. The Doll waited, gagging and shivering. After
a long pause, the light returned. Then Conrad's
body, all sixteen stone of it, dropped through the
gap. The corpse landed in front of the Doll, bounced
and rolled on top of him. With difficulty, he heaved
the carcass aside. Before he'd caught his breath,
bright torchlight shone in his eyes. He heard Rawhead singing, 'Got myself a crying, talking, sleeping,
walking living doll . . .'

Rawhead emitted a low, gentle chuckle that was
peculiarly free of malice. The Doll yelled empty
threats. Then both laughter and light began to fade.
The Doll continued to struggle. All around him, the

bodies shifted and sighed. He looked up at the hole in the wall, now defined by a faint, winking glow. A heavy door slammed. Suddenly there was no light at all.

The smell of the dead burned his throat and nostrils. The flies roared in his ears. The darkness was absolute. While he tried to think of a plan, he felt something cold and wet crawling across his hand. The Doll began to scream.

14

I killed him,' he said presently. 'I could stand it no longer.'
'The Screaming Skull', F. Marion Crawford

When Billy heard the bell ringing, he felt sure that something had gone badly wrong. At any moment, he expected police cars to arrive, lights flashing and sirens wailing. But the toll died abruptly and was followed by nothing. Not a cry, or a single shot. There was no sign of the all-clear signal that Rawhead had told him to watch for.

Billy was standing at the far edge of the cornfield behind the church. He felt safe here. Newey's gun was in his right hand and his eyes were on the church. But he found the waiting agonizing. Ten minutes after the bell had ceased, he disobeyed his orders and started walking towards the churchyard.

At the perimeter fence he stopped, parted the branches of a bramble hedge and peered through into the churchyard. The graves lay quiet and undisturbed. The church was dark and still. A calm breeze blew from the field, whispering in the ripening corn and ruffling the hair at the nape of his neck. It was a scene of pastoral beauty from a Samuel Palmer lithograph. All that was missing were the rustic figures and the harvest moon.

He was circling the hedge in a clockwise direction when he heard the sound of running footsteps. A gigantic shadow flew out of the darkness and crashed into Billy. Billy grunted and rolled to the ground, dropping his gun as he fell. The man he had collided with remained standing.

Billy tried to find the gun and failed. He looked up to see Chef gazing down at him. From the ground, Chef seemed enormous, a long-boned giant with a sad face. He was holding a gun loosely in his left hand. Chef could see that Billy was dazed and unarmed. But he didn't seem interested in killing him. After surveying Billy dispassionately, he turned and fled over the fields towards the road. For a big man, he moved quickly. He kept running until he was out of sight.

By the time Billy had found his gun, Rawhead was standing next to him, staring at Chef's retreating form. His Remington was pointing at the ground.

'Who was it?' asked Rawhead.

Billy told him. Rawhead nodded with satisfaction.

'You're not going after him?'

Rawhead shook his head. 'He'll be more use to us alive.'

They entered the house. Nothing seemed out of place. Rawhead surprised Billy by filling a bucket with water and mopping the kitchen floor. 'What happened?'

'Nothing. I scared them all away.'

'Do you expect me to believe that?'

'Go and pack. We're going to Manchester.'

'Why?'

'To find that girlfriend of yours.'

Billy went upstairs and threw his possessions into a bag. When he was in the bathroom, he thought he heard a muffled yell. It seemed to be coming from the washbasin. He walked out onto the landing and heard the noise again, so faint that it might have been the wind. He called out to Rawhead, who ascended the stairs slowly, gripping the handrail. He halted on the landing below and looked up at Billy through the banister rail. The lean, hard face was watchful. 'What is it?'

'That noise.'

'What noise?'

'The fucking screaming I told you about. It's back. Can't you hear it?'

Billy held his breath while Rawhead listened. There was a long silence. 'No. I can't hear anything.'

Rawhead snorted and began to go downstairs. Billy watched him, wondering how the back of a man's head could look so aggressive. Billy decided to be direct. 'They're in the cellar, aren't they? The men you killed.'

Billy saw Rawhead hesitate. Without answering, he resumed his descent.

Billy waited in the Mercedes Sprinter while Rawhead locked up the house. He couldn't quite believe what had happened. A posse of criminals had travelled all the way from Manchester to kill them both. One of them had fled, the rest had vanished, and not a single shot had been fired. Rather than feeling comforted, Billy was now more convinced than ever that he was in the company of a monster.

Rawhead sent the van skidding down the winding lanes to Kimbolton. The dawn was an hour away. They drove at eighty miles an hour, tyres screeching on the sharp bends. After driving in silence for three hours, they entered Alderley Edge. Billy guessed that Rawhead had no intention of waiting for Priest to launch a fresh attack. He planned to strike again, while Priest was vulnerable.

It was still early as they motored down the dirt track that led to Rawhead's Romany home. Rawhead ran over a wood pigeon on the way. Billy felt a sickening bump as the wheels turned the bird to paste. Billy felt this was unlucky – even more unlucky than the murder of three men in a quiet country parish.

They parked the Sprinter beside the caravan. Rawhead brewed some tea and they sipped it in silence. Although Rawhead had not slept for days, he offered Billy the bed and sat beside him, keeping watch. Billy awoke just before noon to see Rawhead still sitting there, scrutinizing him coldly.

Now it was Rawhead's turn to rest. He lay down without a word and closed his eyes, not so much falling asleep as losing consciousness. Billy occupied the chair he'd vacated. As Rawhead slumbered, he rambled feverishly. 'She'll let you down, Billy.' Then, 'She left you once, she'll do it again.'

Billy tried to convince himself that Rawhead was delirious, that he could have been talking about anyone.

Malcolm Priest was floating in his swimming pool when he heard a voice.

'Boss? Boss?'

He raised himself onto one elbow and saw a tall, lithe young man wearing a lightweight suit. The young man looked like a dancer. His face was dark, his hair an unfeasible shade of honey blond.

'Who the fuck are you?' demanded Priest.

'Boner,' the young man answered. 'I work for you.'

'No, you don't.' Priest sat up on the lilo, saw the newcomer eyeing his big tits and pregnant belly. 'I've never seen you before in my fucking life.'

'I was hired by Mister Chef, like.'

'Jesus Christ!' Squinting, Priest leaned forward slightly. 'Are you a nigger?'

'No way!' asserted Boner indignantly. 'I'm a Paki.'

Priest was so startled that he almost fell off the lilo. 'A fucking Paki?'

'Relax, man. We're all on the same side.'

'Don't give me that! You cheeky black bastard. What's Chef doing hiring Pakistanis?'

Unoffended, Boner held out his arm like a compère at the London Palladium. 'There's someone to see you, Mr Priest, sir.'

A man and a woman strolled into view. The man was about forty-five, slightly paunchy, with a neat side-parting and deep-set eyes. The woman was in her late twenties, with a pointed nose, sturdy legs and enormous childbearing hips. Both of the visitors were wearing cheap, ill-fitting suits, so Priest knew them to be police officers.

'Not just a Paki,' Priest hissed at Boner, 'but a Paki who hasn't got the brains to ask for a search warrant!'

The officers nodded to Boner. Boner smiled back and excused himself. Priest now found himself half-naked, on a lilo adrift in a swimming pool, watched by a pair of amused, fully-clothed detectives. Yet he was uncowed. 'What the fuck do you want?'

'Mr Priest? I'm DI Broadhurst,' said the male officer, still smiling. 'This is my colleague, Detective Constable Mather. We'd like a word, if we may.'

'Why? Don't I pay you fucking leeches enough?'

The smile on Broadhurst's face melted away. His eyes seemed to recede further into his skull. 'We're with the Cheshire Constabulary, Mr Priest. As far as I'm aware, you don't pay us anything.'

Half an hour after the police had left, Chef returned. Priest, a chilled bottle of Theakston's in his left hand, saw the Chrysler Voyager coming up the drive and met Chef at the door. When he saw that Chef was alone, he guessed the worst. His response was a stream of abuse. 'You fucking big fucking loser! Call yourself a leader? You couldn't organize a wank in a monastery.'

Chef was exhausted. His long face looked longer still. His dark complexion had acquired a yellowish, heart-attack hue. Silently, he walked past Priest and entered the games room. Priest followed him, watching from the doorway as Chef poured neat brandy into a tumbler.

'They're dead, aren't they?' demanded Priest. He was shaking his head. 'Three more fucking gone!'

Chef downed half the brandy before sinking slowly into a wicker chair. He seemed to have lost weight overnight. He turned his melancholy eyes to Priest and shrugged his preposterously large shoulders.

Priest said, 'Are you telling me you don't even fucking know?'

'Malcolm, they may well be dead. I don't know. All I can tell you is all three went in and not one came back.'

'Not even the Doll?'

'No.'

'Why didn't you go in after 'em?'

Chef smiled bitterly. 'I *imagined* I'd be more use to you alive.'

'Don't fucking flatter yourself. You useless twat.'

Chef took a sip of brandy. He threw back his head and closed his eyes, savouring the relief as the alcohol quickened his blood.

'I've just had the fucking CID here. They were sniffing around after that crappy little Jesus who fingered Billy Dye.'

Chef opened his eyes. 'Who put 'em onto us?'

Priest shrugged. 'Probably that fucking Paki you fucking hired without my fucking permission.'

'Yes, I hired him.' Chef downed his drink and got up to pour another. 'I didn't have much choice, Malcolm. There's nobody left. Rawhead's killed everybody.'

Chef returned to his chair. Priest entered the room and stood over him. 'And why's that? Way I see it, kebab-dick, it's all down to you. You hired Rawhead, which is why I've got no firm left and the spacks are breathing down my fucking neck.'

'It was the Doll who killed the Jesus. You hired him, not me. I never liked the glassy-eyed creep.'

Priest hurled his beer bottle at Chef's head. Chef ducked and the bottle shattered against a wall, leaving an obscene brown stain.

'Don't you dare fucking contradict me!' boomed Priest. 'This is all down to you!'

Priest waited for Chef to retaliate. When he saw that Chef wasn't about to fight back, he began to relax. His manner became intimate, almost friendly. 'I'm going to hire some proper people. Don't care how much it costs. A crack team of professionals. They can do what you failed to do.'

'Malcolm, why don't you just face facts? It's over. He's beaten us.'

'Beaten you, maybe.'

Chef let out a sigh that contained all the weariness and frustration of his life.

'See?' said Priest. 'That's the difference between us. You're a quitter. I never give up. That's why I'm number one. You're number two.'

Chef knew in his heart that if Rawhead was simply left alone, he wouldn't waste any more energy on the Priesthood or its members. Conversely, if Priest antagonized this maniac further, no one was safe. Not Chef, or his family.

Priest turned his back on Chef and walked over to a photograph on the far wall. It was a picture of the Priest family at Southport in the early sixties. Mr and Mrs Priest were sitting in deckchairs. Young Malcolm and his teenage sister were crouched at their feet, grinning cheesily at the camera. Even at the age of eight, Malcolm had bigger tits than his mother.

Chef watched Priest steadily. One eyelid flickered slightly. Apart from that, he showed no outward sign of the pressure he was under.

'I'm Malcolm Priest.' Priest opened a box on the mantelpiece and took out a Montecristo No. 2. He thrust the cigar between his pale lips. Turning, he grinned into Chef's eyes. 'They know my name in Las Vegas, Miami, you fucking name it. You? They don't even know who you are in Oldham.'

Fourteen years ago, no one insulted Chef. No one would have dared. When he joined forces with Priest, that all changed. Every day, a constant stream of abuse. *Greasy, lazy, spunk-bubble, camel-breath.* Chef had taken more from Malcolm Priest than he'd taken from anyone. 'Malcolm, who do you think you're talking to? Everyone who knows you knows me. We built up this organization together. Remember?'

'Shut your fucking noise and give me a light. You *cunt.*'

Chef took his lighter from his pocket. With a

casual flick of his thumb, he produced a flame. He held the flame up to Priest's cigar. Priest started to inhale. Without warning, Chef moved the lighter to one side and set fire to Priest's hair. At first, Priest didn't seem to grasp what was happening. Then he cursed sharply, dancing and slapping his head. 'What're you fucking doing?'

In a single motion, Chef flung his brandy at Priest's shirt and lit the spreading stain. Fresh flames sprang forth. Having put out his hair, Priest now tried to tear off the shirt. While he was tearing at the buttons, his trousers caught fire. Shrieking, Priest rolled about on the floor in the hope of extinguishing himself.

Chef reached calmly into his pocket and extracted a small bottle of lighter fluid that he'd been saving for a special occasion. He unscrewed the lid and poured the contents of the bottle over Manchester's number one. The fire took hold. Priest screamed and threshed, an incandescent manikin. Black smoke poured out of him.

When Boner came running, Priest was no longer moving and Chef was putting out little fires on the carpet with the aid of a soda siphon. The room reeked of rancid fat. Boner stared at the oily, blazing body and raised unsteady eyes to Chef.

'What the fuck happened?'

When Chef turned, he was holding a gun in his hand. 'Spontaneous combustion.'

As if to challenge this verdict, the burning body twitched and moaned. Chef aimed his Smith & Wesson at Priest's head and fired once. The moaning stopped. Boner was impressed.

'Heavy shit.'

'That's exactly what he is,' said Chef calmly, 'and it'll take four strong men to get rid of the body. Arrange it for me.'

Boner chose his next words carefully.

'Anything else, *boss*?' he asked.

Chef thought for a moment. 'No.' He sank down into his chair, weary but relieved. 'That'll be all for now.'

While Rawhead slept, Billy walked into Alderley to buy food, paracetamol and brandy. On his way back from the supermarket, he entered a phone box and tried to call Nikki. He got Nikki's mother, who had never liked him. 'Oh, it's you, is it?' she said. 'I was wondering when you'd get in touch.'

Resisting the temptation to abuse the old bitch, Billy asked for Nikki.

'She's just gone out.'

Relief charged through him like a narcotic. 'When? Just now?'

'Five minutes ago. She's only nipped to the shops.'

'And she's all right? She's really all right?'

Nikki's mother tutted. 'As all right as anyone

could be when they're eight months' pregnant and they've been abandoned.'

Billy let this go. 'Thanks. I'll call later.'

Happiness was out there, waiting to be embraced. A life so sweet he could taste it. Its flavour was pine trees, freshly baked bread, creosote on fences, a salty wind blowing from a rolling ocean. All the scents and flavours he had taken for granted at twenty and never noticed since. Fuck Rawhead. Fuck all bullies and killers and bastards. Billy was going to live again. He had made up his mind.

In his exuberance, he decided to call his agent. The phone was answered by Sophie, Rosie's assistant. She recognized Billy's voice instantly and was astonished.

'Good God! I thought you'd vanished off the face of the earth.'

Billy made some excuse about travelling to France to research a new book and asked to speak to Rosie. There was a long silence on the line.

'You haven't heard?'

Billy swallowed hard. 'What?'

'Oh, it's so awful. You don't know about this?' The girl's voice quavered with emotion.

He knew what was coming. 'Has something happened?'

'Rosie's been murdered.'

'Shit. *Shit.*' There was a long silence, which Billy broke. 'They found her body?'

'Well. Yes and no. You really don't know anything about this?'

'No.'

'Oh God.' She sighed, not wanting to go over the same grisly facts again. 'They only found the head.'

Sophie began to talk about how terrible it had been for Rosie's family. But Billy had stopped listening. He was busily making mental calculations. Rosie Silkman had a small head on a large frame. Her head constituted approximately a tenth of her body. Billy replaced the receiver. He knew what had happened: Rawhead had killed his agent and carried off most of the corpse, leaving her with her usual ten per cent.

Because Rawhead had been his protector, Billy had tried to convince himself that his friend was a man of honour, a better class of murderer. He now knew this to be a fallacy. As far as Billy could see, the only difference between Rawhead and Malcolm Priest was that Rawhead could spell.

Rawhead liked to kill people. Especially people who had sinned against Billy Dye. He thought of Rawhead refusing to drink Nikki's health. *She left you once, she'll do it again.* If Rawhead could murder his agent and his publisher, what hope was there for a woman who had broken Billy's heart?

Billy didn't go back, not at first. He walked to the brink of the Edge and sat there for a long time. He watched the aircraft winging backwards and forwards over the Cheshire Plain. It was a dull day. Stray drops of rain blew down on the wind. Billy knew what he had to do. It was only a question of finding the courage.

When he returned to the caravan, Rawhead was smiling in his sleep. It was a subtle, winning smile that reminded Billy of the boy he'd once known. The bottle of morphine stood on its shelf, alongside hypodermics in sealed sterile packets. Trembling with fear, Billy unwrapped a fresh needle. He injected all the morphine that remained, about five milligrams, into a vein in Rawhead's left arm.

Rawhead did not stir. Billy waited until Rawhead was snoring before leaving the caravan. In the back of the Voyager, he found a petrol can. He re-entered the caravan to splash the fuel over the floor and walls.

In the village, he'd bought a pack of safety matches for the Calor gas stove. He took a book from a shelf – *Weaveworld* by Clive Barker. He struck a match and set the book alight. Deliberately not looking at the man on the bed, Billy backed out of the caravan onto the steps. He dropped the burning book in through the open doorway. There was an angry whoosh. A great tongue of flame reared up like a fire demon. In seconds the caravan was violently ablaze.

Billy left the door wide open. That way, he could tell himself it wasn't really murder. He felt himself blushing with guilt and shame. If Steve had cried out at that point, Billy would have gone back for him. But no cry came. Trembling, he climbed into the van and started up the engine.

At the entrance to the field he rolled down the car window and looked back. The Romany caravan was rocking in the heat like a burning cradle. The fire was dazzling, even beautiful. Stray scraps of soot and blistered paint climbed the lurid sky, spinning in dainty arcs. Billy put his foot down hard and sent the Sprinter van hurtling up the track. He was crying so much he could barely see to drive. It was a miracle he didn't do himself an injury.

15

I began to think I was safe.
'Green Tea', Sheridan Le Fanu

Billy Dye went back to his old, new life. He became a father, a role he took to with unexpected enthusiasm. Nikki and the baby moved into Billy's house on Albert Road. It was a time of glorious hope. Billy found a new agent – a peaceable man who practised yoga – and started work on a book about Manchester criminals, unpromisingly titled *Rawhead*.

The police didn't arrive to question Billy. All he went home to was a pile of angry red bills. No one was watching the house. Overnight, the menace vanished from his life. Billy was relieved. Yet, perversely, he was also disappointed.

Three months passed. One night in early autumn, he was awoken by the sound of a baby crying. He turned over in bed, saw that the beautiful dark woman at his side was sleeping soundly, and got up to attend to the child himself. But when he entered the nursery, his daughter was fast asleep. Puzzled, he looked at her for a few moments, then heard a soft click downstairs. It sounded like the front door closing.

Billy stood on the landing in the dark, listening. It was a dry, frosty night. There was a full moon and the house was aflood with pale blue light. Billy waited until he was shivering with the cold. At last, encouraged by the silence, he went downstairs. Nothing was out of place. There was no one in the house but Billy, Nikki and the baby.

He went upstairs, had a piss and returned to bed. As he drew back the covers, Billy saw a dark object lying on his pillow. Astonished, he picked it up. It was a book. He walked out onto the landing to find that he was holding a first edition of ghost stories by a writer called Montague Rhodes James. There was no inscription, but one corner of the cover was slightly buckled, as if damaged by fire.